P9-CRM-783

BABY-SITTERS
LITTLE SISTER®

KAREN'S SCHOOL PICTURE

**DON'T MISS THE OTHER BABY-SITTERS
LITTLE SISTER GRAPHIC NOVELS!**

KAREN'S WITCH

KAREN'S ROLLER SKATES

KAREN'S WORST DAY

KAREN'S KITTYCAT CLUB

ANN M. MARTIN
BABY-SITTERS LITTLE SISTER®

KAREN'S SCHOOL PICTURE

A GRAPHIC NOVEL BY
KATY FARINA
WITH COLOR BY BRADEN LAMB

An Imprint of
■ SCHOLASTIC

This book is for Ashley Vinsel
A. M. M.

This book is for my friends, my unyielding
pillars of love and support
K. F.

Text copyright © 2022 by Ann M. Martin
Art copyright © 2022 by Katy Farina

All rights reserved. Published by Graphix, an imprint of
Scholastic Inc., *Publishers since 1920.* SCHOLASTIC, GRAPHIX,
BABY-SITTERS LITTLE SISTER, and associated logos are trademarks
and/or registered trademarks of Scholastic Inc.

The publisher does not have any control over and does not assume any
responsibility for author or third-party websites or their content.

No part of this publication may be reproduced, stored in a retrieval system,
or transmitted in any form or by any means, electronic, mechanical, photocopying,
recording, or otherwise, without written permission of the publisher. For information
regarding permission, write to Scholastic Inc., Attention: Permissions
Department, 557 Broadway, New York, NY 10012.

This book is a work of fiction. Names, characters, places, and
incidents are either the product of the author's imagination or are used
fictitiously, and any resemblance to actual persons, living or dead, business
establishments, events, or locales is entirely coincidental.

Library of Congress Control Number: 2021937361

ISBN 978-1-338-76252-5 (hardcover)
ISBN 978-1-338-76251-8 (paperback)

10 9 8 7 6 5 4 3 2 1   22 23 24 25 26

Printed in China   62
First edition, January 2022

Edited by Cassandra Pelham Fulton and David Levithan
Book design by Shivana Sookdeo
Creative Director: Phil Falco
Publisher: David Saylor

CHAPTER 1

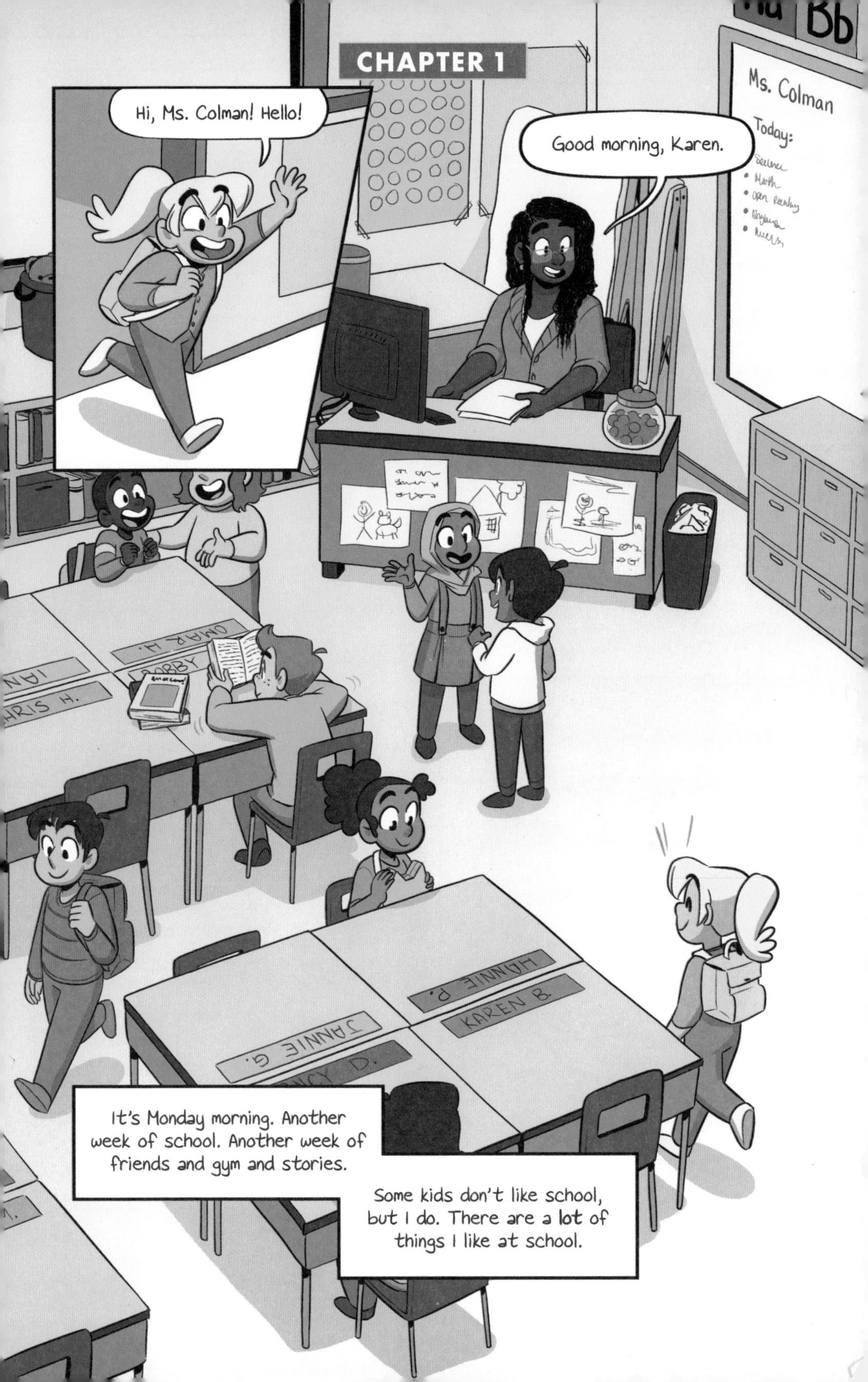
Hi, Ms. Colman! Hello!
Ms. Colman
Today:
Good morning, Karen.
OMAR H.
HANNIE P.
KAREN B.
JANNIE G.
It's Monday morning. Another week of school. Another week of friends and gym and stories.
Some kids don't like school, but I do. There are a **lot** of things I like at school.

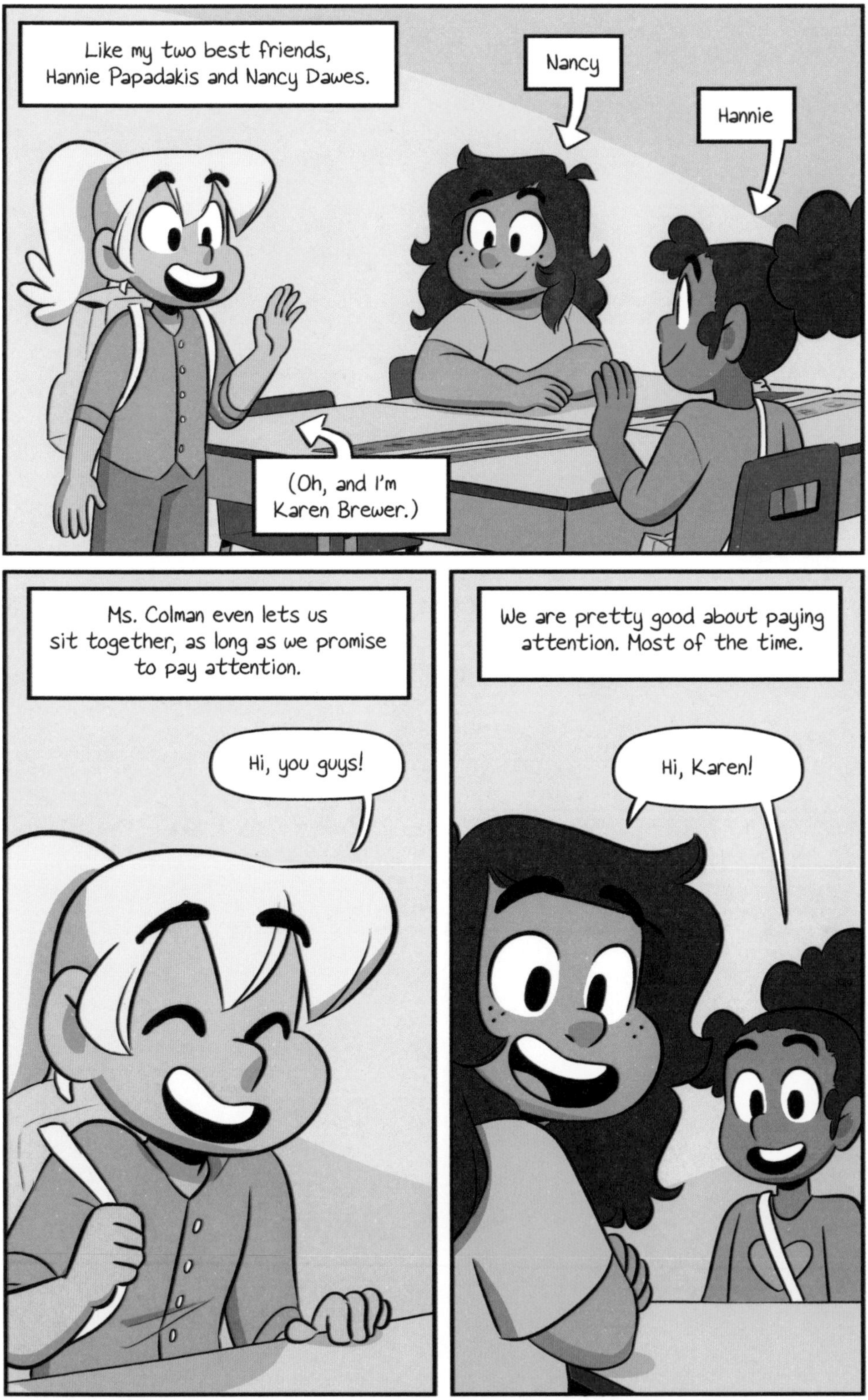

Like my two best friends, Hannie Papadakis and Nancy Dawes.
Nancy
Hannie
(Oh, and I'm Karen Brewer.)
Ms. Colman even lets us sit together, as long as we promise to pay attention.
Hi, you guys!
We are pretty good about paying attention. Most of the time.
Hi, Karen!

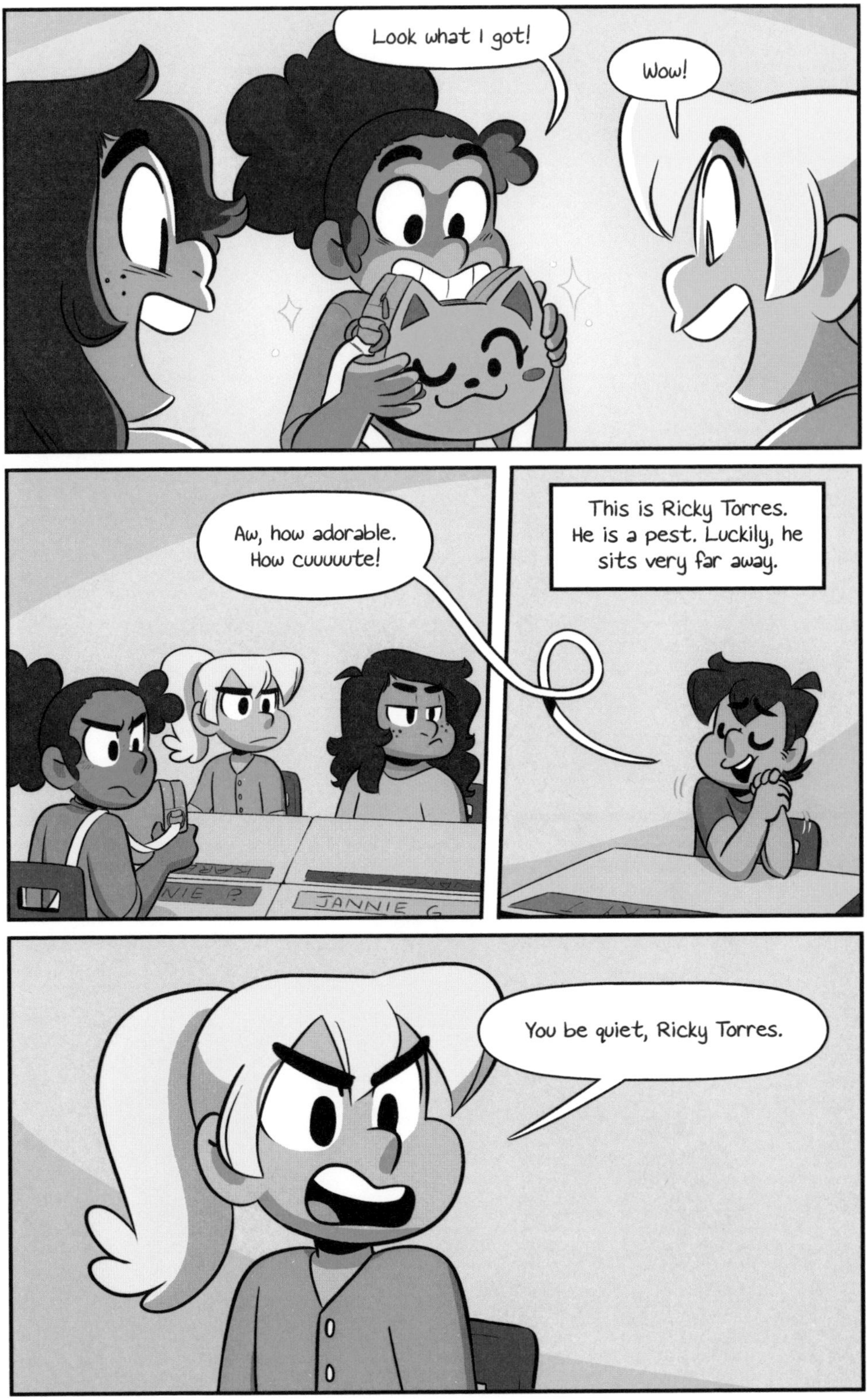
Look what I got!
Wow!
Aw, how adorable. How cuuuuute!
JANNIE G
This is Ricky Torres. He is a pest. Luckily, he sits very far away.
You be quiet, Ricky Torres.

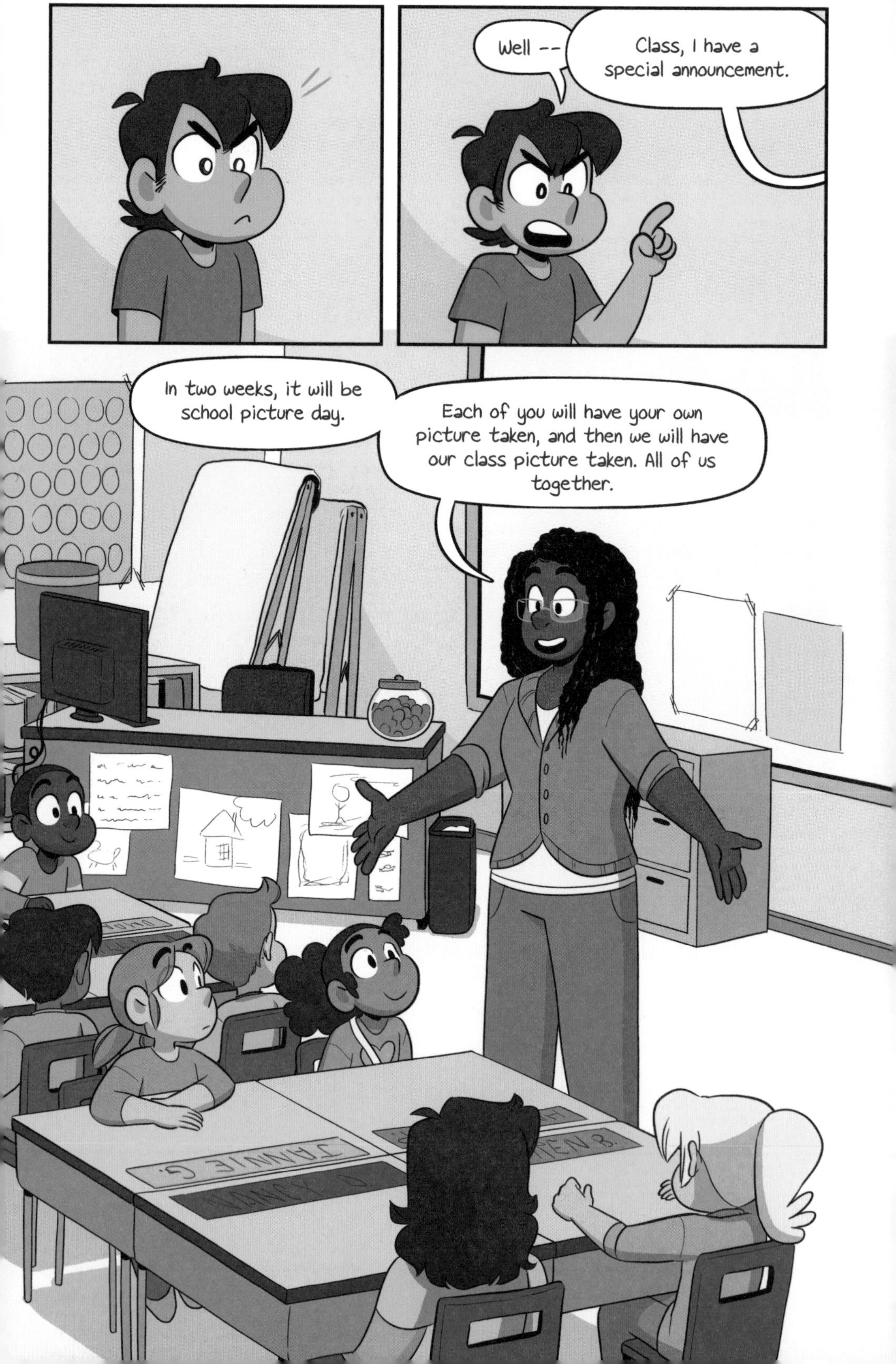
Well --
Class, I have a special announcement.
In two weeks, it will be school picture day.
Each of you will have your own picture taken, and then we will have our class picture taken. All of us together.

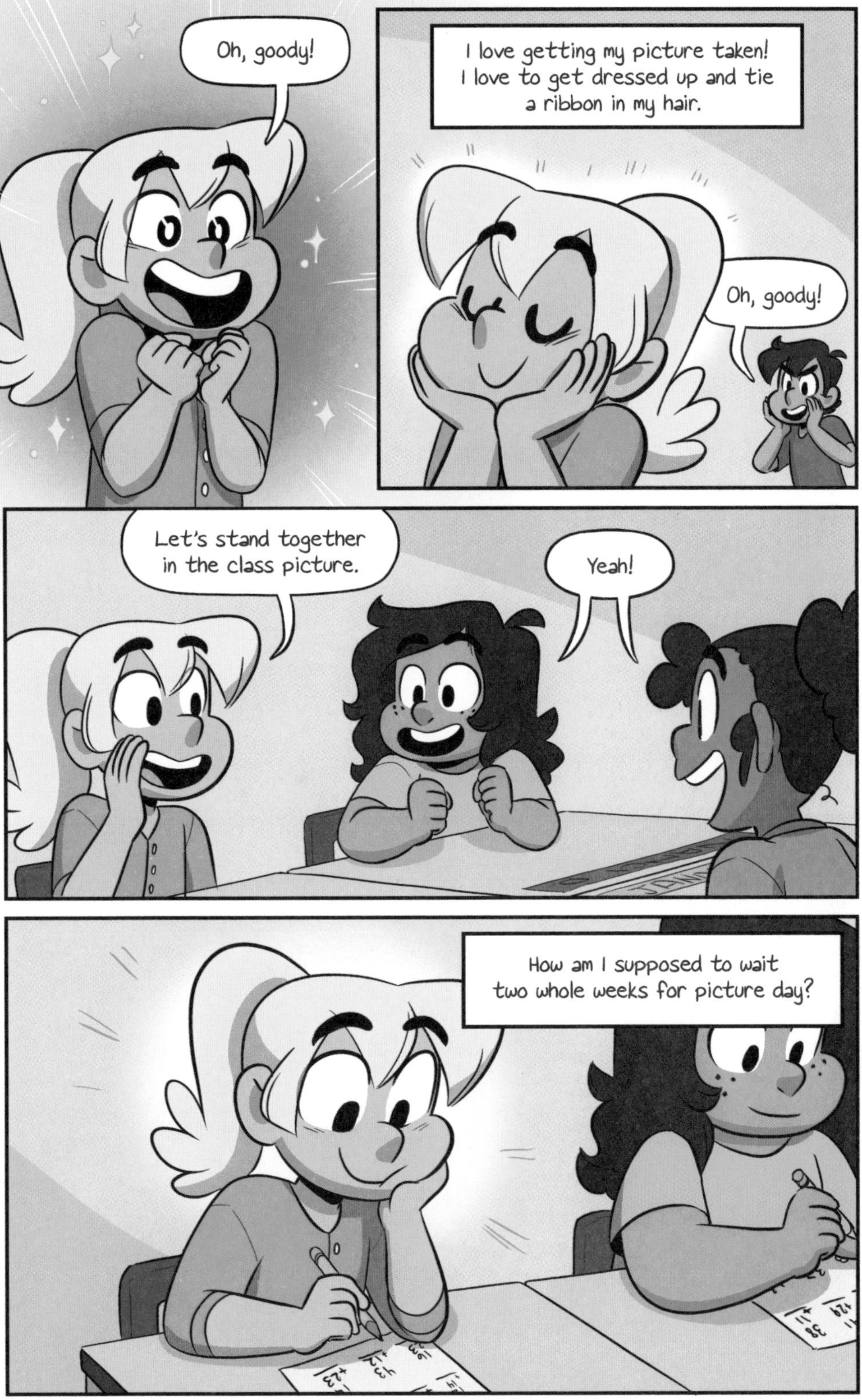
Oh, goody!
I love getting my picture taken! I love to get dressed up and tie a ribbon in my hair.
Oh, goody!
Let's stand together in the class picture.
Yeah!
How am I supposed to wait two whole weeks for picture day?

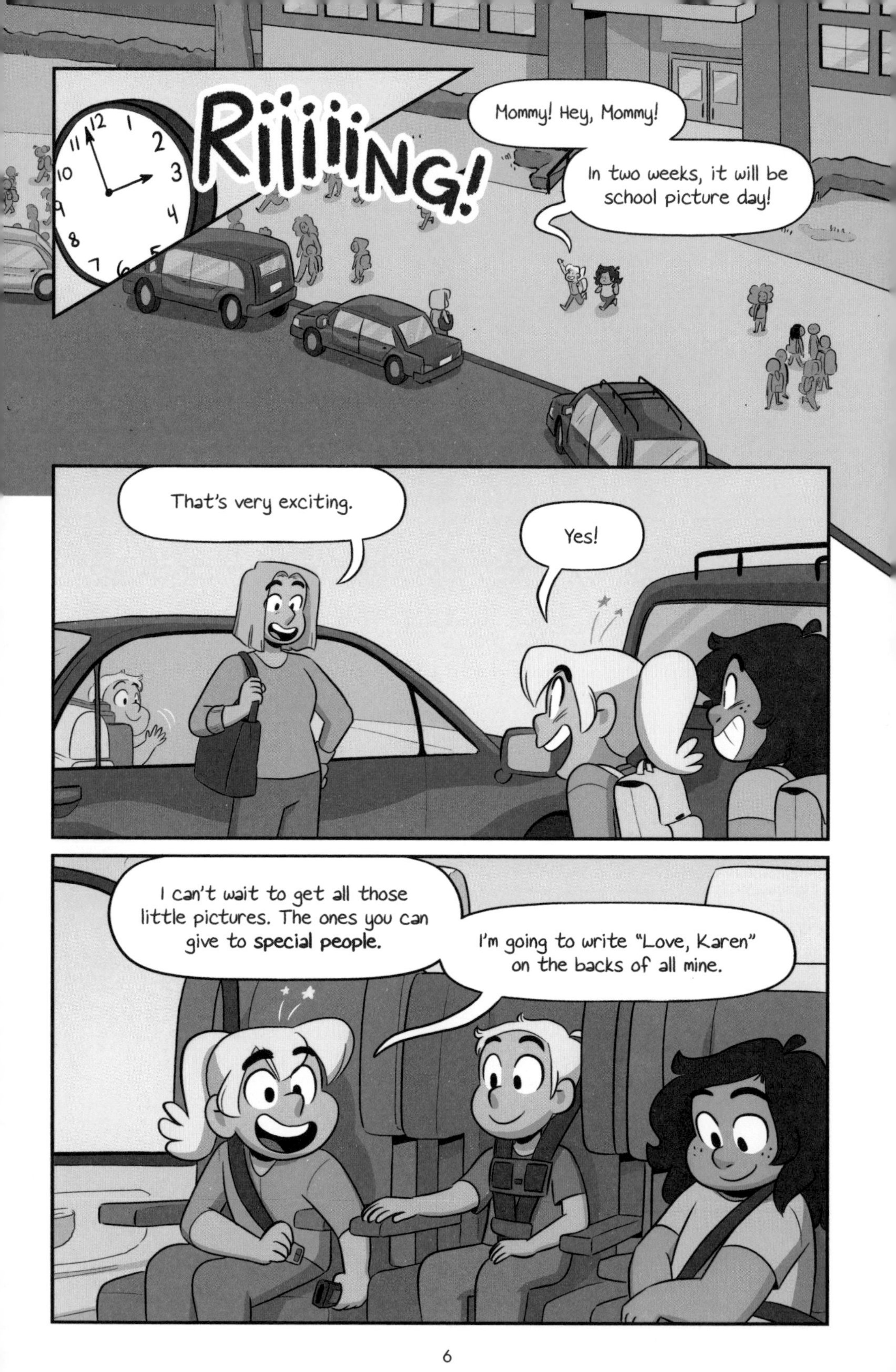
RiiiiNG!
Mommy! Hey, Mommy!
In two weeks, it will be school picture day!
That's very exciting.
Yes!
I can't wait to get all those little pictures. The ones you can give to **special people.**
I'm going to write "Love, Karen" on the backs of all mine.

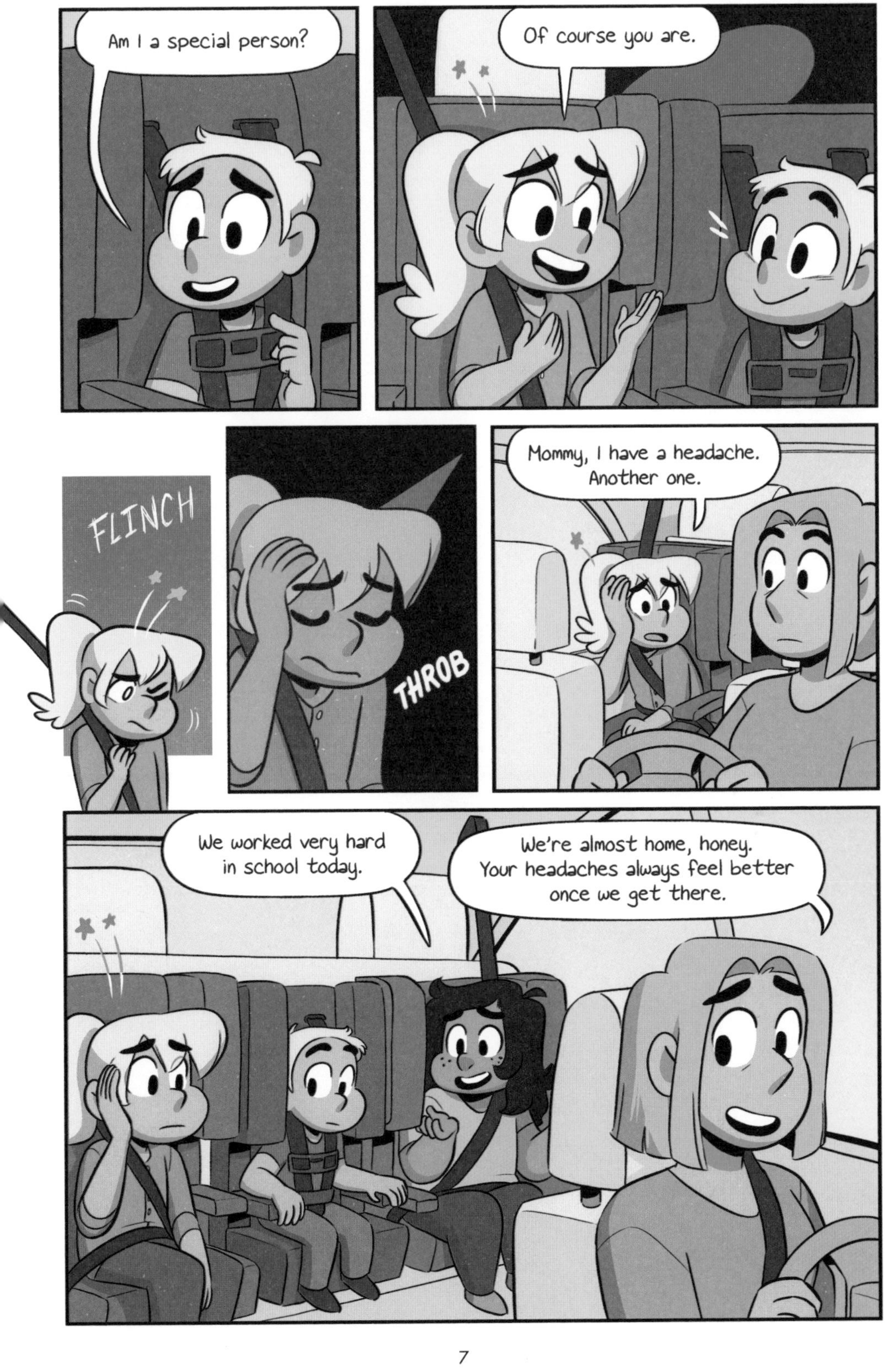

Am I a special person?
Of course you are.
FLINCH
THROB
Mommy, I have a headache. Another one.
We worked very hard in school today.
We're almost home, honey. Your headaches always feel better once we get there.

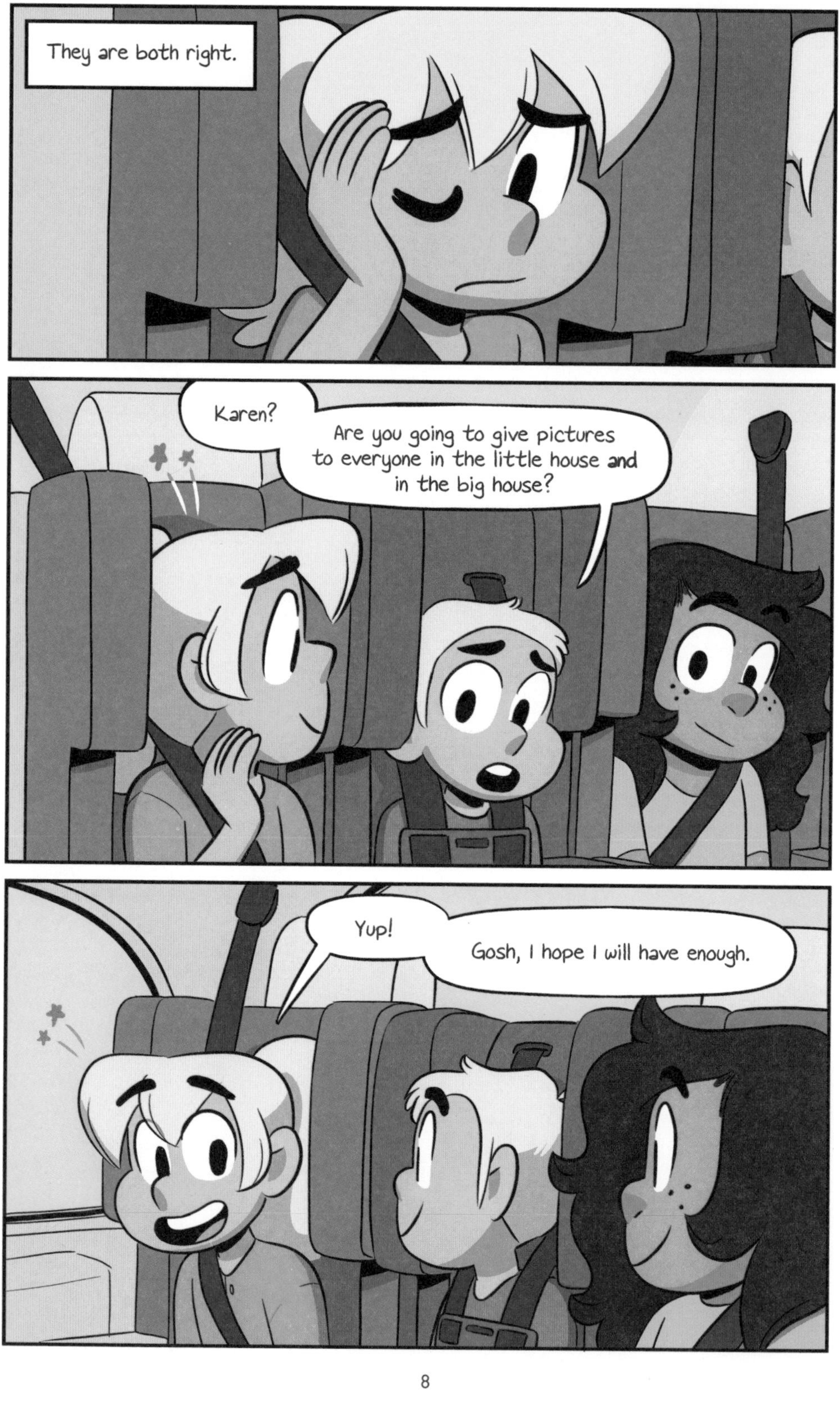
They are both right.
Karen?
Are you going to give pictures to everyone in the little house and in the big house?
Yup!
Gosh, I hope I will have enough.

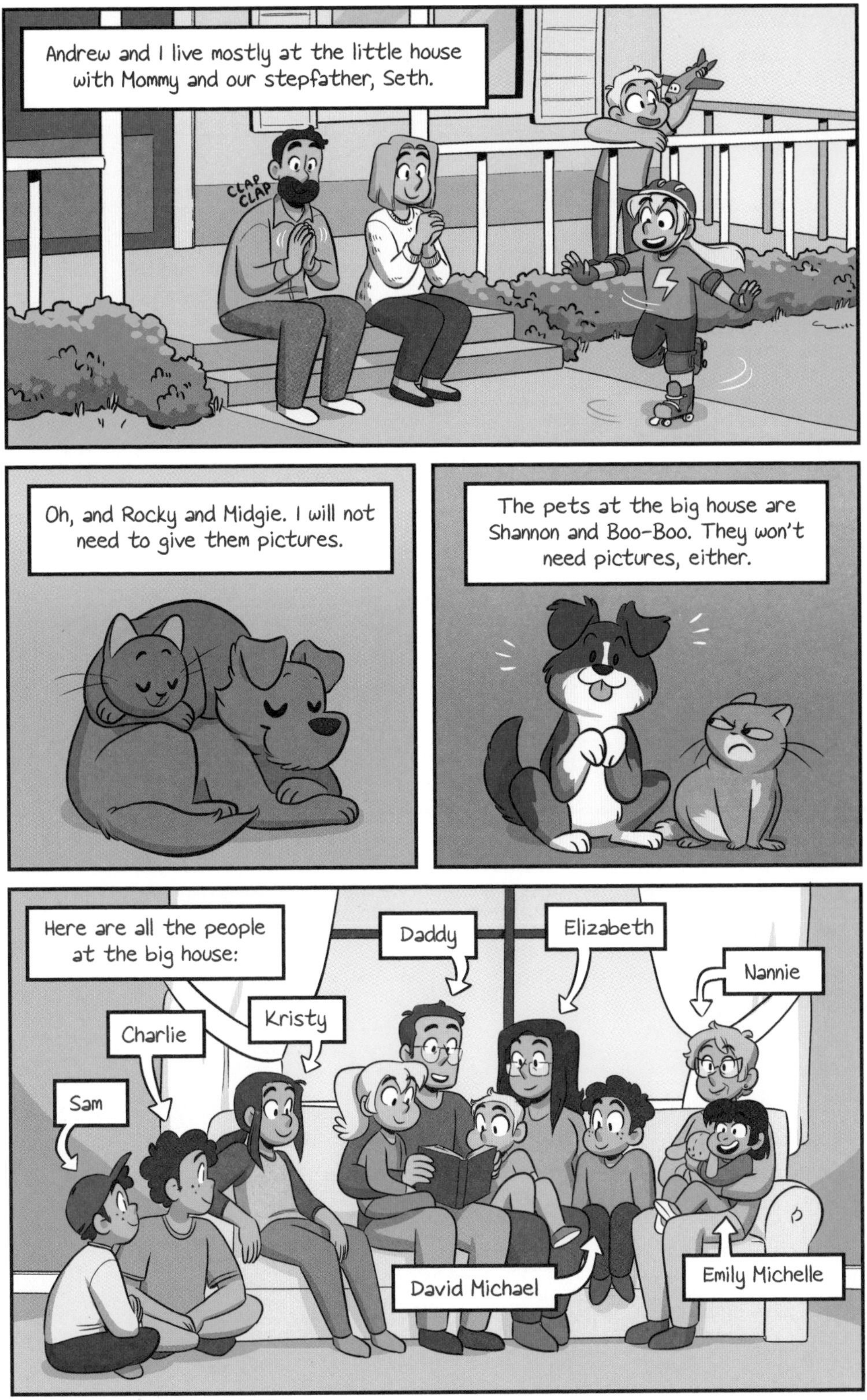

Andrew and I live mostly at the little house with Mommy and our stepfather, Seth.
CLAP CLAP
Oh, and Rocky and Midgie. I will not need to give them pictures.
The pets at the big house are Shannon and Boo-Boo. They won't need pictures, either.
Here are all the people at the big house:
Daddy
Elizabeth
Nannie
Charlie
Kristy
Sam
David Michael
Emily Michelle

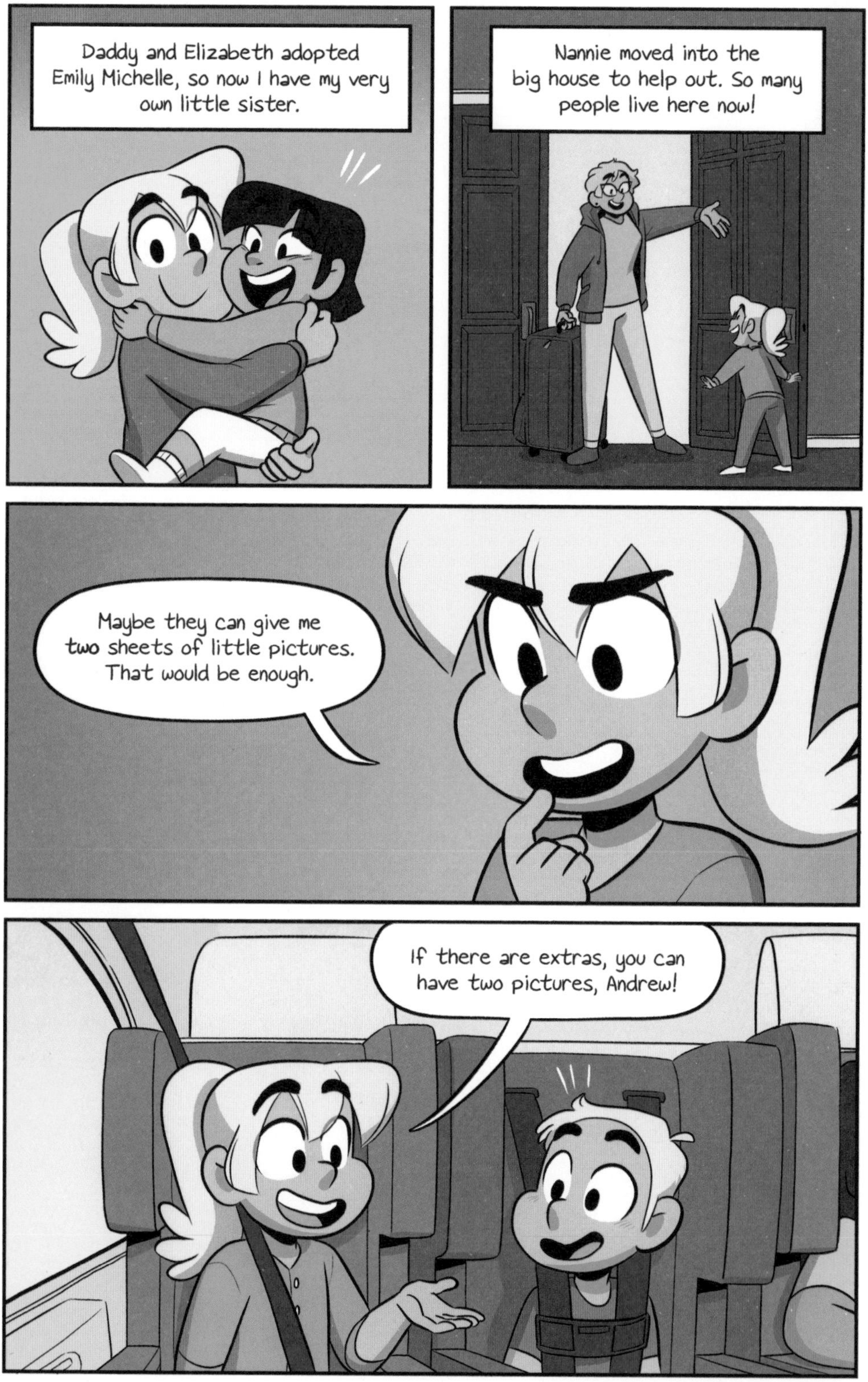
Daddy and Elizabeth adopted Emily Michelle, so now I have my very own little sister.
Nannie moved into the big house to help out. So many people live here now!
Maybe they can give me two sheets of little pictures. That would be enough.
If there are extras, you can have two pictures, Andrew!

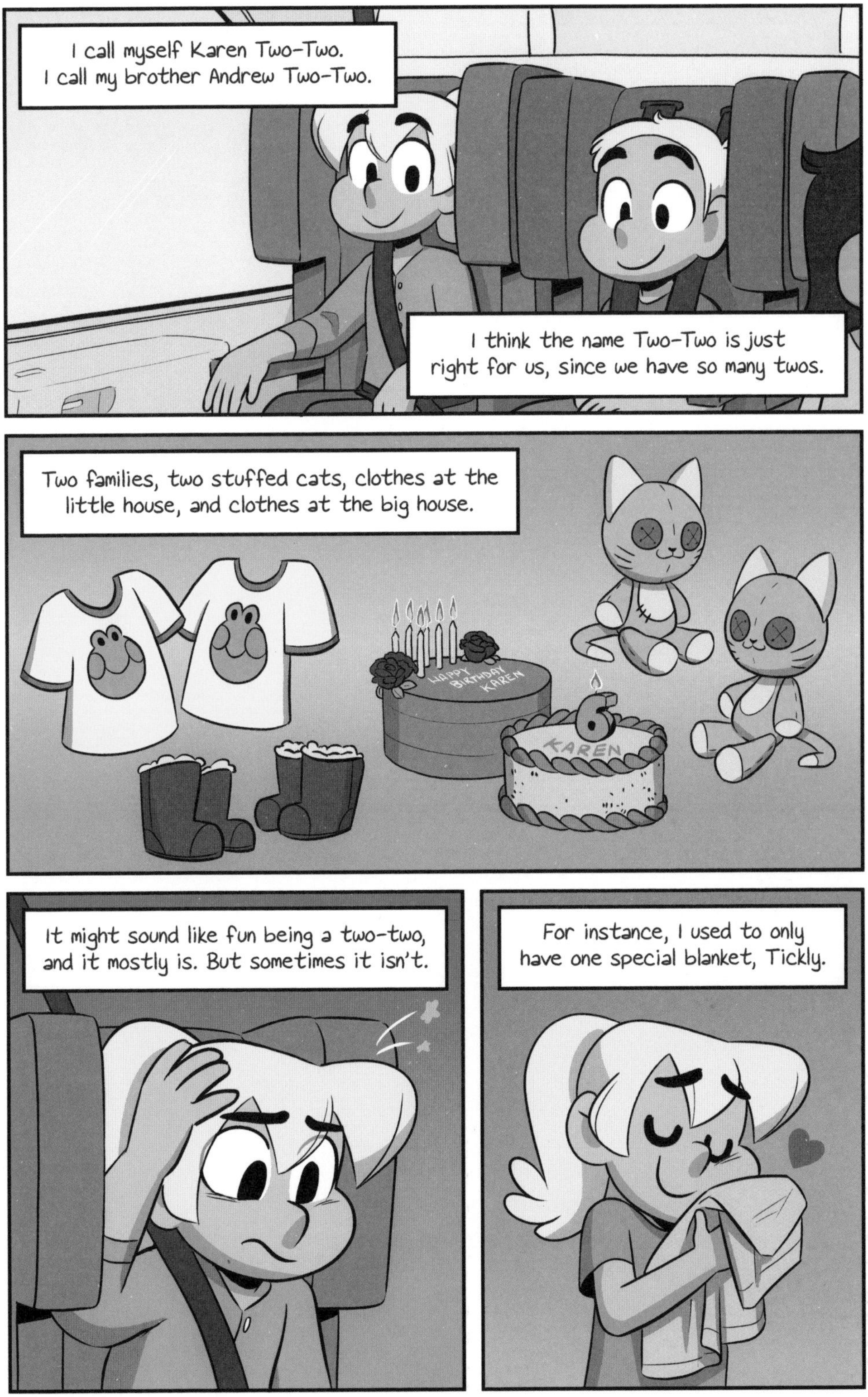
I call myself Karen Two-Two.
I call my brother Andrew Two-Two.
I think the name Two-Two is just right for us, since we have so many twos.
Two families, two stuffed cats, clothes at the little house, and clothes at the big house.
HAPPY BIRTHDAY KAREN
KAREN
It might sound like fun being a two-two, and it mostly is. But sometimes it isn't.
For instance, I used to only have one special blanket, Tickly.

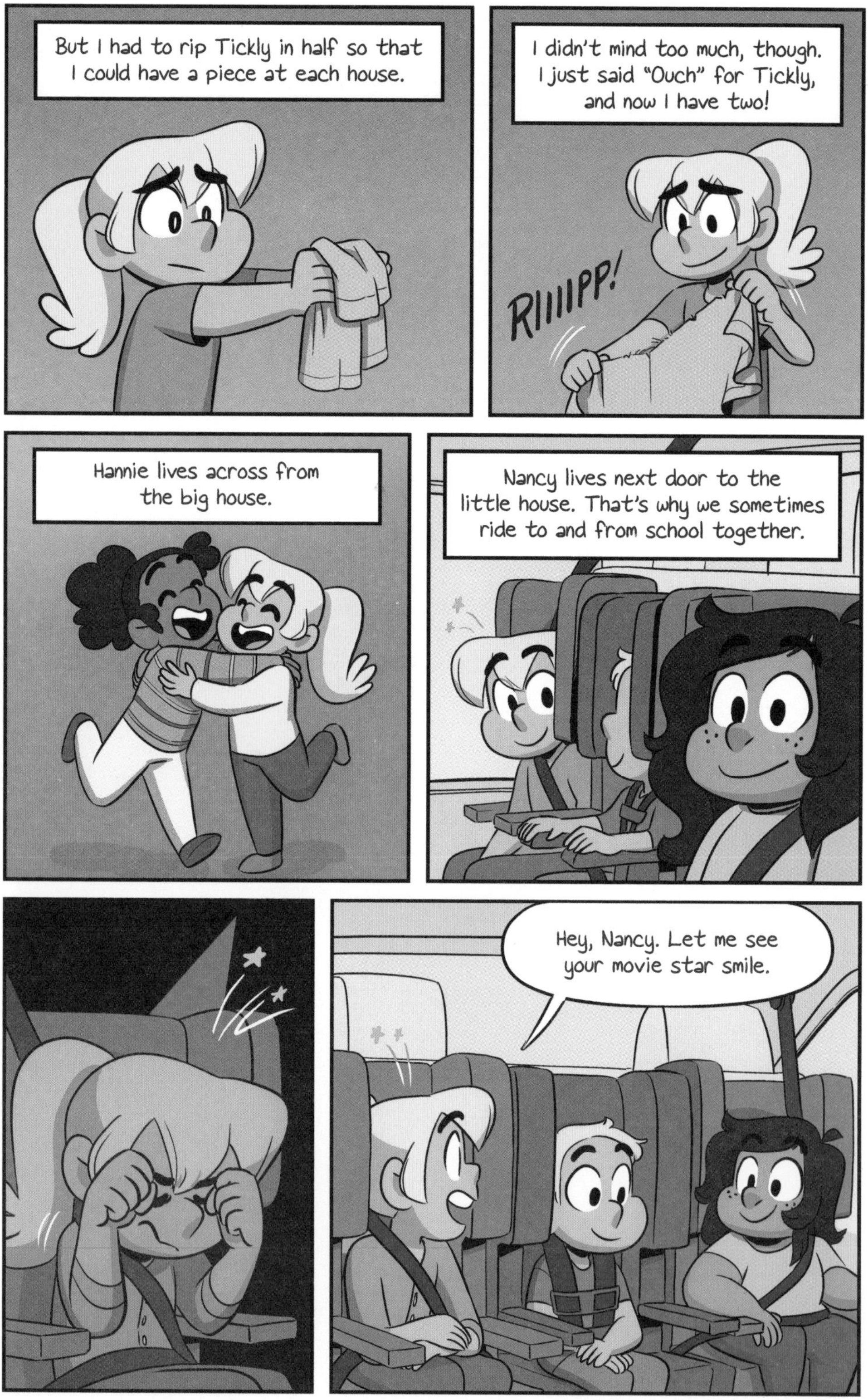
But I had to rip Tickly in half so that I could have a piece at each house.
I didn't mind too much, though. I just said "Ouch" for Tickly, and now I have two!
RIIIIPP!
Hannie lives across from the big house.
Nancy lives next door to the little house. That's why we sometimes ride to and from school together.
Hey, Nancy. Let me see your movie star smile.

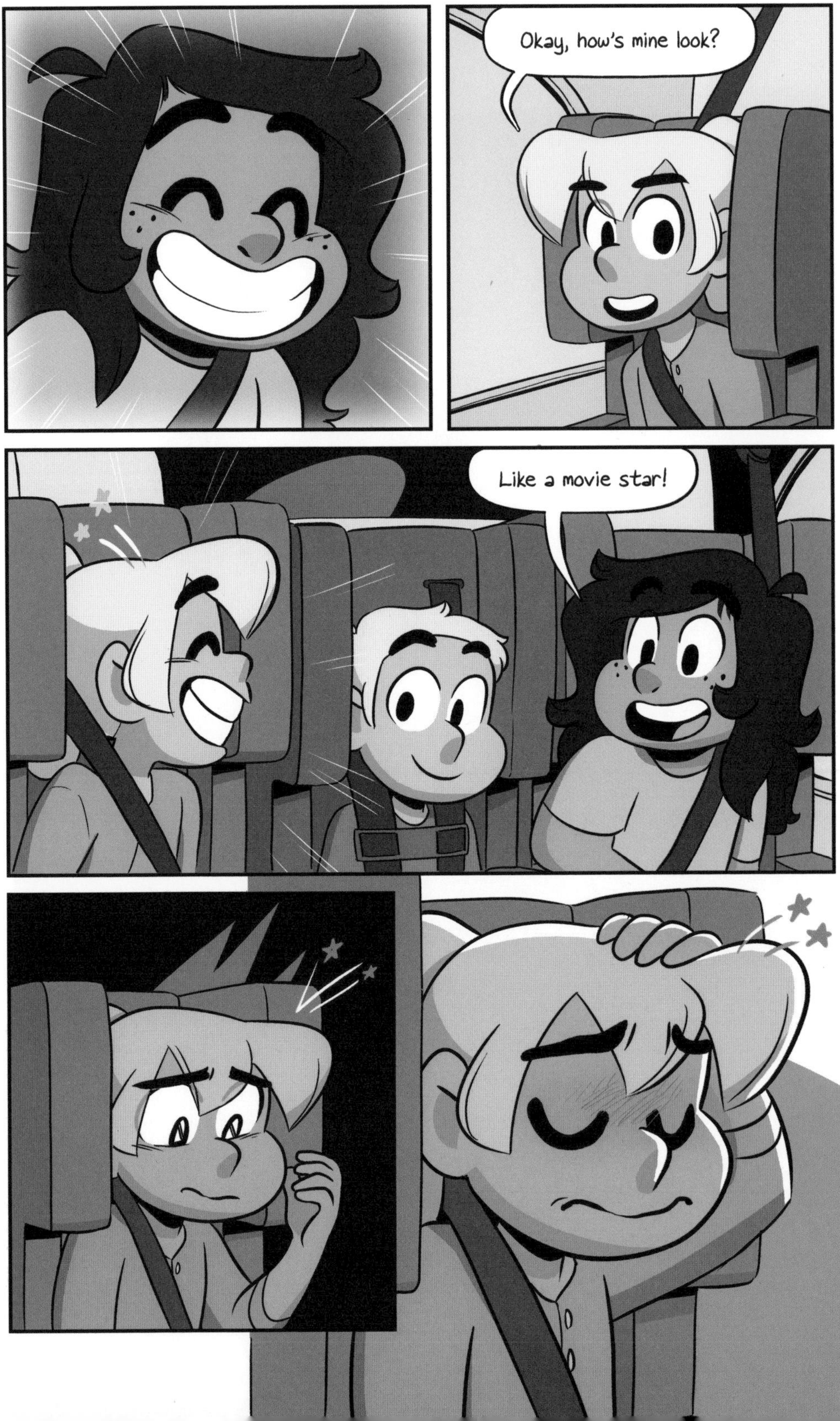
Okay, how's mine look?
Like a movie star!

CHAPTER 2

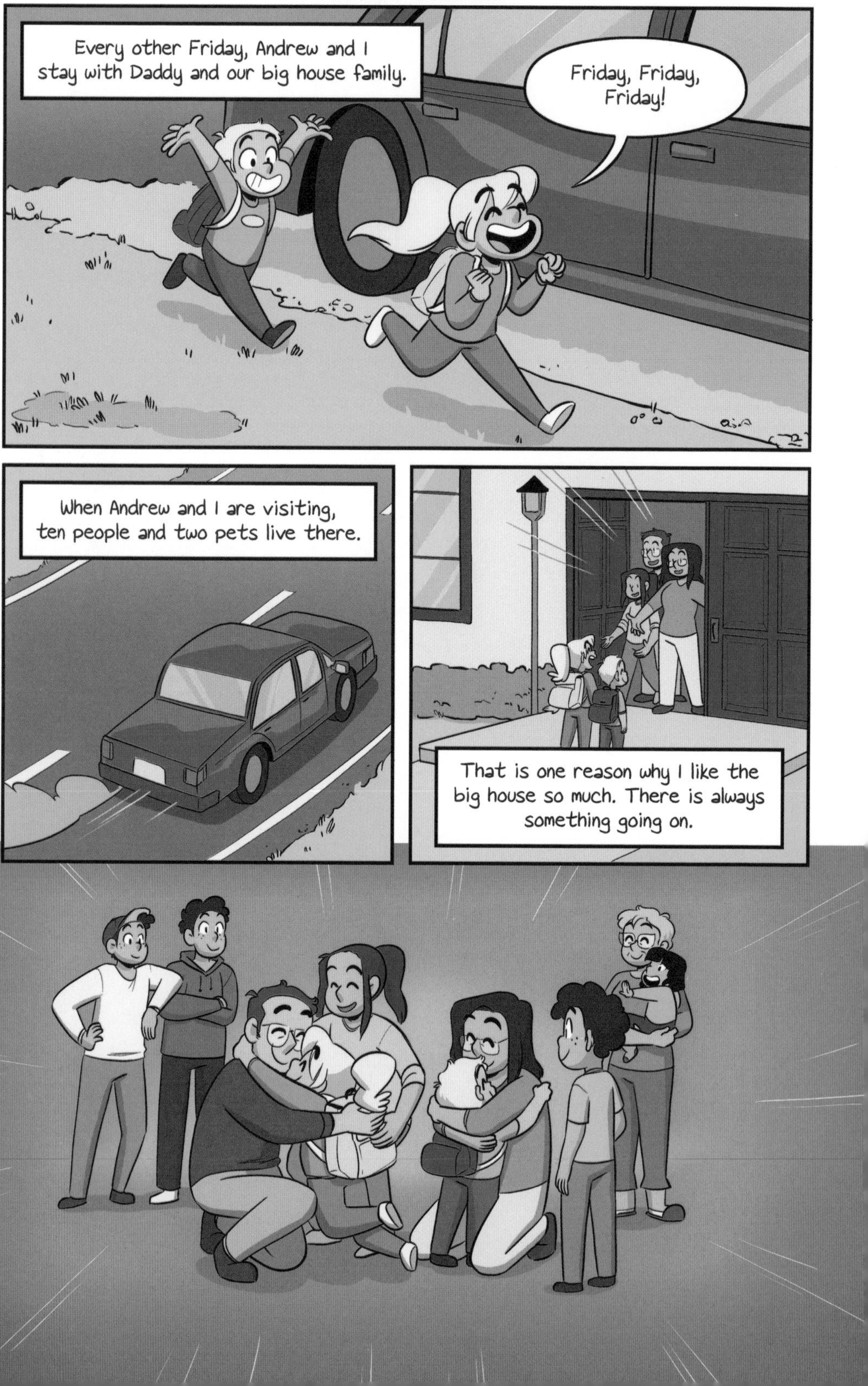
Every other Friday, Andrew and I stay with Daddy and our big house family.
Friday, Friday, Friday!
When Andrew and I are visiting, ten people and two pets live there.
That is one reason why I like the big house so much. There is always something going on.

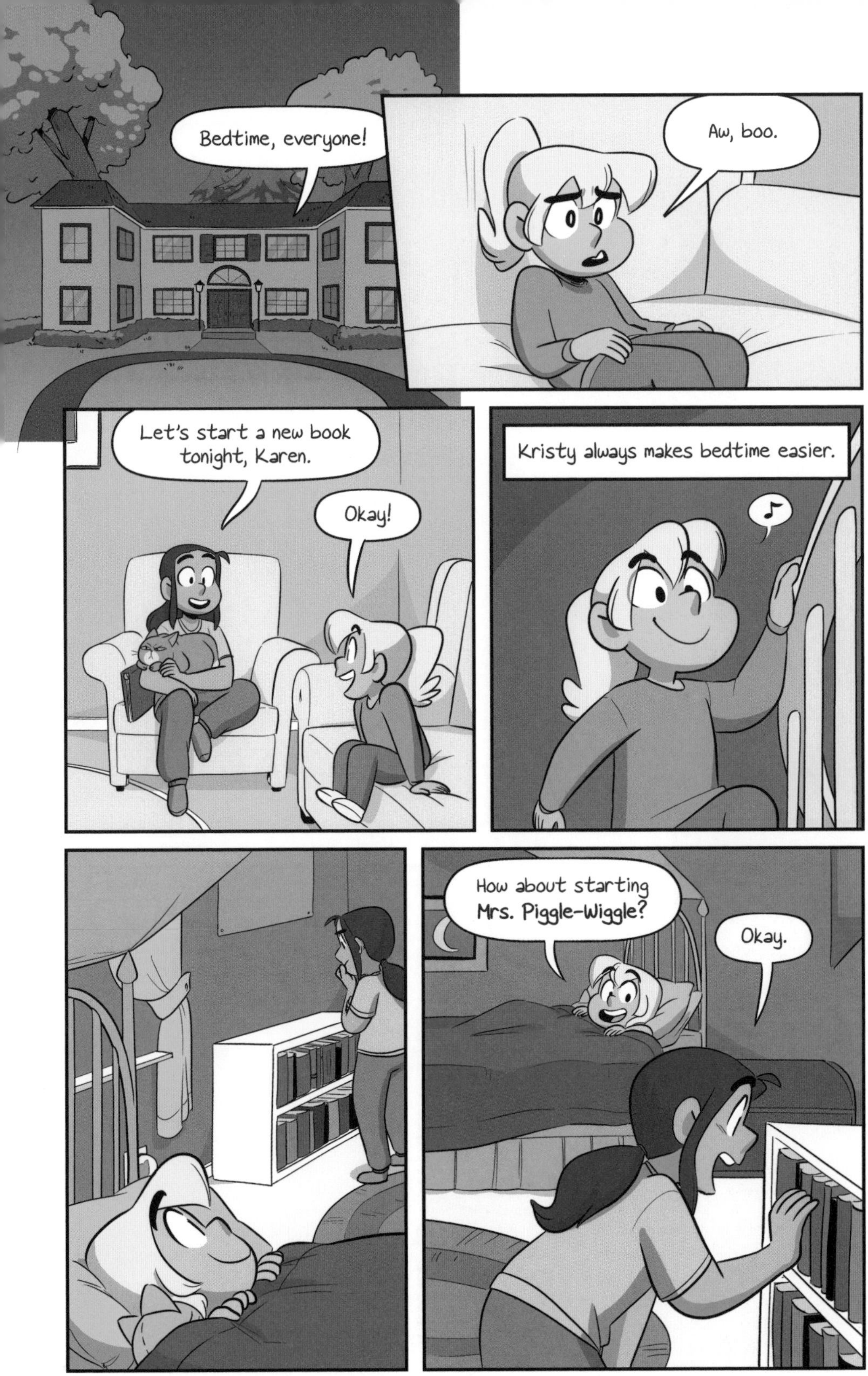

Bedtime, everyone!
Aw, boo.
Let's start a new book tonight, Karen.
Okay!
Kristy always makes bedtime easier.
♪
How about starting Mrs. Piggle-Wiggle?
Okay.

Do you want to read first?

Yeah.

...when they were

...just might sha...

Kristy, I can't read anymore. My eyes hurt. So does my head.

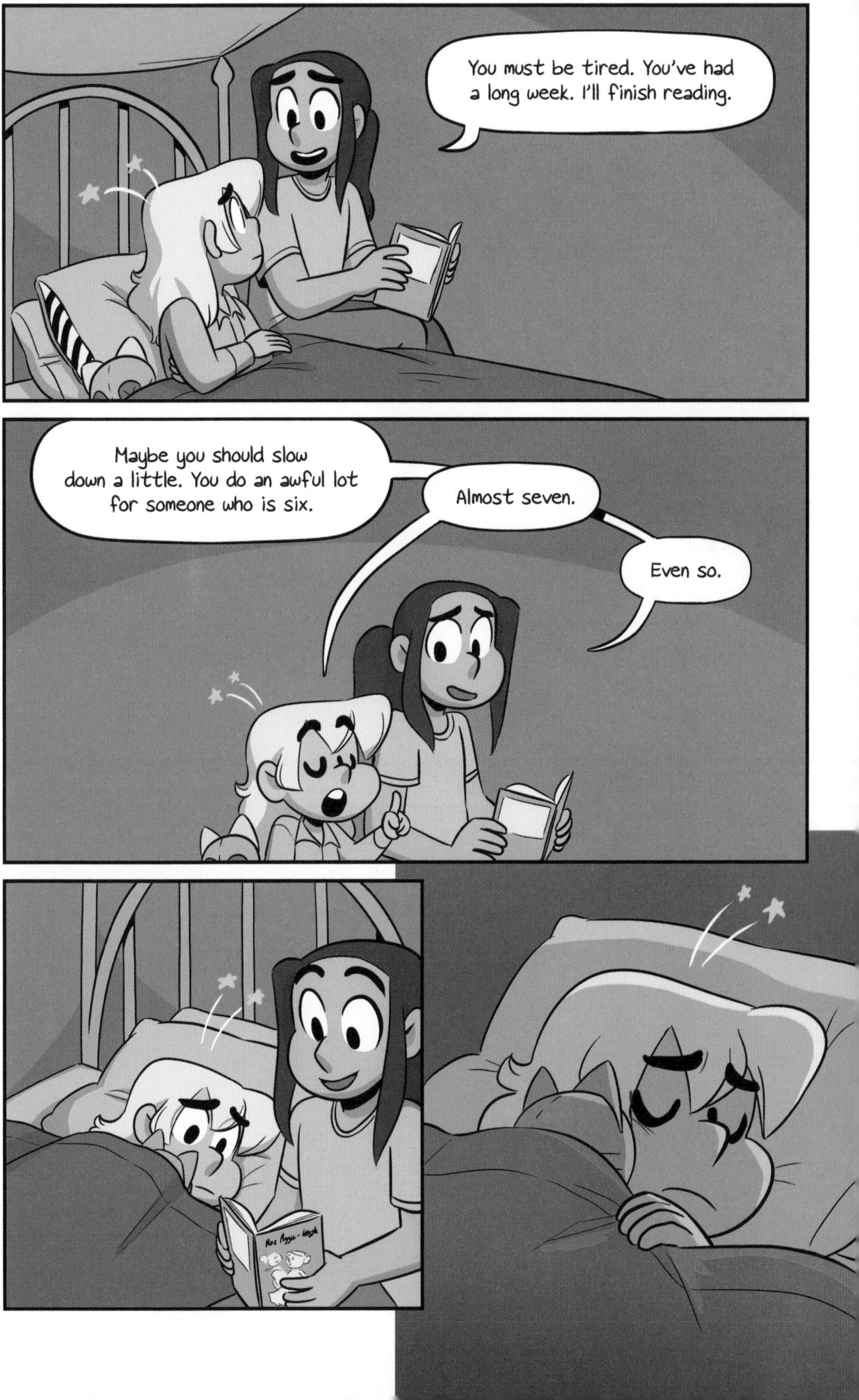
You must be tired. You've had a long week. I'll finish reading.
Maybe you should slow down a little. You do an awful lot for someone who is six.
Almost seven.
Even so.

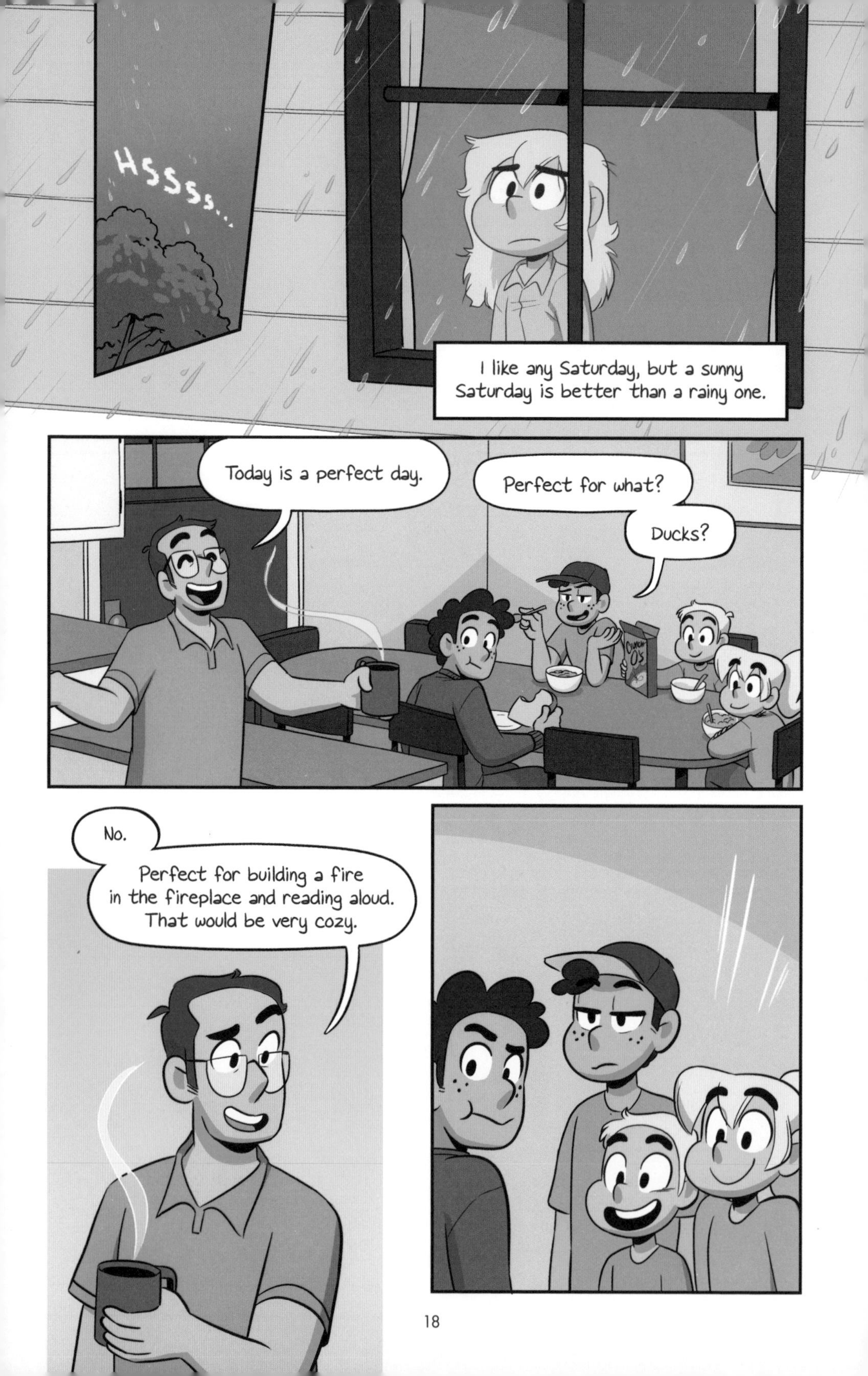
HSSSS...
I like any Saturday, but a sunny Saturday is better than a rainy one.
Today is a perfect day.
Perfect for what?
Ducks?
Crunch O's
No.
Perfect for building a fire in the fireplace and reading aloud. That would be very cozy.

What are we going to read?

A book called Mrs. Frisby and the Rats of NIMH.

We can take turns reading. I'll start. Then, anyone who wants to can take a turn.

When the other rats moved to the rose bush...

as she ran from the same as the have

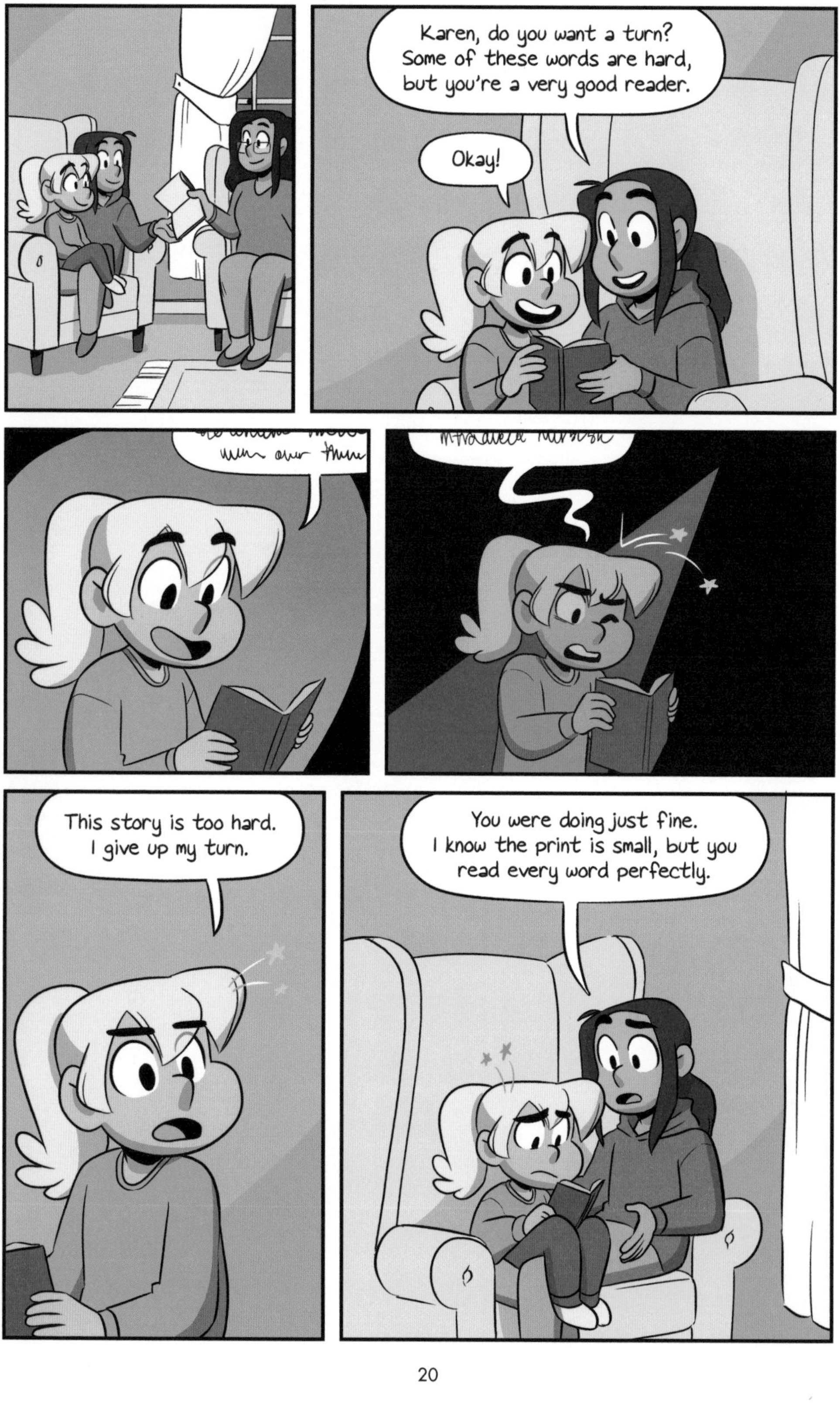
Karen, do you want a turn? Some of these words are hard, but you're a very good reader.
Okay!
This story is too hard. I give up my turn.
You were doing just fine. I know the print is small, but you read every word perfectly.

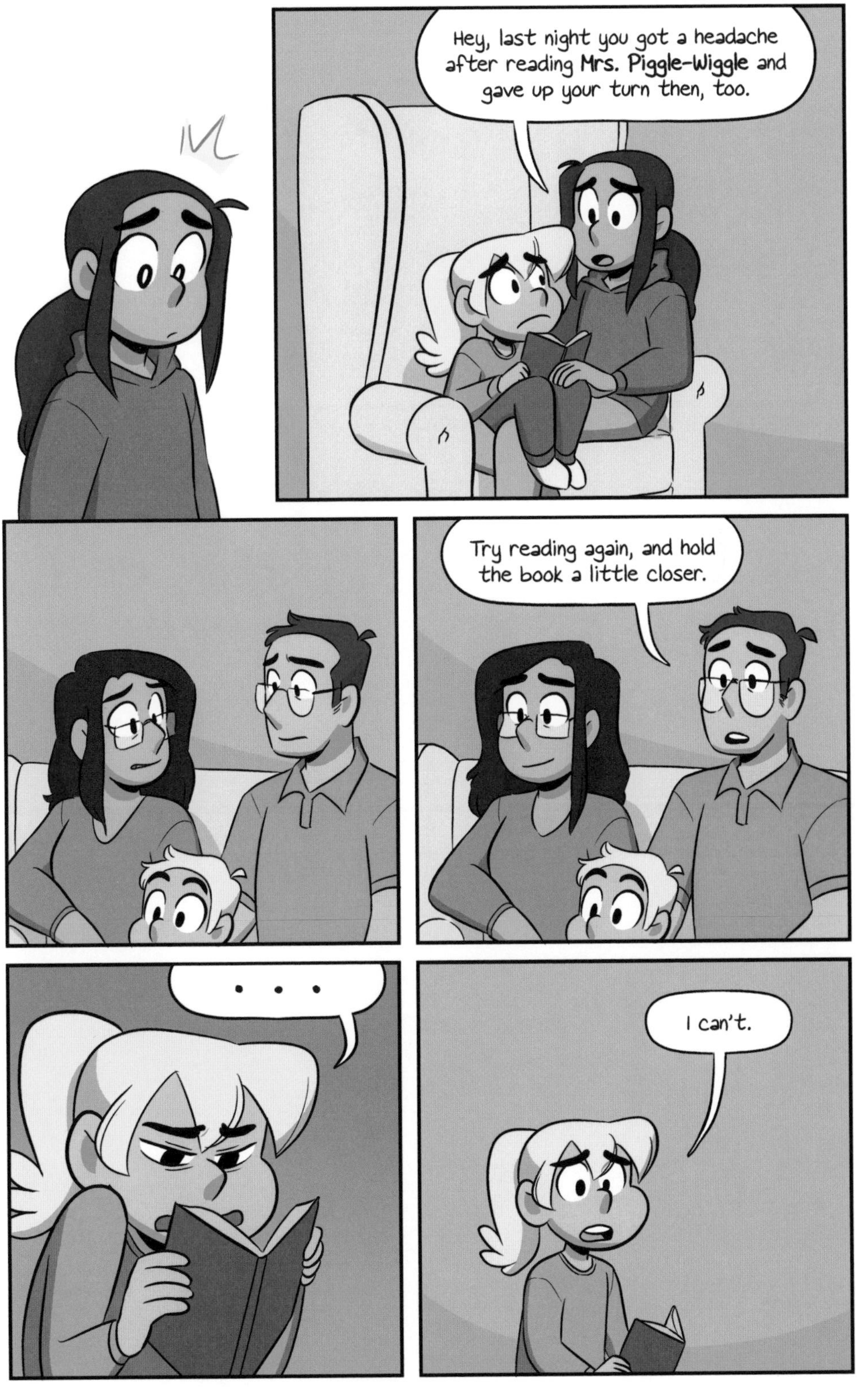
Hey, last night you got a headache after reading Mrs. Piggle-Wiggle and gave up your turn then, too.
Try reading again, and hold the book a little closer.
. . .
I can't.

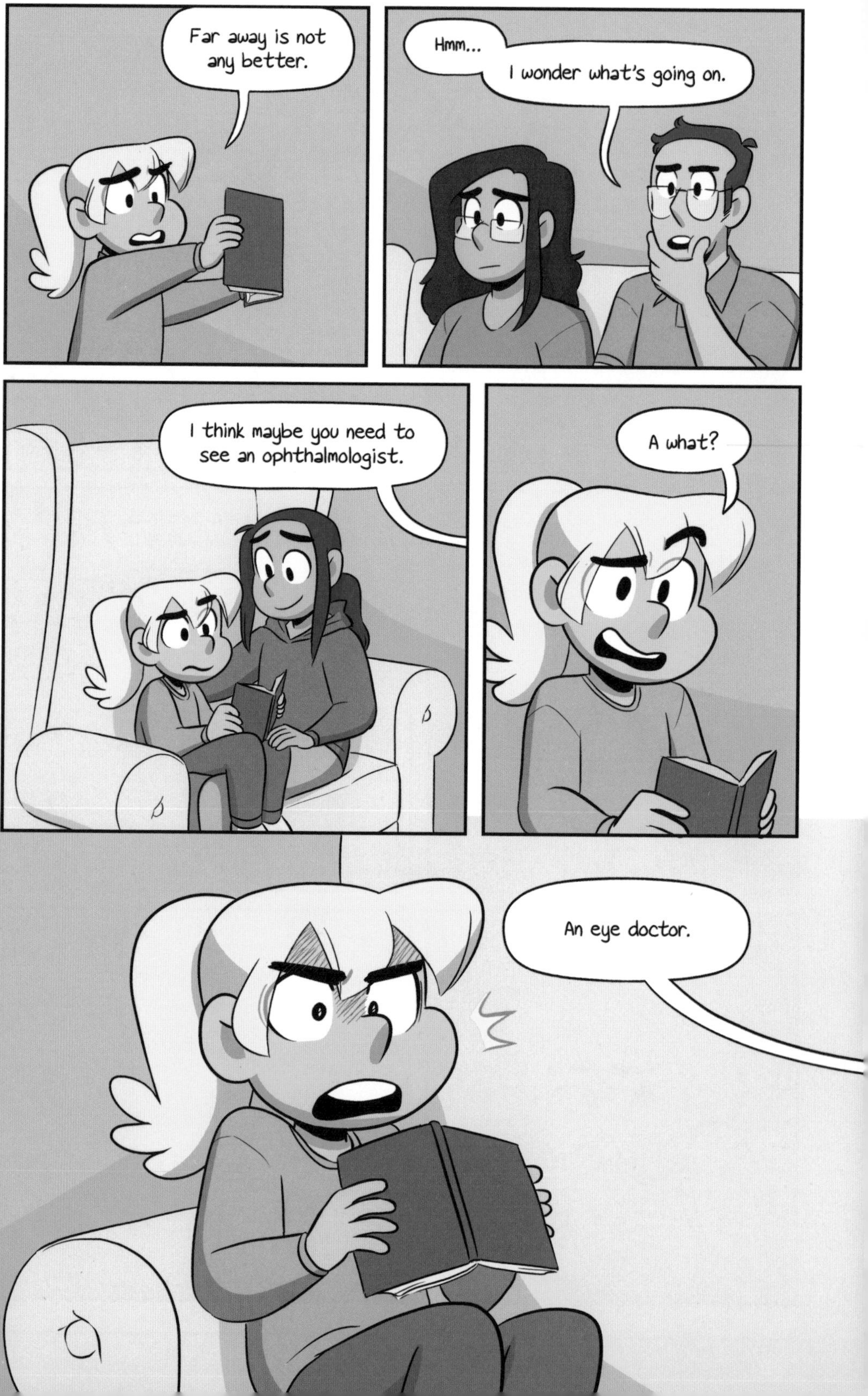
Far away is not any better.
Hmm...
I wonder what's going on.
I think maybe you need to see an ophthalmologist.
A what?
An eye doctor.

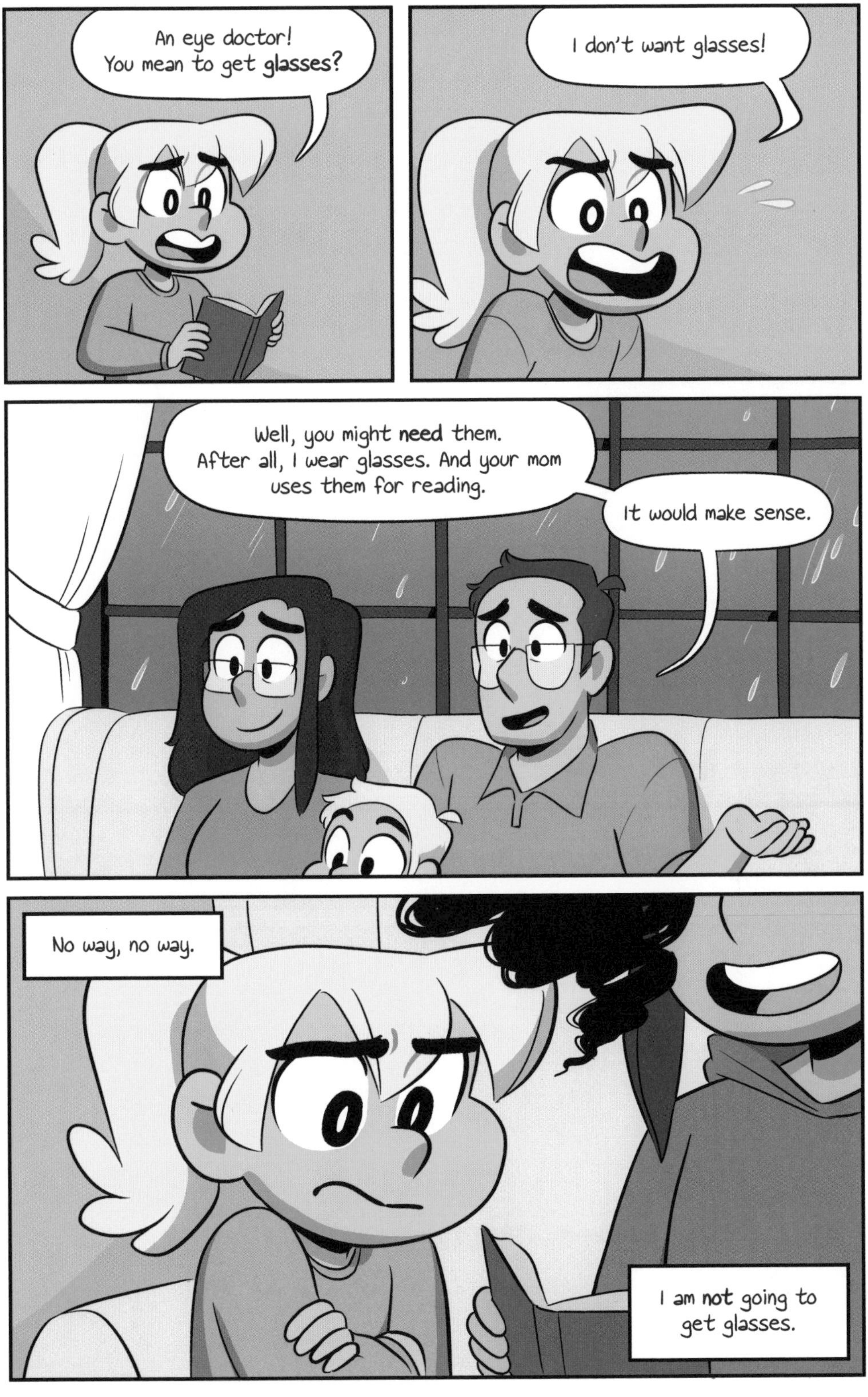
An eye doctor! You mean to get **glasses**?
I don't want glasses!
Well, you might **need** them. After all, I wear glasses. And your mom uses them for reading.
It would make sense.
No way, no way.
I am **not** going to get glasses.

CHAPTER 3

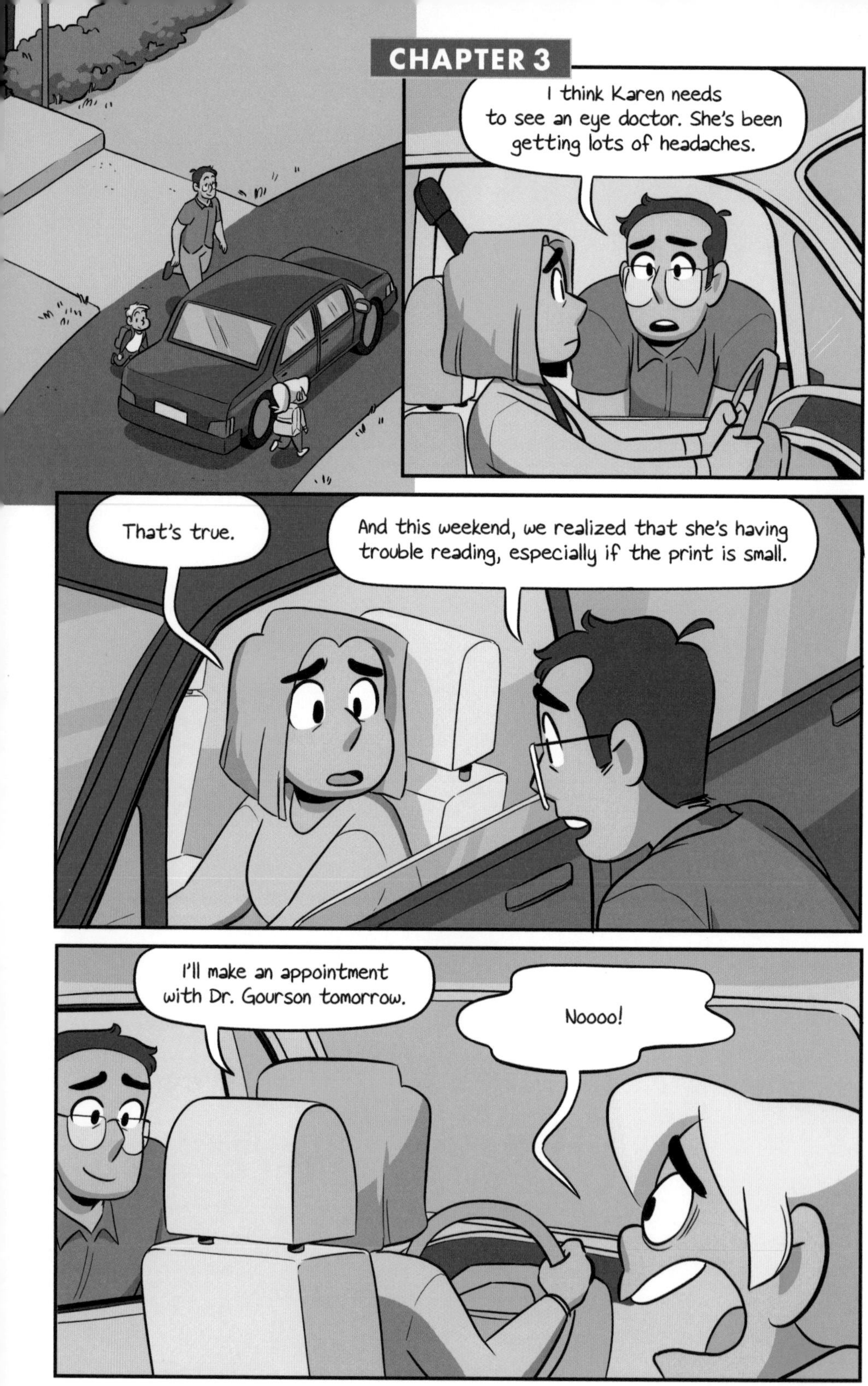
I think Karen needs to see an eye doctor. She's been getting lots of headaches.
That's true.
And this weekend, we realized that she's having trouble reading, especially if the print is small.
I'll make an appointment with Dr. Gourson tomorrow.
Noooo!

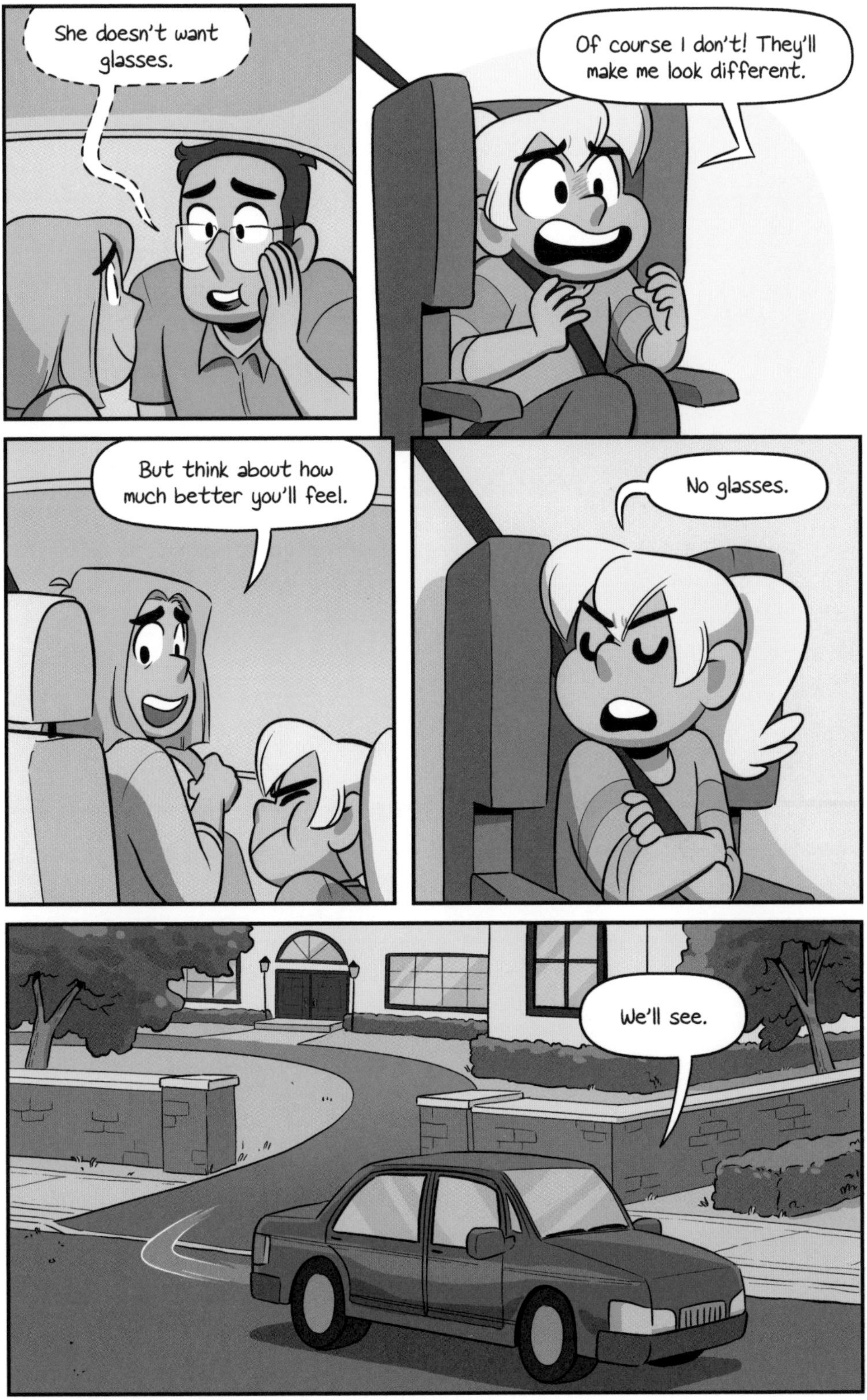
She doesn't want glasses.
Of course I don't! They'll make me look different.
But think about how much better you'll feel.
No glasses.
We'll see.

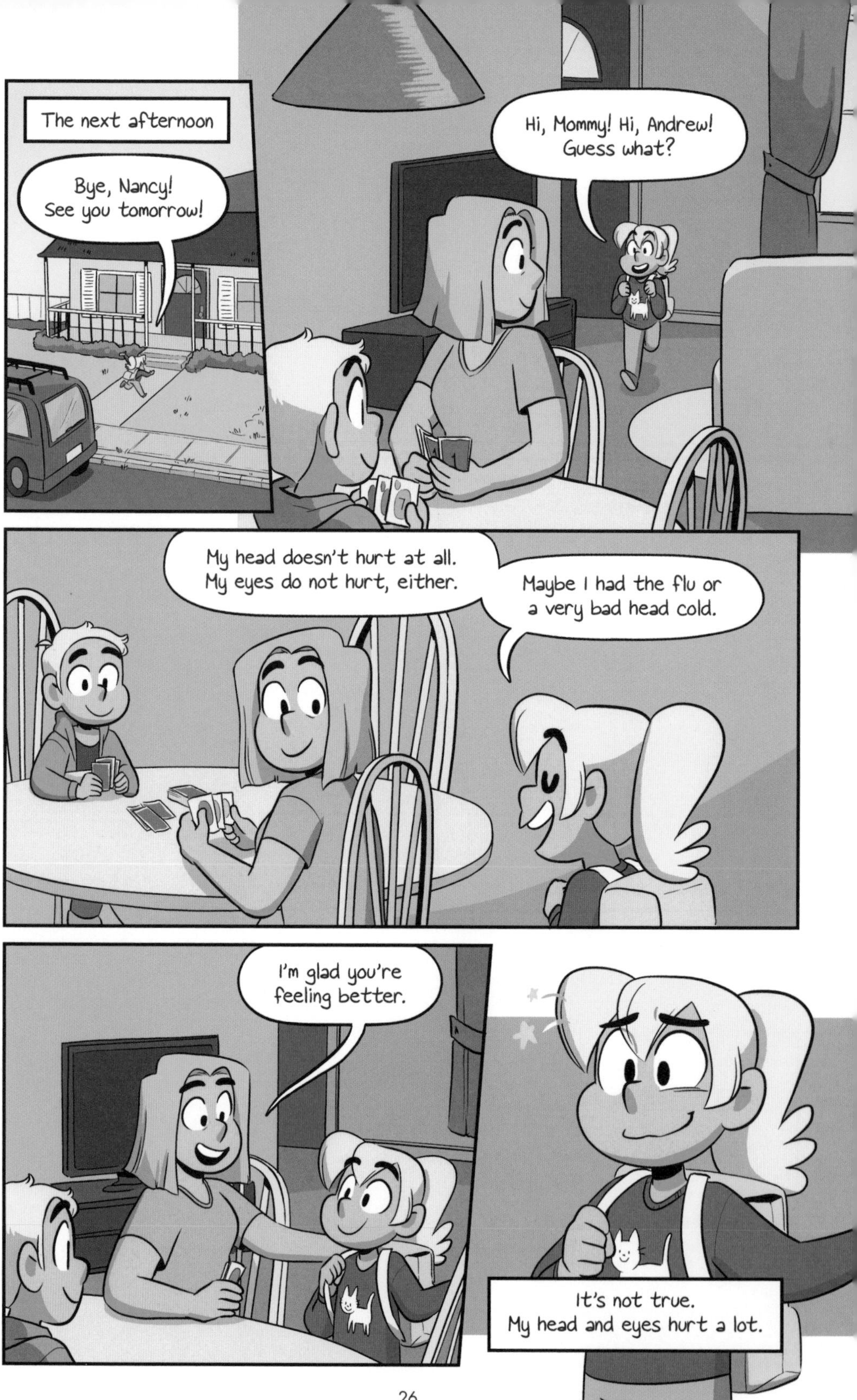
The next afternoon
Bye, Nancy! See you tomorrow!
Hi, Mommy! Hi, Andrew! Guess what?
My head doesn't hurt at all. My eyes do not hurt, either.
Maybe I had the flu or a very bad head cold.
I'm glad you're feeling better.
It's not true. My head and eyes hurt a lot.

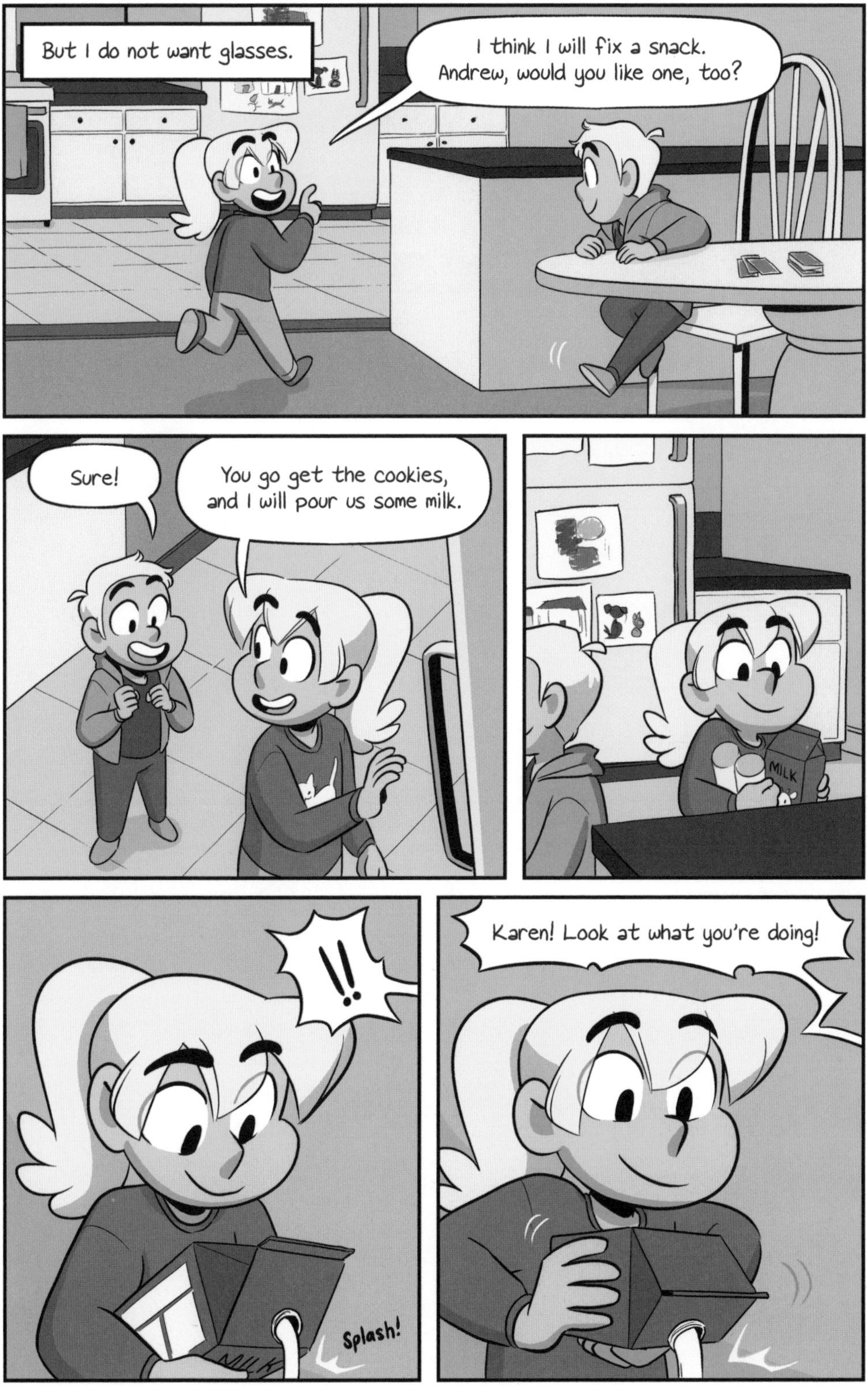
But I do not want glasses.
I think I will fix a snack. Andrew, would you like one, too?
Sure!
You go get the cookies, and I will pour us some milk.
MILK
!!
MILK
Splash!
Karen! Look at what you're doing!

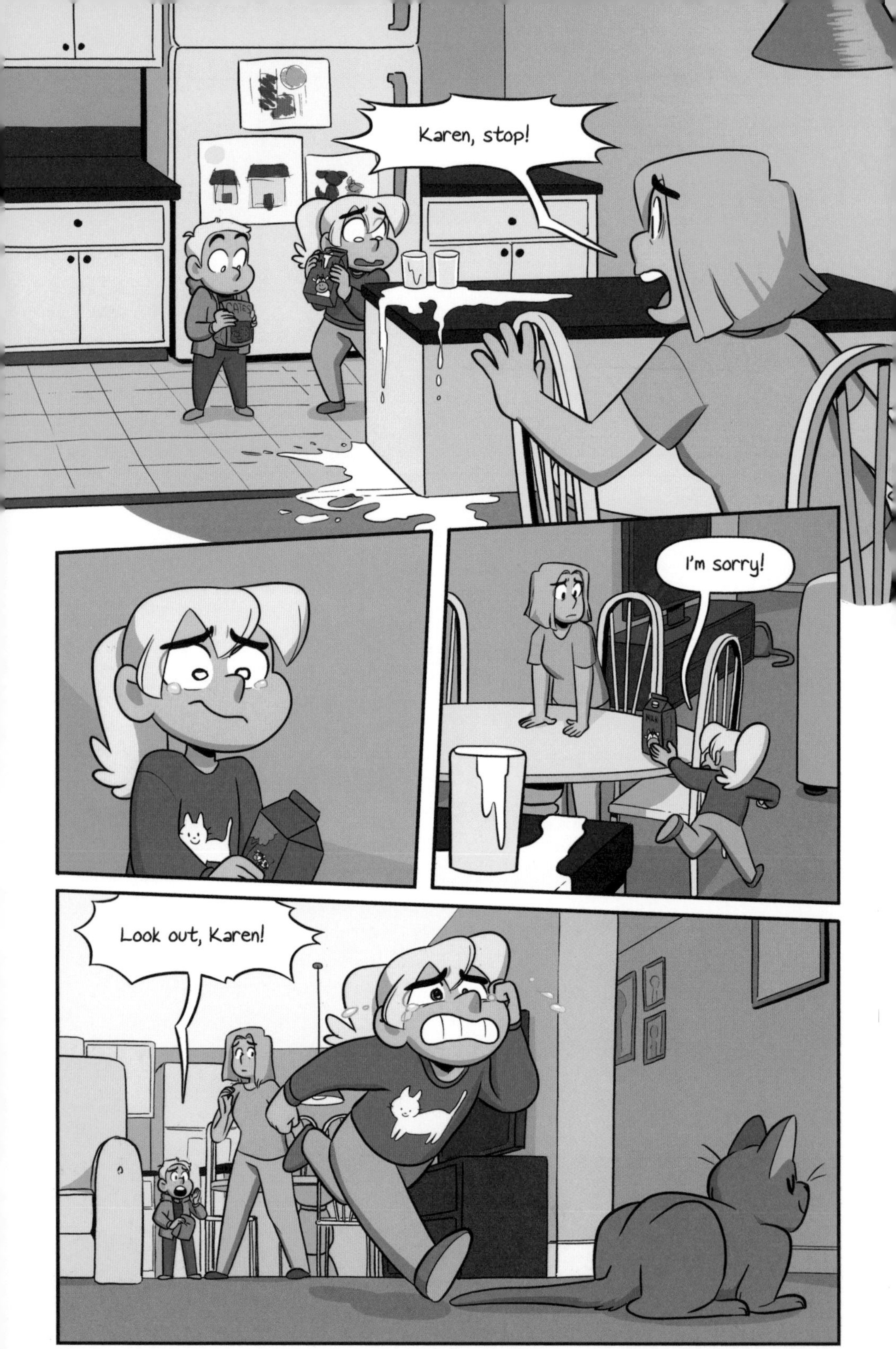
Karen, stop!
I'm sorry!
Look out, Karen!

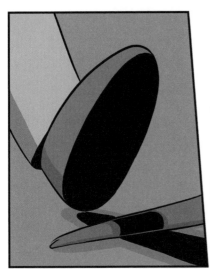

MREOW!

Rocky, oh no! I'm sorry!

SOB SOB SOB

I feel awful.

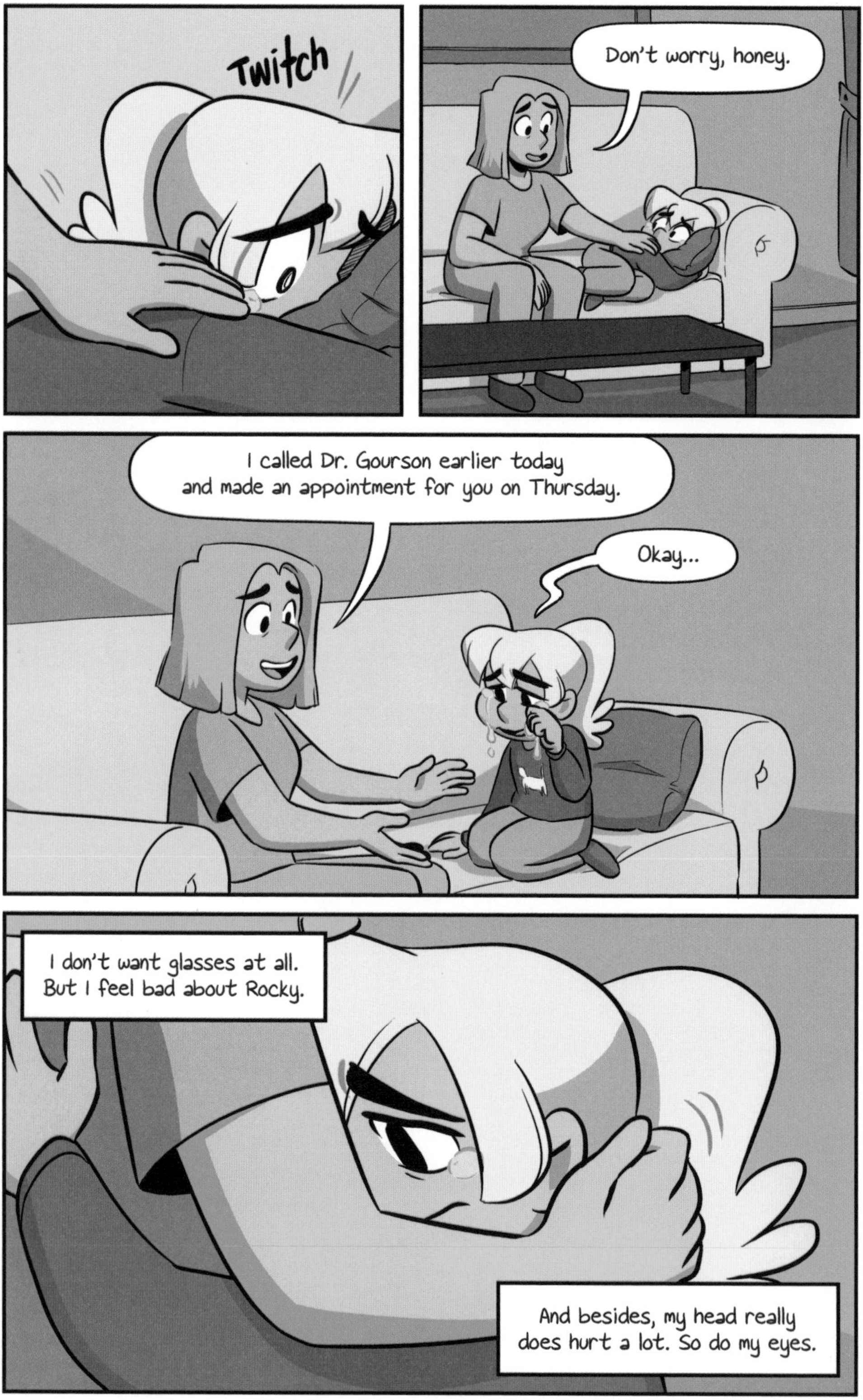
Twitch
Don't worry, honey.
I called Dr. Gourson earlier today and made an appointment for you on Thursday.
Okay...
I don't want glasses at all. But I feel bad about Rocky.
And besides, my head really does hurt a lot. So do my eyes.

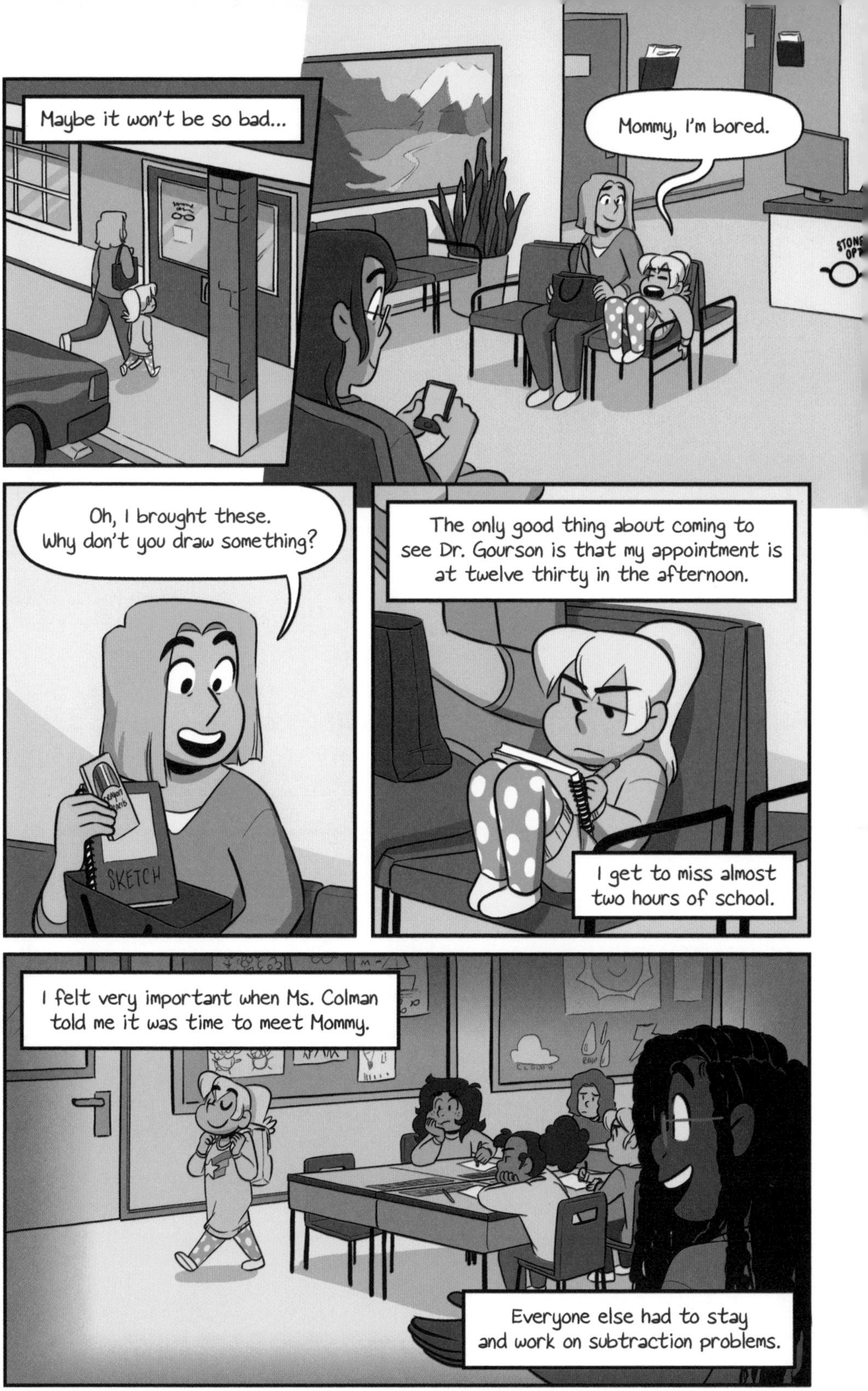

Maybe it won't be so bad...
Mommy, I'm bored.
Oh, I brought these. Why don't you draw something?
SKETCH
The only good thing about coming to see Dr. Gourson is that my appointment is at twelve thirty in the afternoon.
I get to miss almost two hours of school.
I felt very important when Ms. Colman told me it was time to meet Mommy.
Everyone else had to stay and work on subtraction problems.

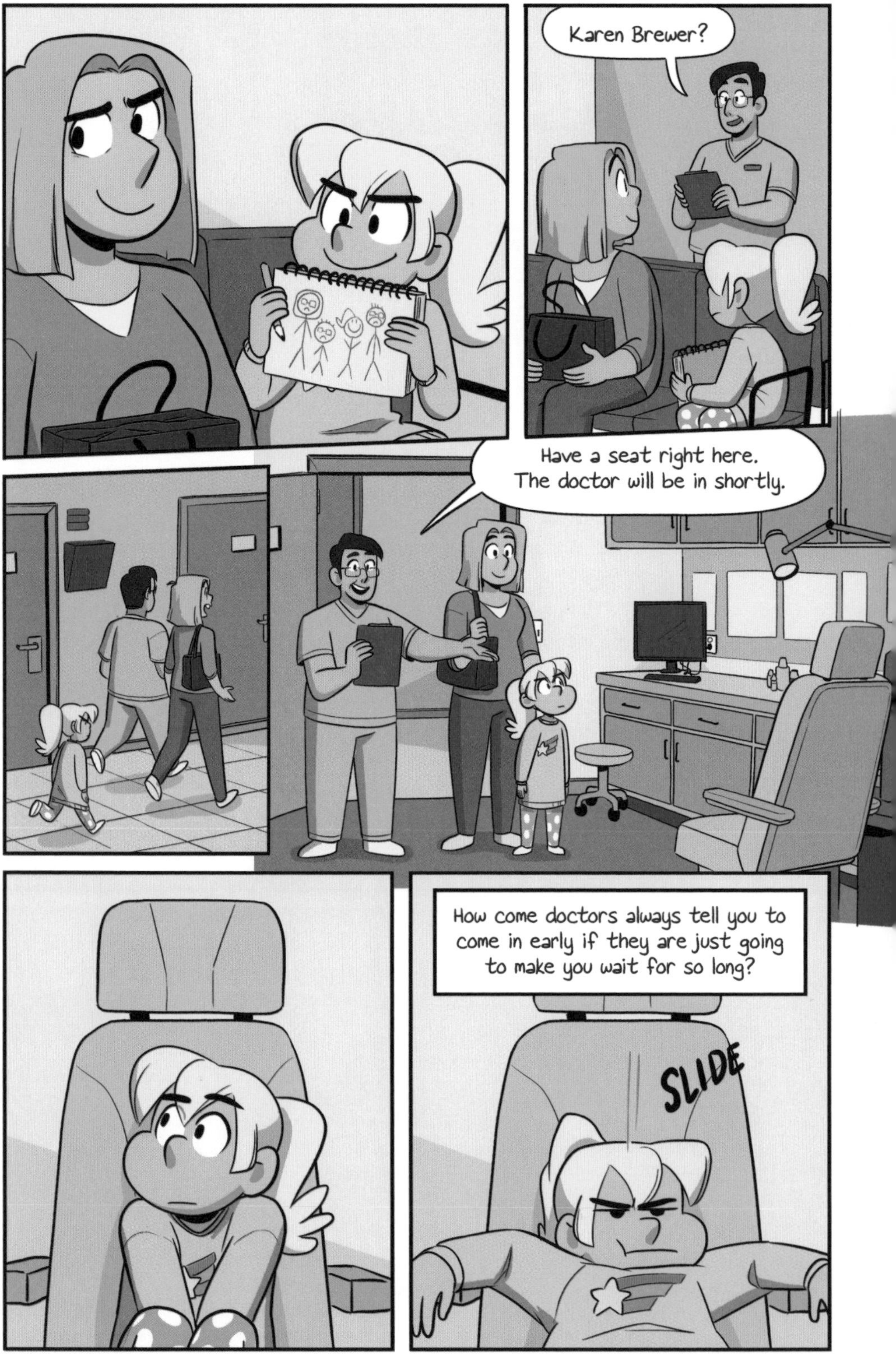
Karen Brewer?
Have a seat right here.
The doctor will be in shortly.
How come doctors always tell you to come in early if they are just going to make you wait for so long?
SLIDE

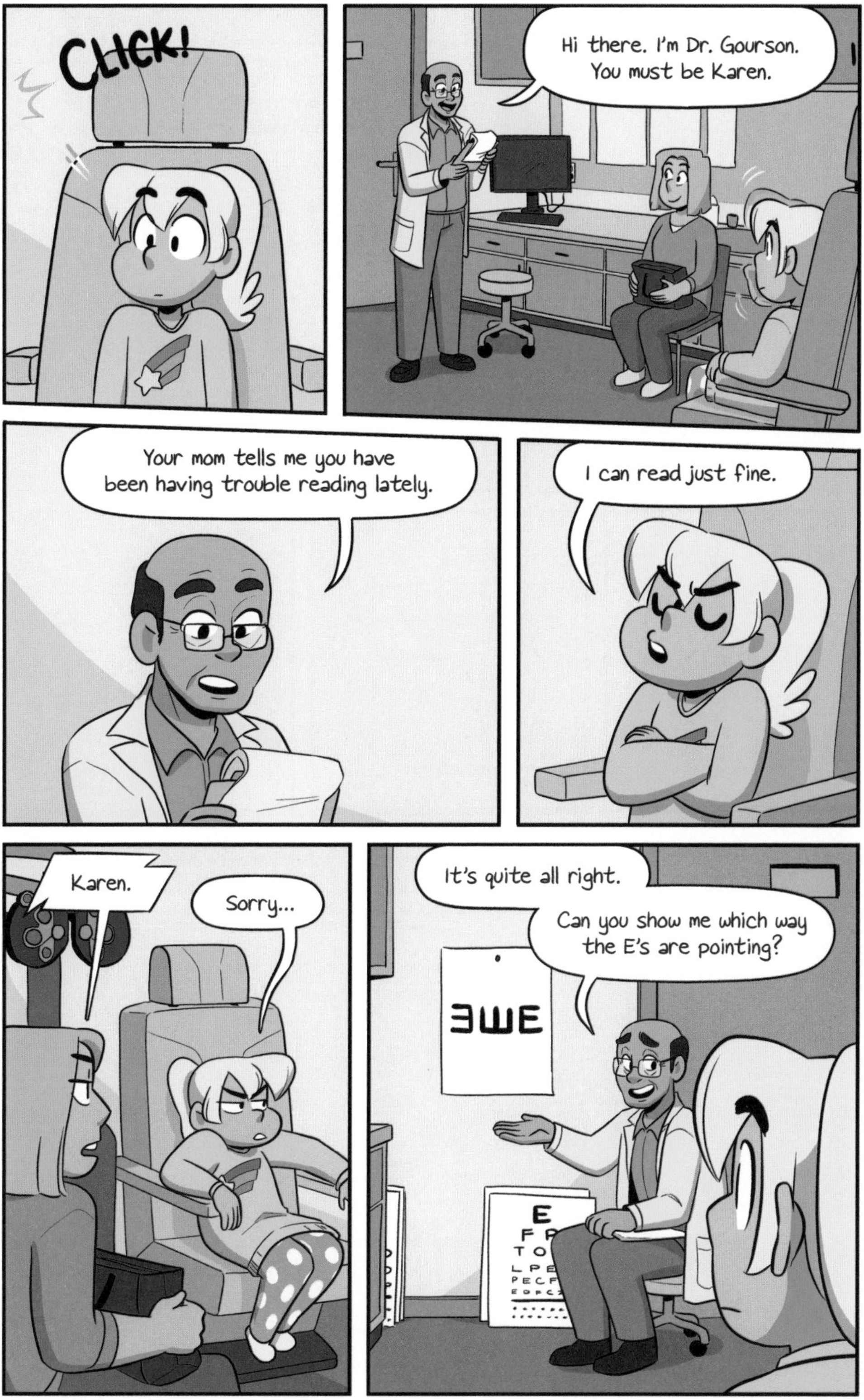
CLICK!
Hi there. I'm Dr. Gourson. You must be Karen.
Your mom tells me you have been having trouble reading lately.
I can read just fine.
Karen.
Sorry...
It's quite all right.
Can you show me which way the E's are pointing?

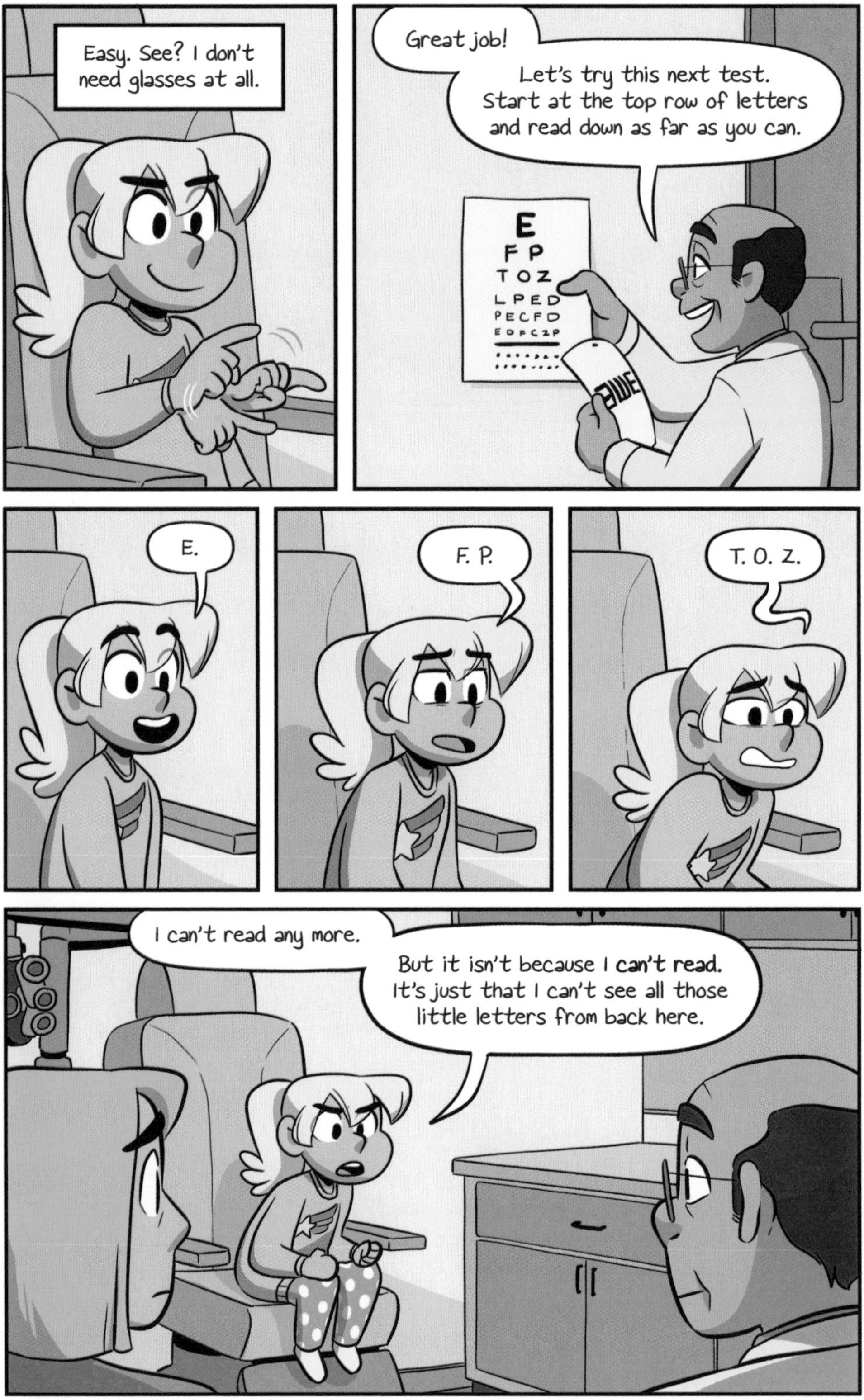

Easy. See? I don't need glasses at all.
Great job!
Let's try this next test. Start at the top row of letters and read down as far as you can.
E
F P
T O Z
L P E D
P E C F D
E D F C Z P
E.
F. P.
T. O. Z.
I can't read any more.
But it isn't because I **can't read.** It's just that I can't see all those little letters from back here.

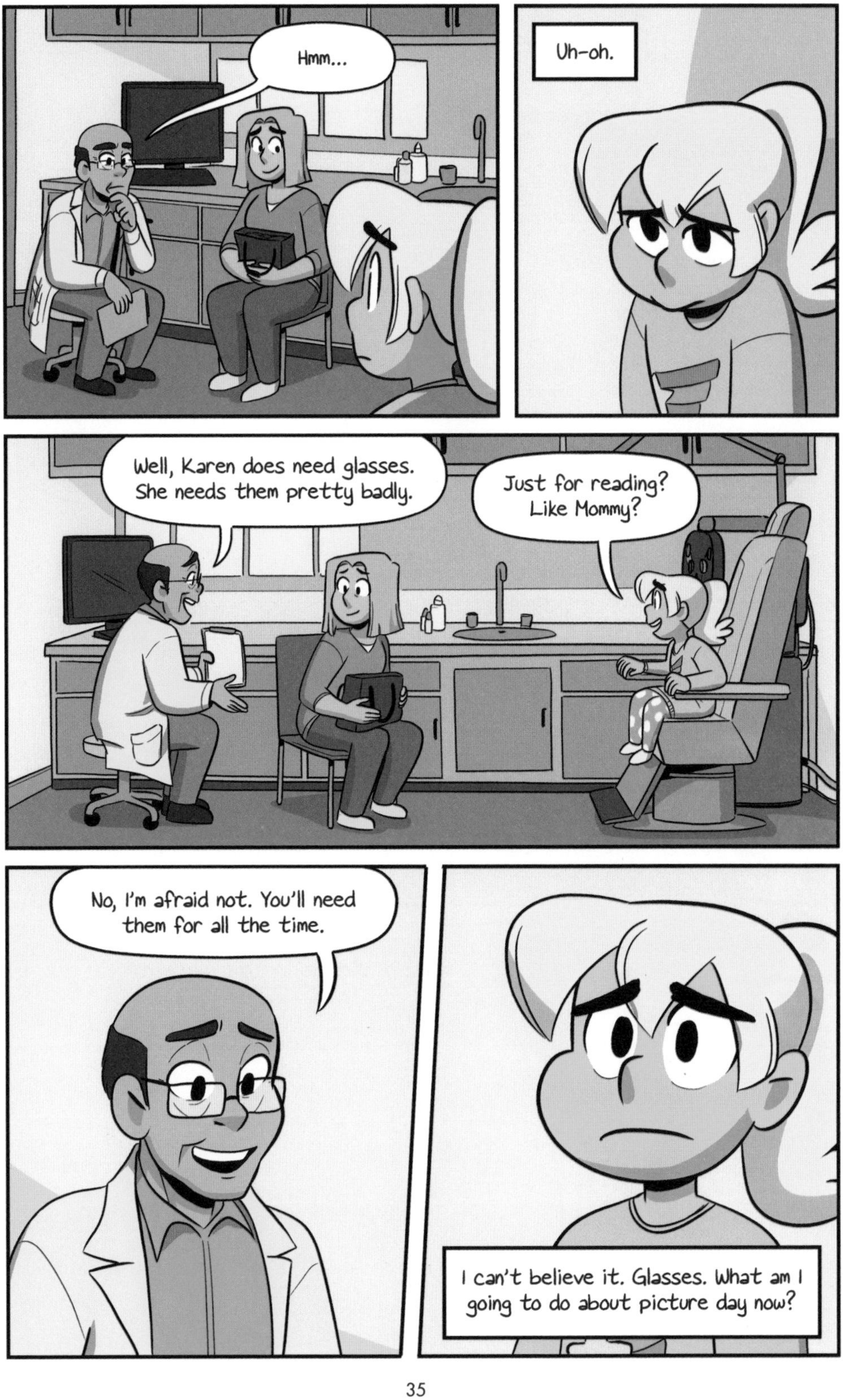
Hmm...
Uh-oh.
Well, Karen does need glasses. She needs them pretty badly.
Just for reading? Like Mommy?
No, I'm afraid not. You'll need them for all the time.
I can't believe it. Glasses. What am I going to do about picture day now?

CHAPTER 4

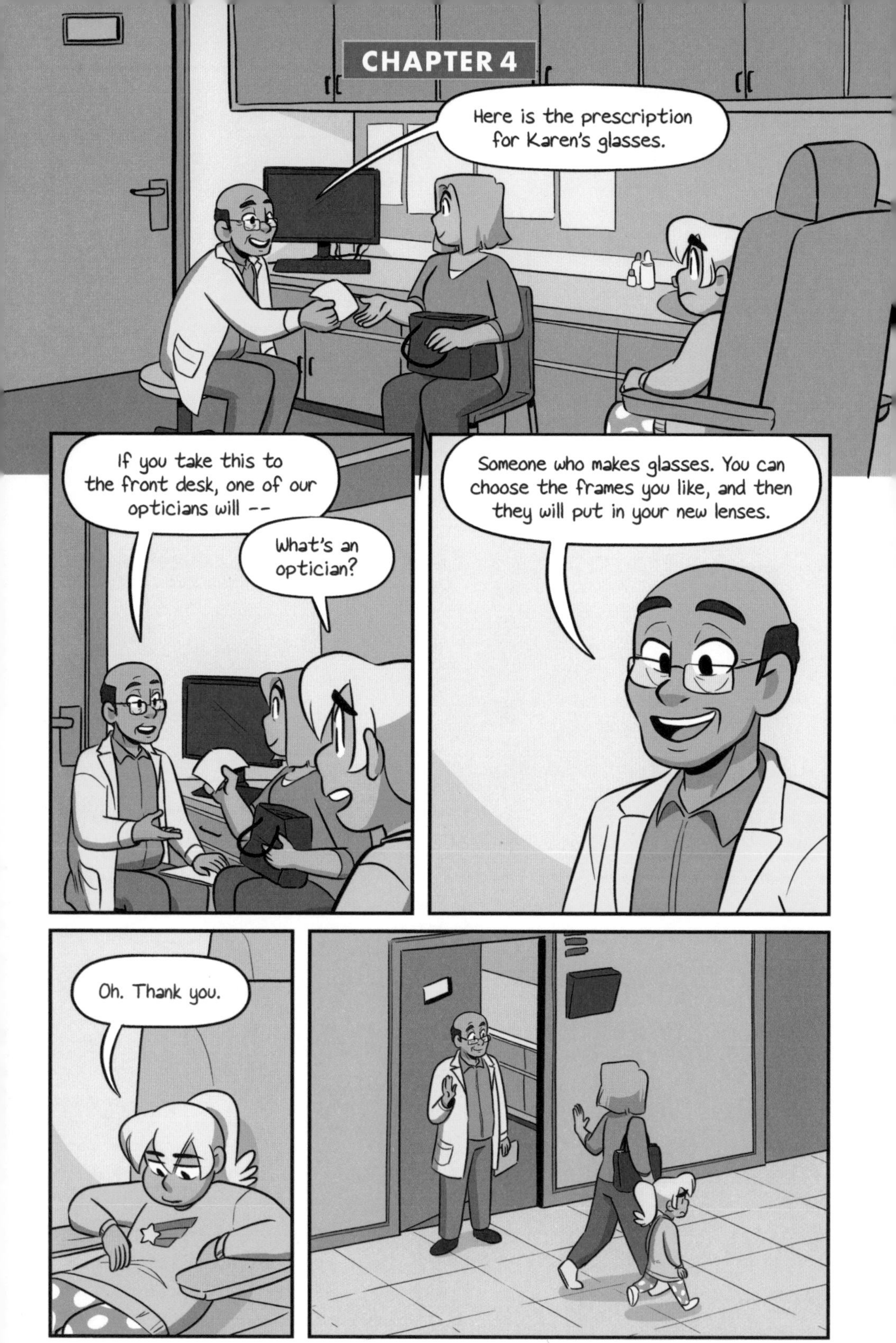
Here is the prescription for Karen's glasses.
If you take this to the front desk, one of our opticians will --
What's an optician?
Someone who makes glasses. You can choose the frames you like, and then they will put in your new lenses.
Oh. Thank you.

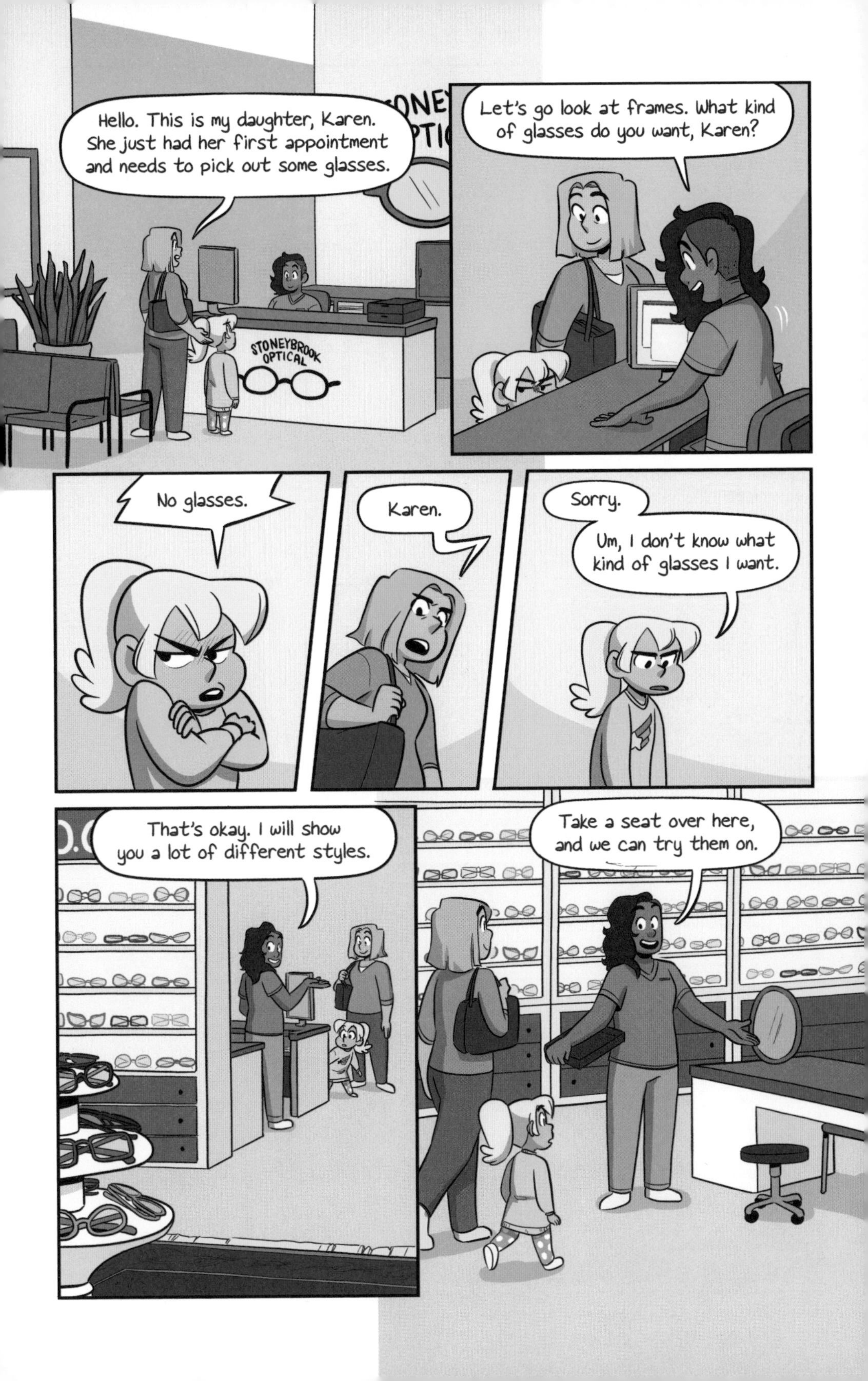
Hello. This is my daughter, Karen. She just had her first appointment and needs to pick out some glasses.
STONEYBROOK OPTICAL
Let's go look at frames. What kind of glasses do you want, Karen?
No glasses.
Karen.
Sorry.
Um, I don't know what kind of glasses I want.
That's okay. I will show you a lot of different styles.
Take a seat over here, and we can try them on.

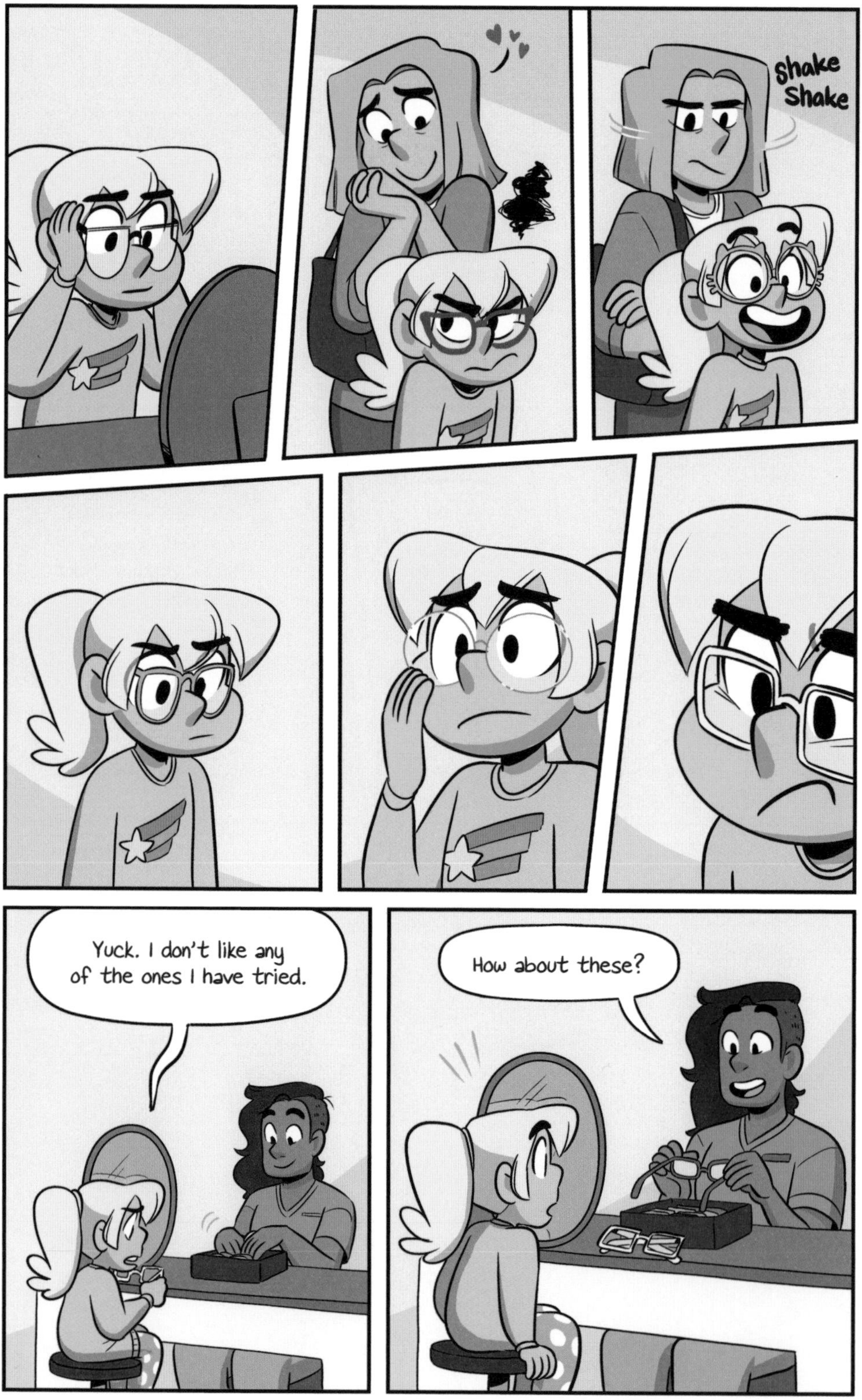
Shake Shake
Yuck. I don't like any of the ones I have tried.
How about these?

Pink! I can have pink glasses?!

I'll take them!

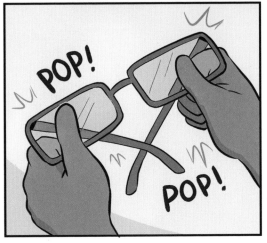

POP!

POP!

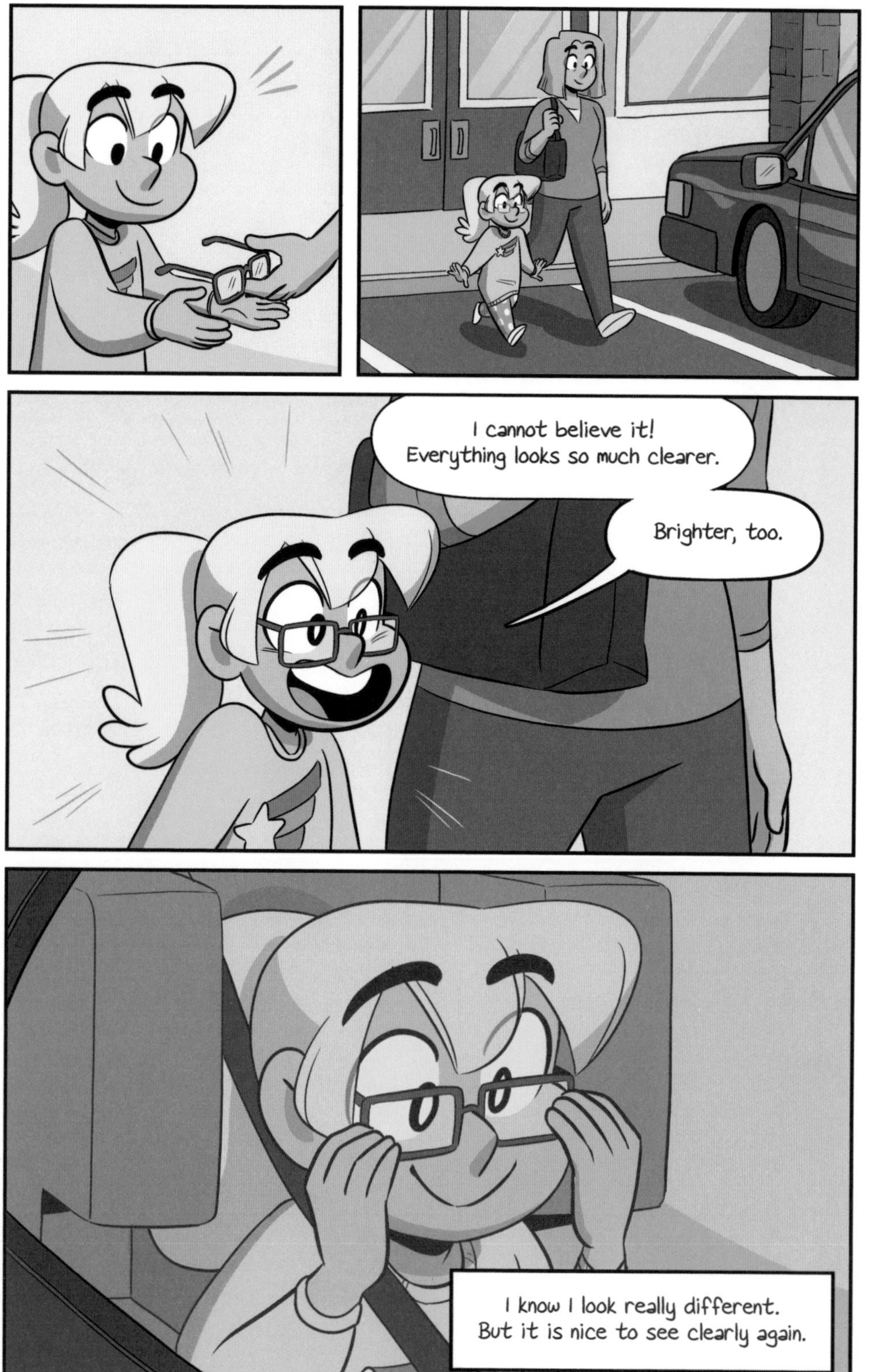
I cannot believe it!
Everything looks so much clearer.
Brighter, too.
I know I look really different.
But it is nice to see clearly again.

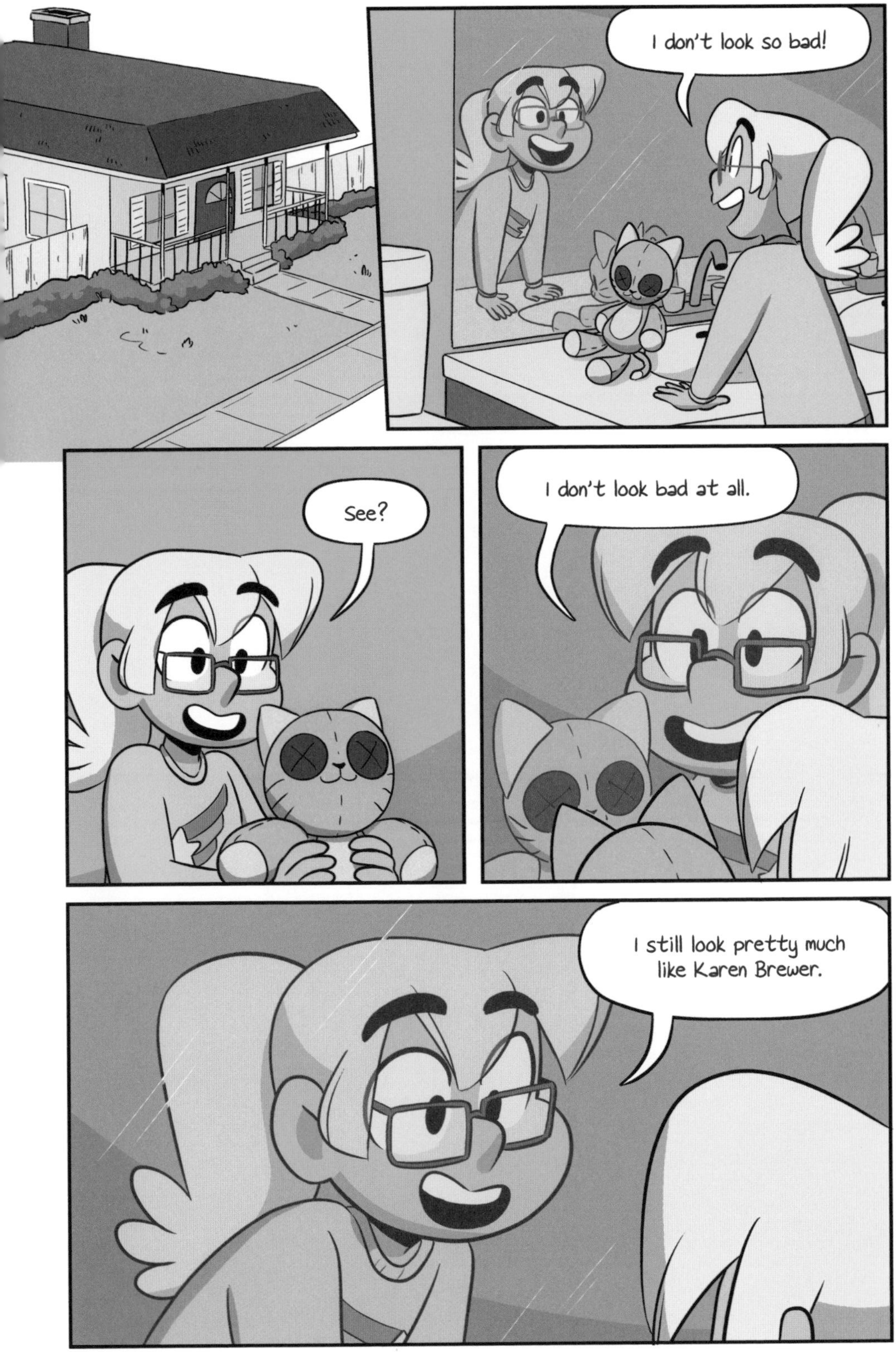
I don't look so bad!
See?
I don't look bad at all.
I still look pretty much like Karen Brewer.

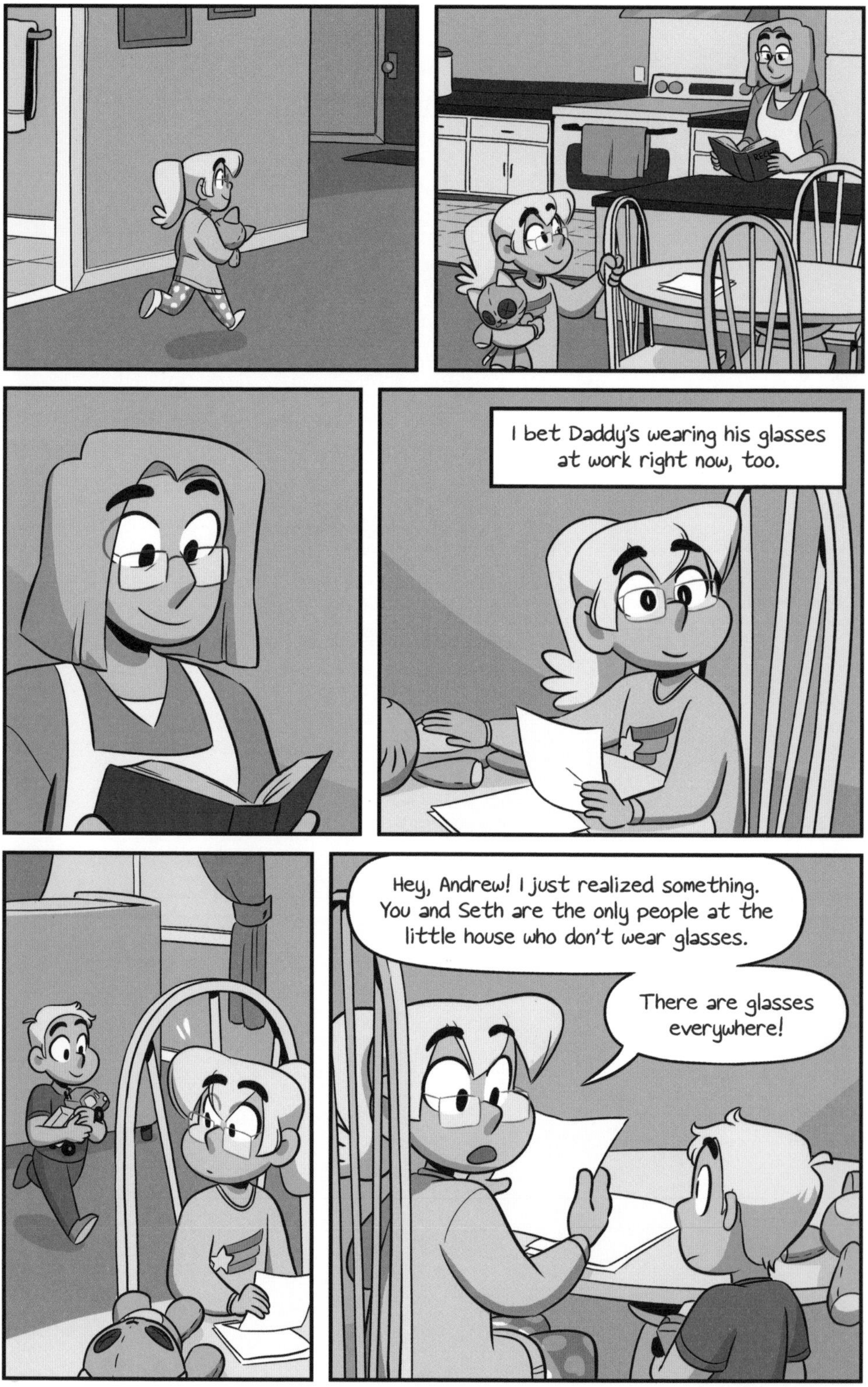

REGARD
I bet Daddy's wearing his glasses at work right now, too.
Hey, Andrew! I just realized something. You and Seth are the only people at the little house who don't wear glasses.
There are glasses everywhere!

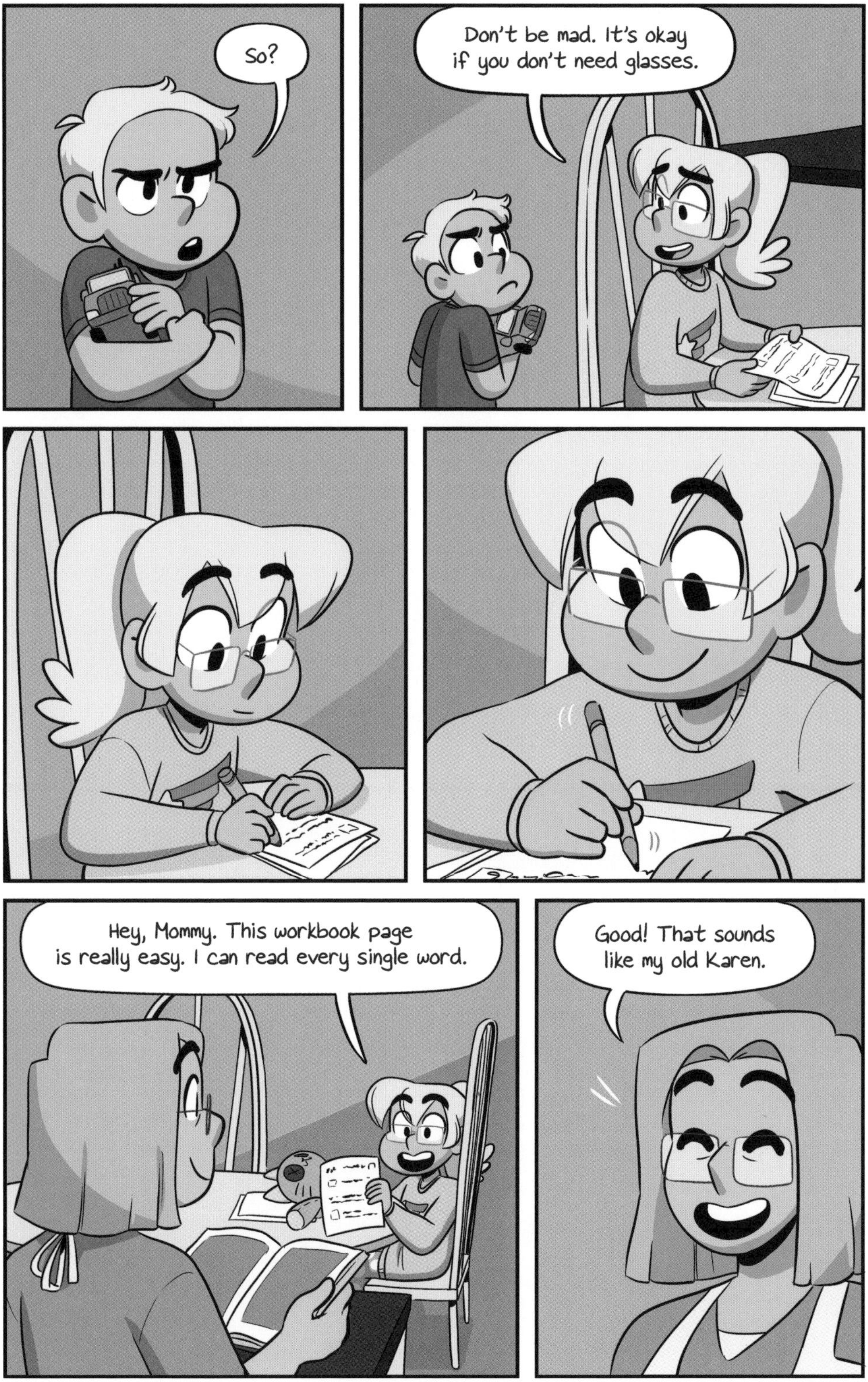
So?
Don't be mad. It's okay if you don't need glasses.
Hey, Mommy. This workbook page is really easy. I can read every single word.
Good! That sounds like my old Karen.

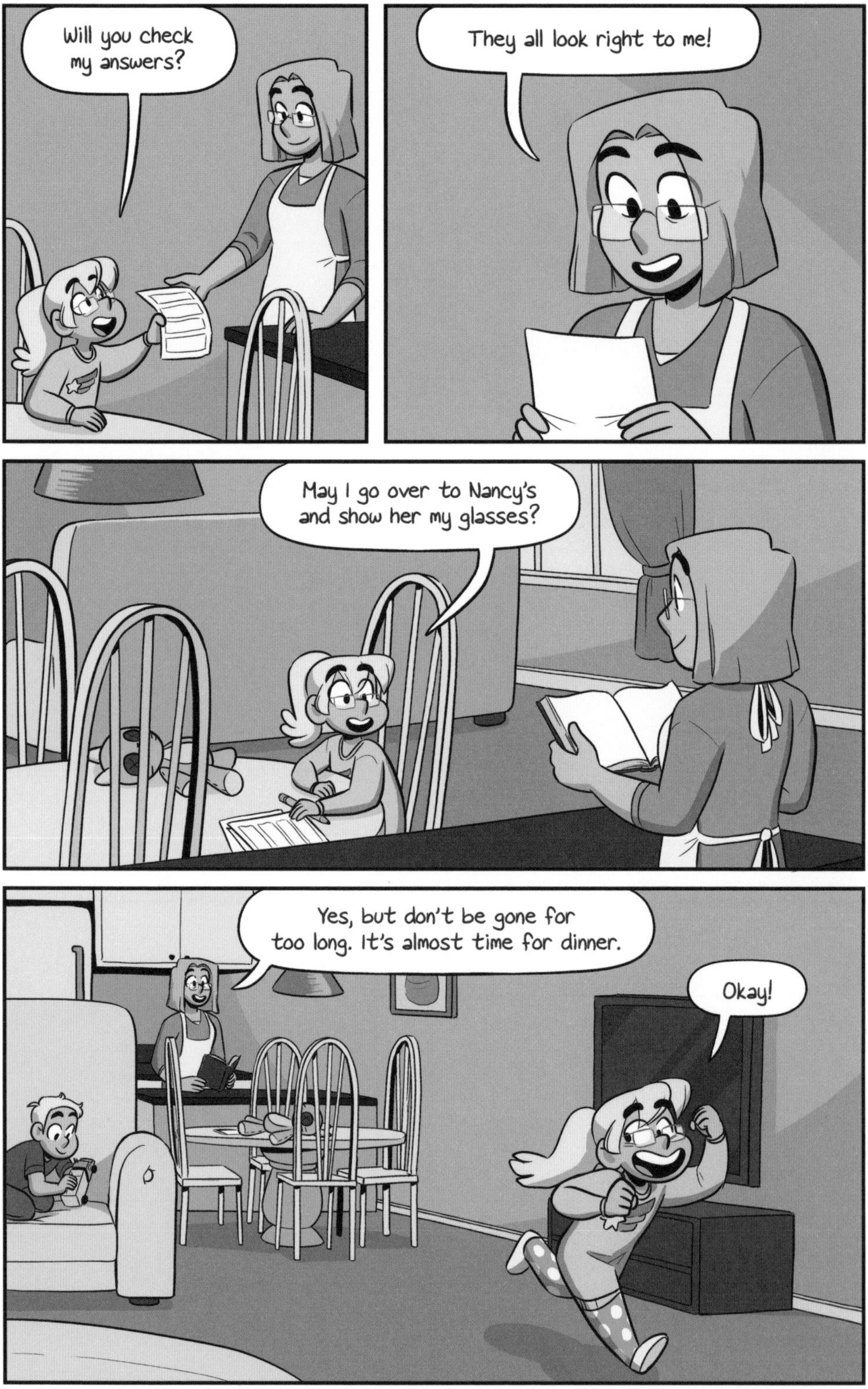
Will you check my answers?
They all look right to me!
May I go over to Nancy's and show her my glasses?
Yes, but don't be gone for too long. It's almost time for dinner.
Okay!

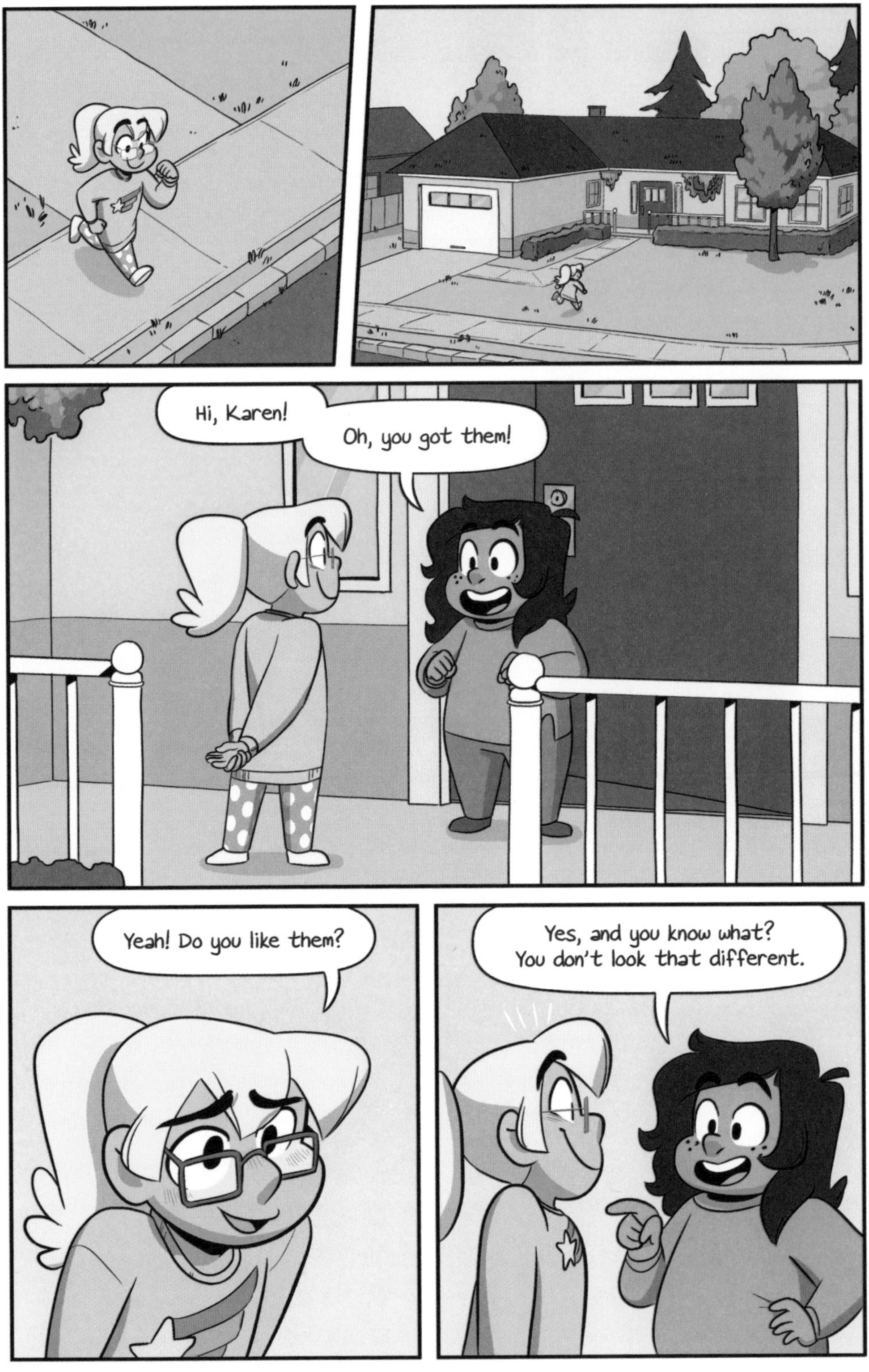
Hi, Karen!
Oh, you got them!
Yeah! Do you like them?
Yes, and you know what? You don't look that different.

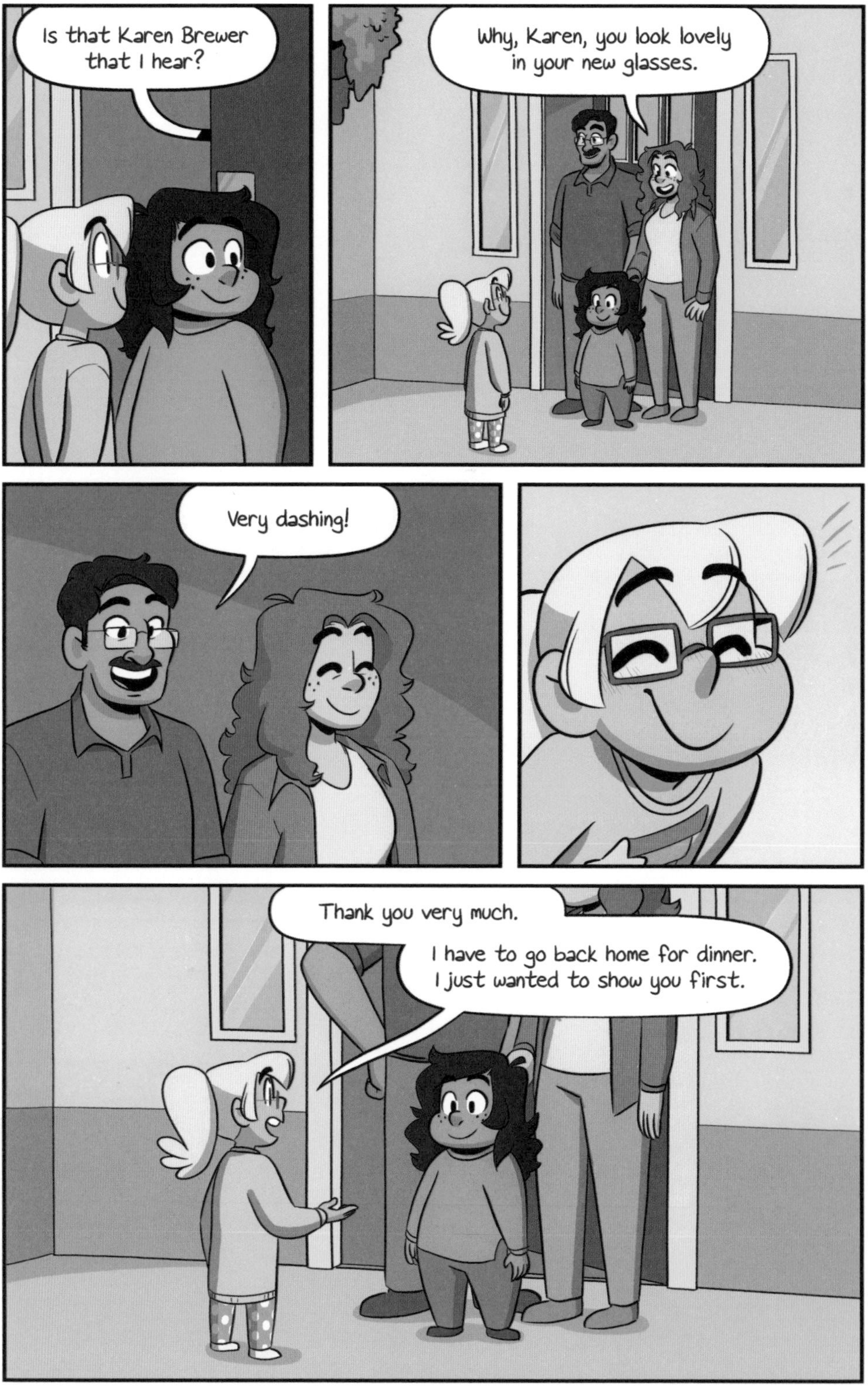
Is that Karen Brewer that I hear?
Why, Karen, you look lovely in your new glasses.
Very dashing!
Thank you very much.
I have to go back home for dinner. I just wanted to show you first.

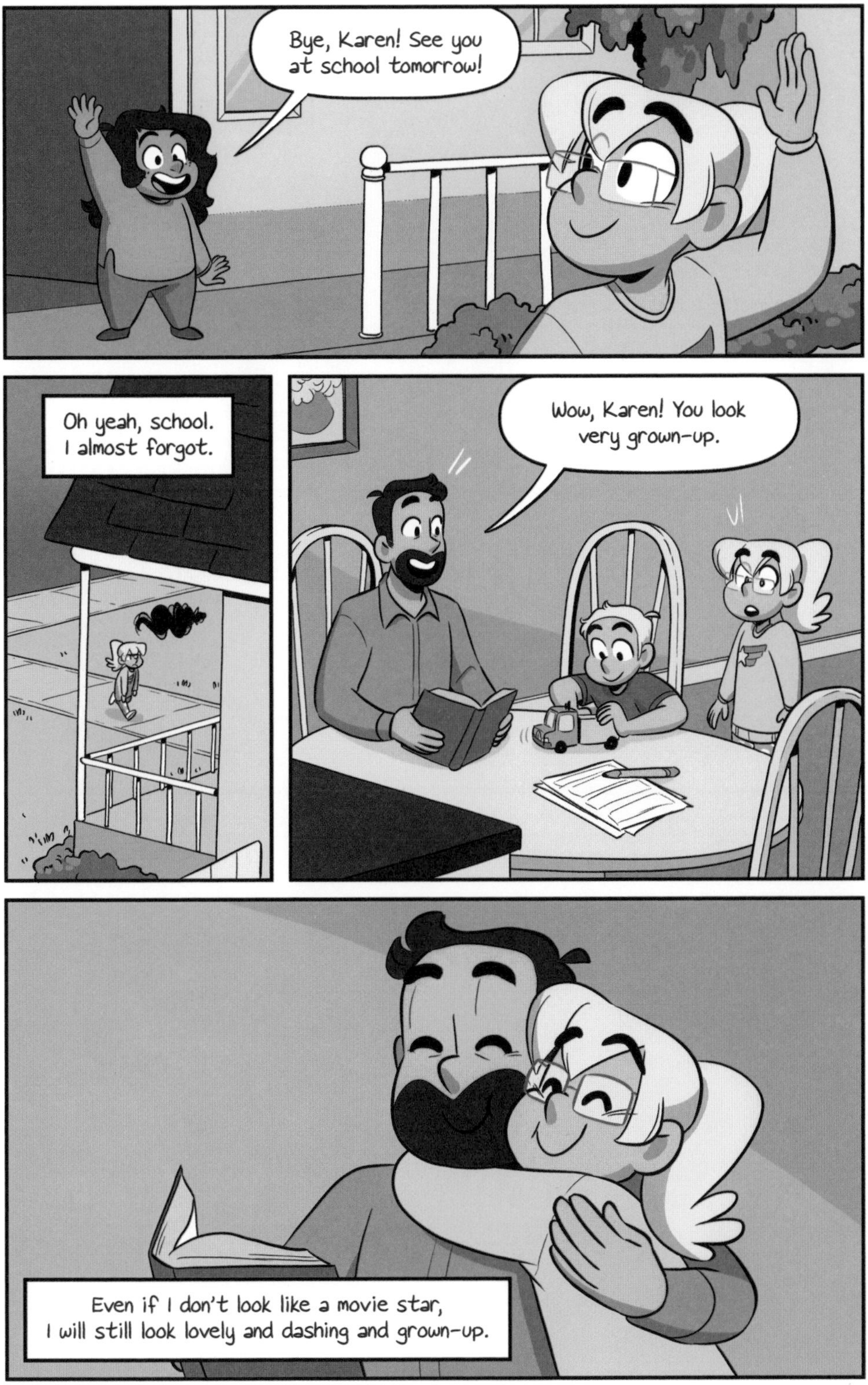
Bye, Karen! See you at school tomorrow!
Oh yeah, school. I almost forgot.
Wow, Karen! You look very grown-up.
Even if I don't look like a movie star, I will still look lovely and dashing and grown-up.

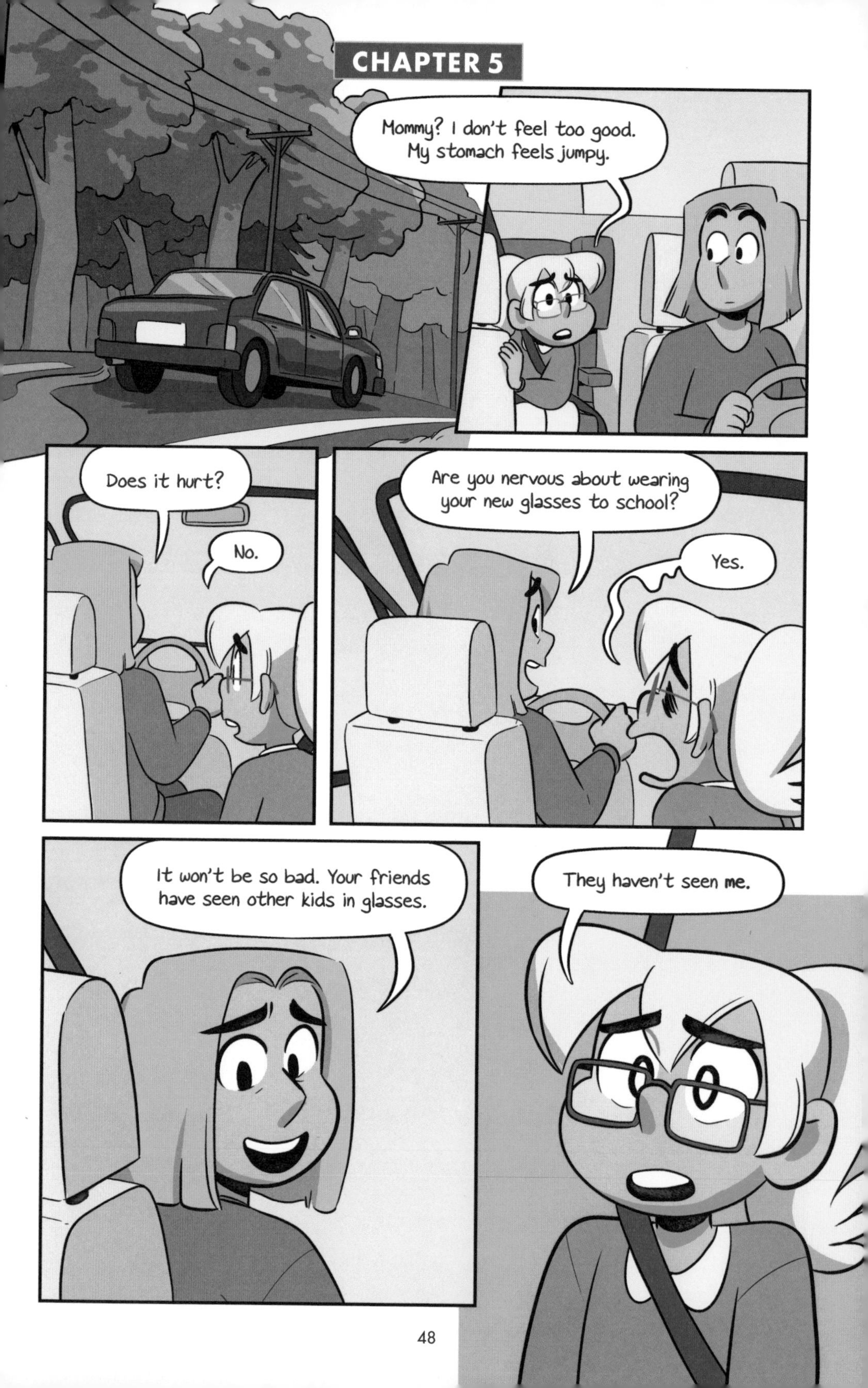
CHAPTER 5
Mommy? I don't feel too good. My stomach feels jumpy.
Does it hurt?
No.
Are you nervous about wearing your new glasses to school?
Yes.
It won't be so bad. Your friends have seen other kids in glasses.
They haven't seen me.

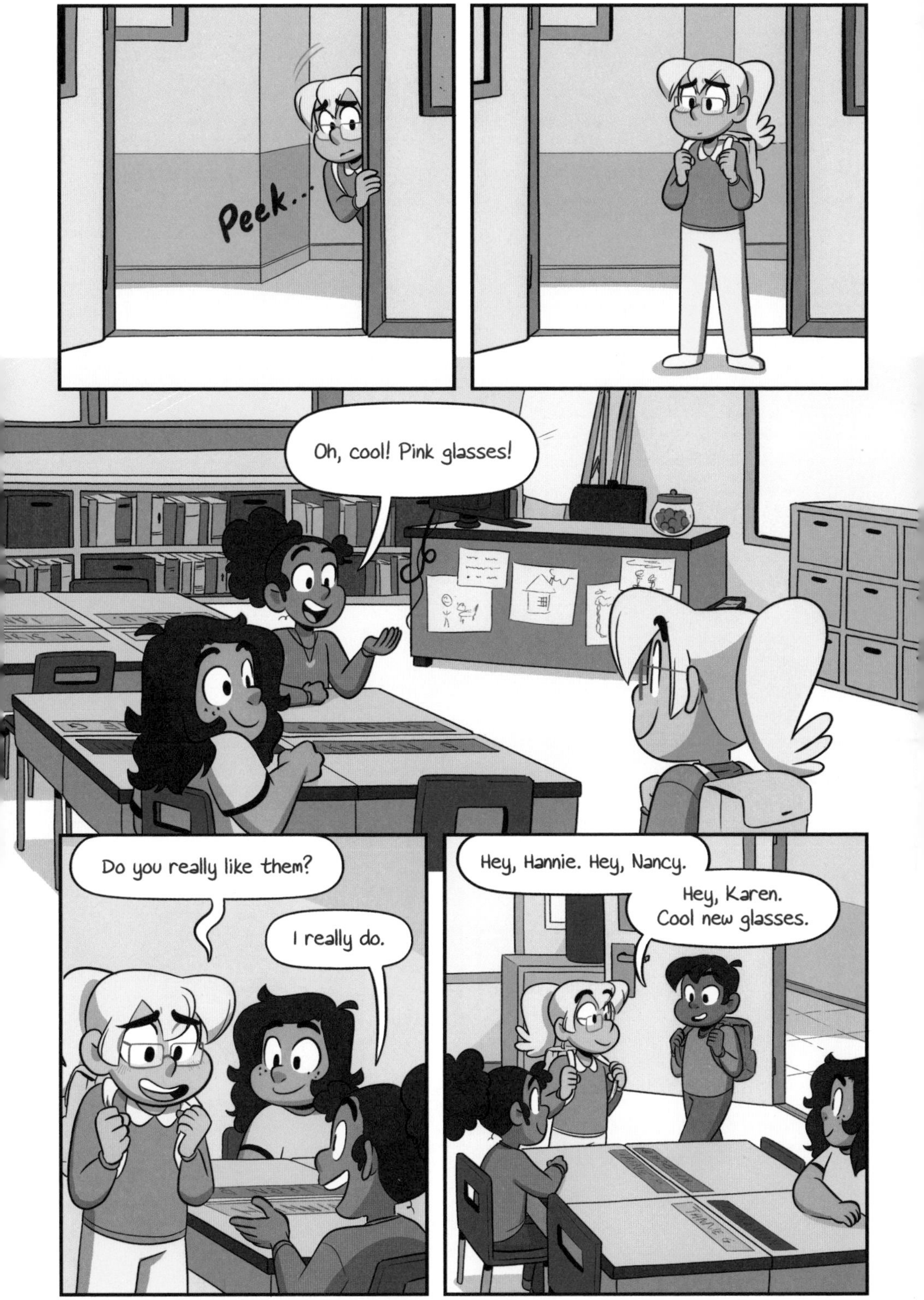
Peek...
Oh, cool! Pink glasses!
Do you really like them?
I really do.
Hey, Hannie. Hey, Nancy.
Hey, Karen.
Cool new glasses.

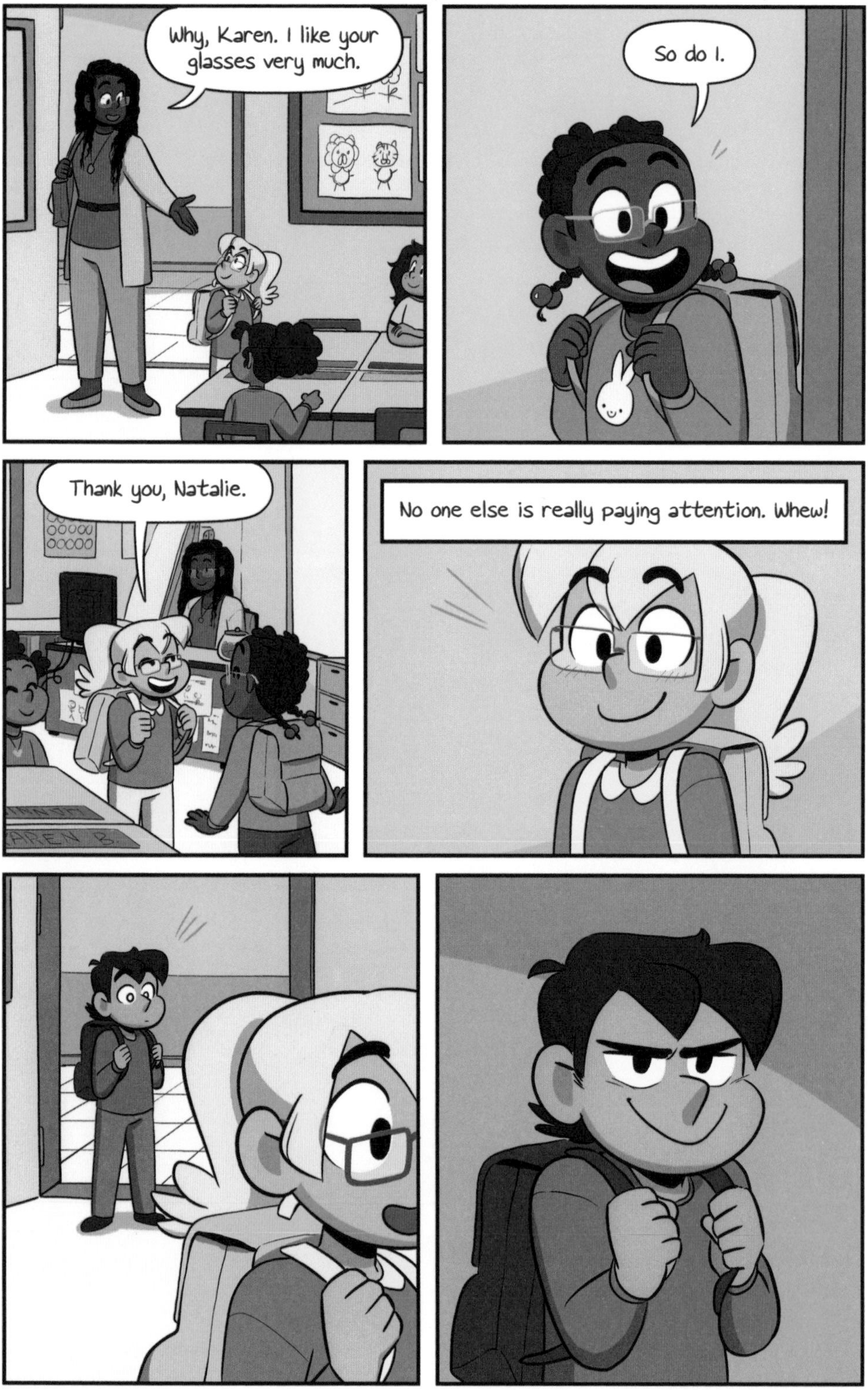
Why, Karen. I like your glasses very much.
So do I.
Thank you, Natalie.
No one else is really paying attention. Whew!
KAREN B.

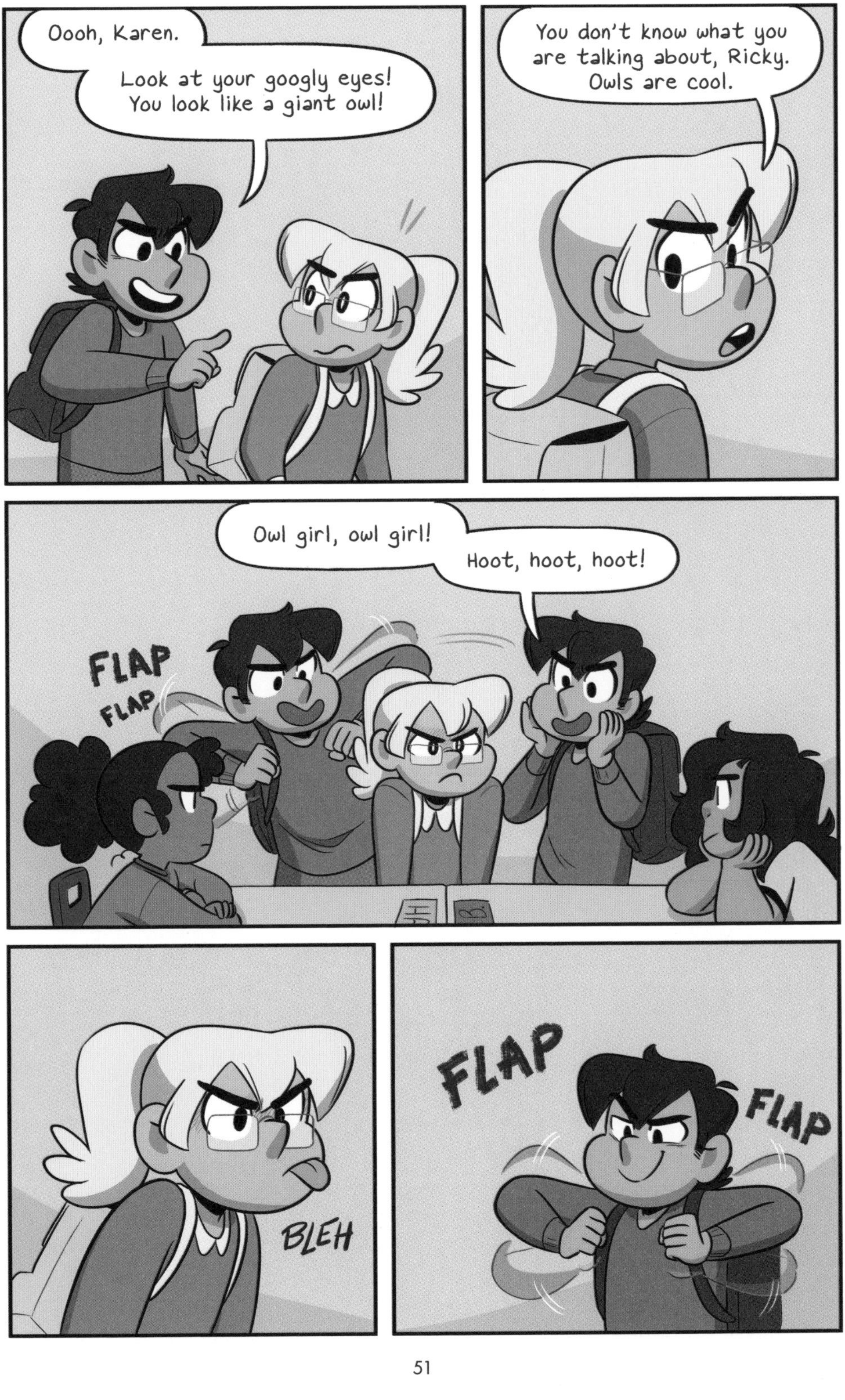
Oooh, Karen.
Look at your googly eyes! You look like a giant owl!
You don't know what you are talking about, Ricky. Owls are cool.
Owl girl, owl girl!
Hoot, hoot, hoot!
FLAP
FLAP
BLEH
FLAP
FLAP

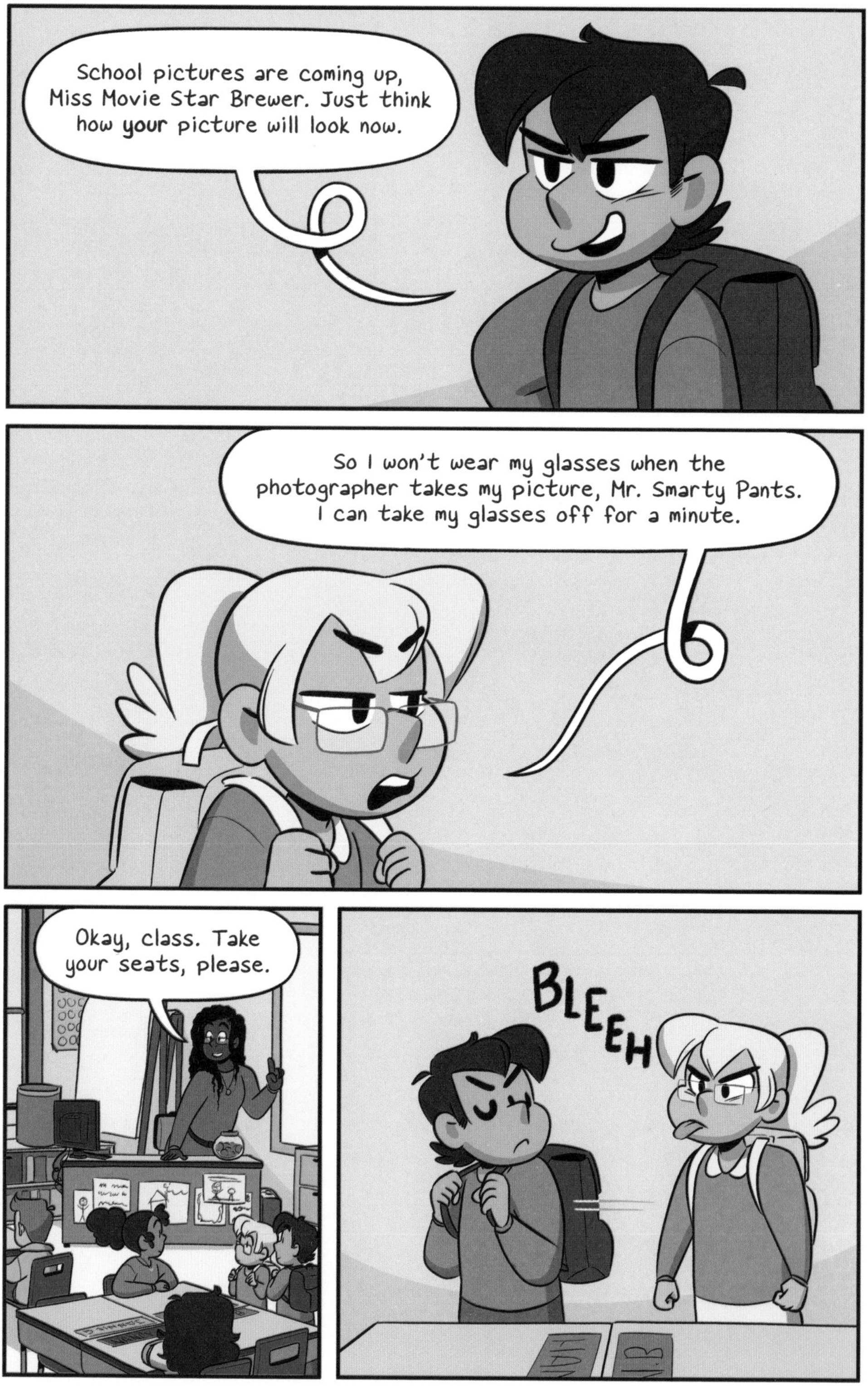
School pictures are coming up, Miss Movie Star Brewer. Just think how **your** picture will look now.
So I won't wear my glasses when the photographer takes my picture, Mr. Smarty Pants. I can take my glasses off for a minute.
Okay, class. Take your seats, please.
BLEEH

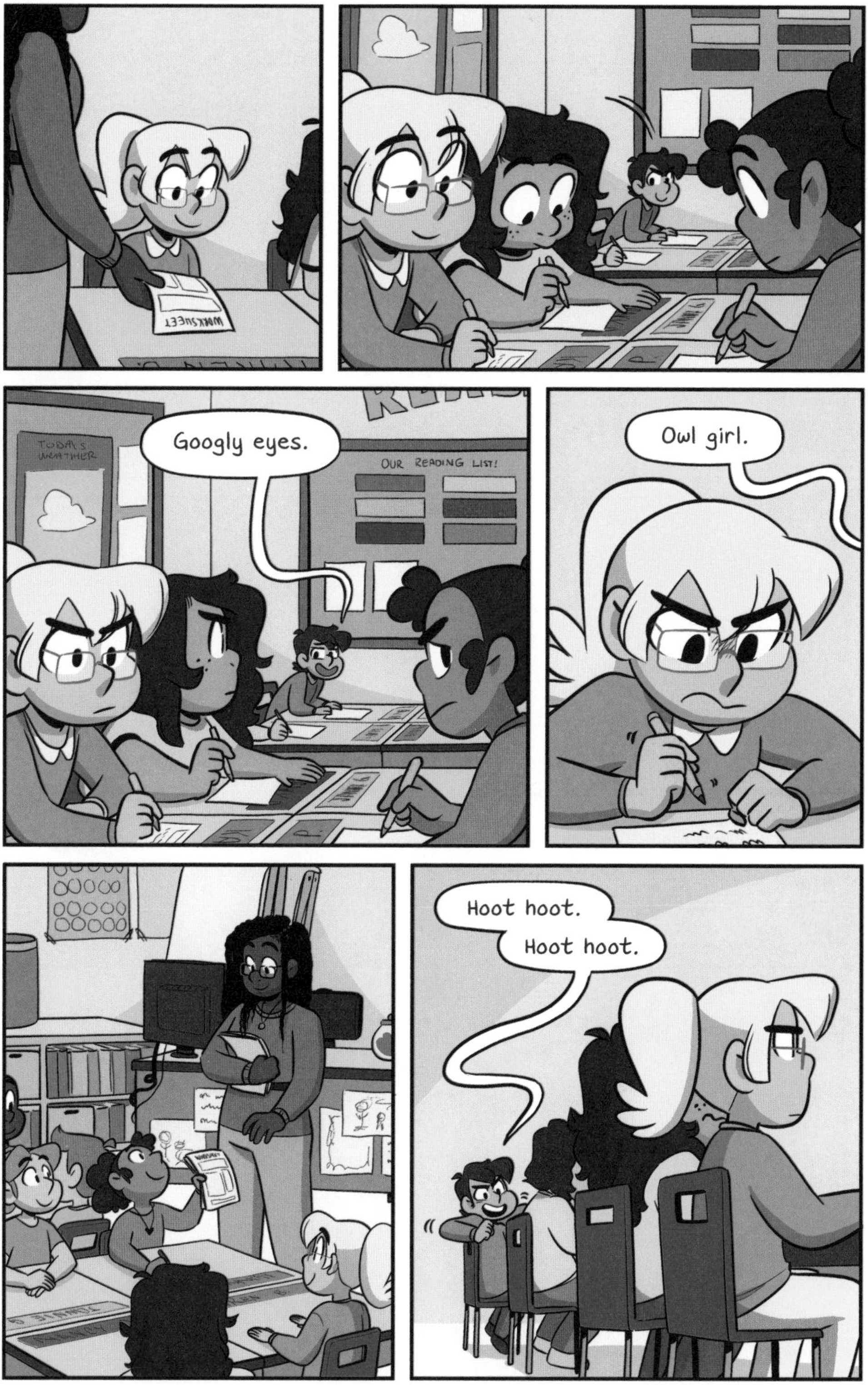
TODAY'S WEATHER
OUR READING LIST!
Googly eyes.
Owl girl.
Hoot hoot.
Hoot hoot.

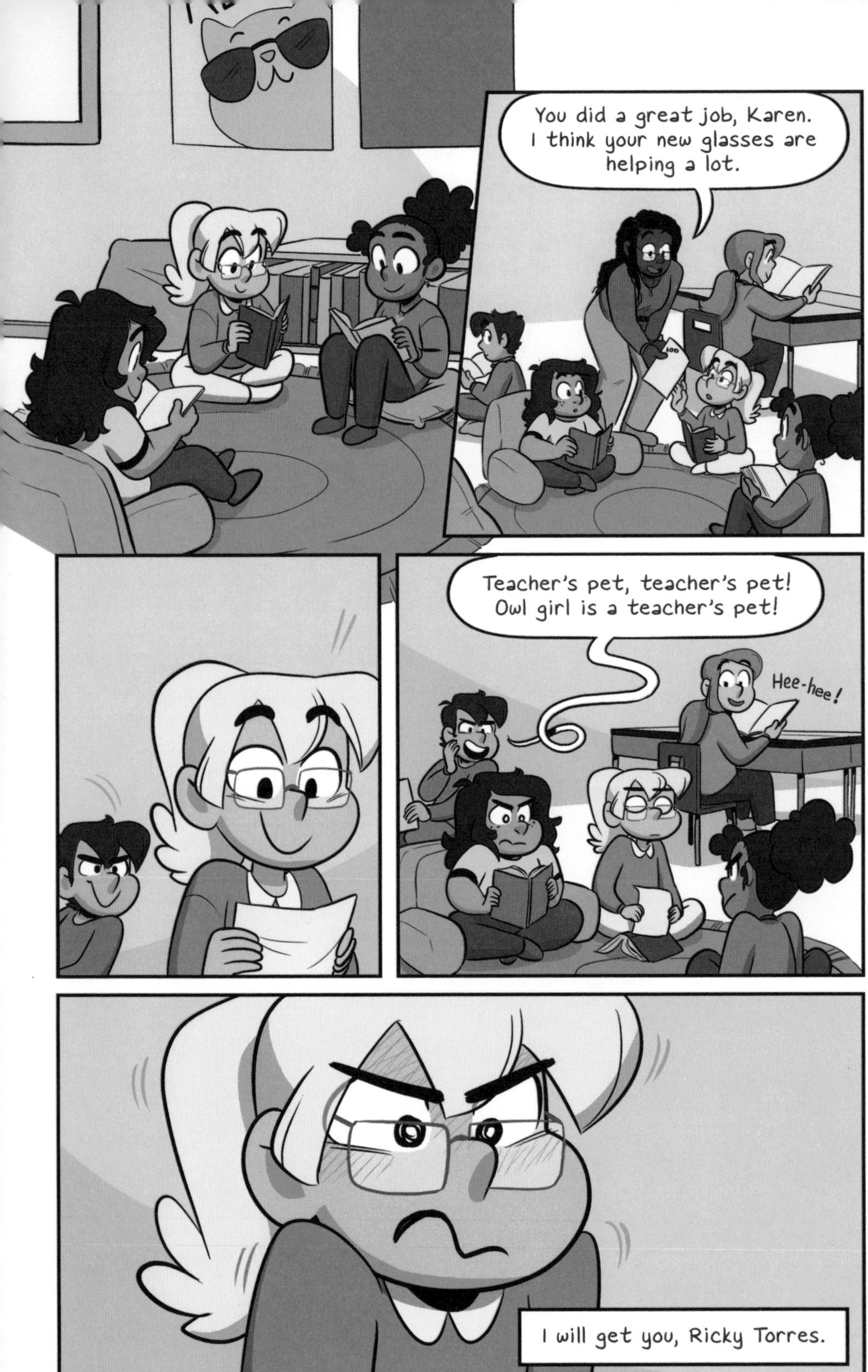
You did a great job, Karen. I think your new glasses are helping a lot.
Teacher's pet, teacher's pet! Owl girl is a teacher's pet!
Hee-hee!
I will get you, Ricky Torres.

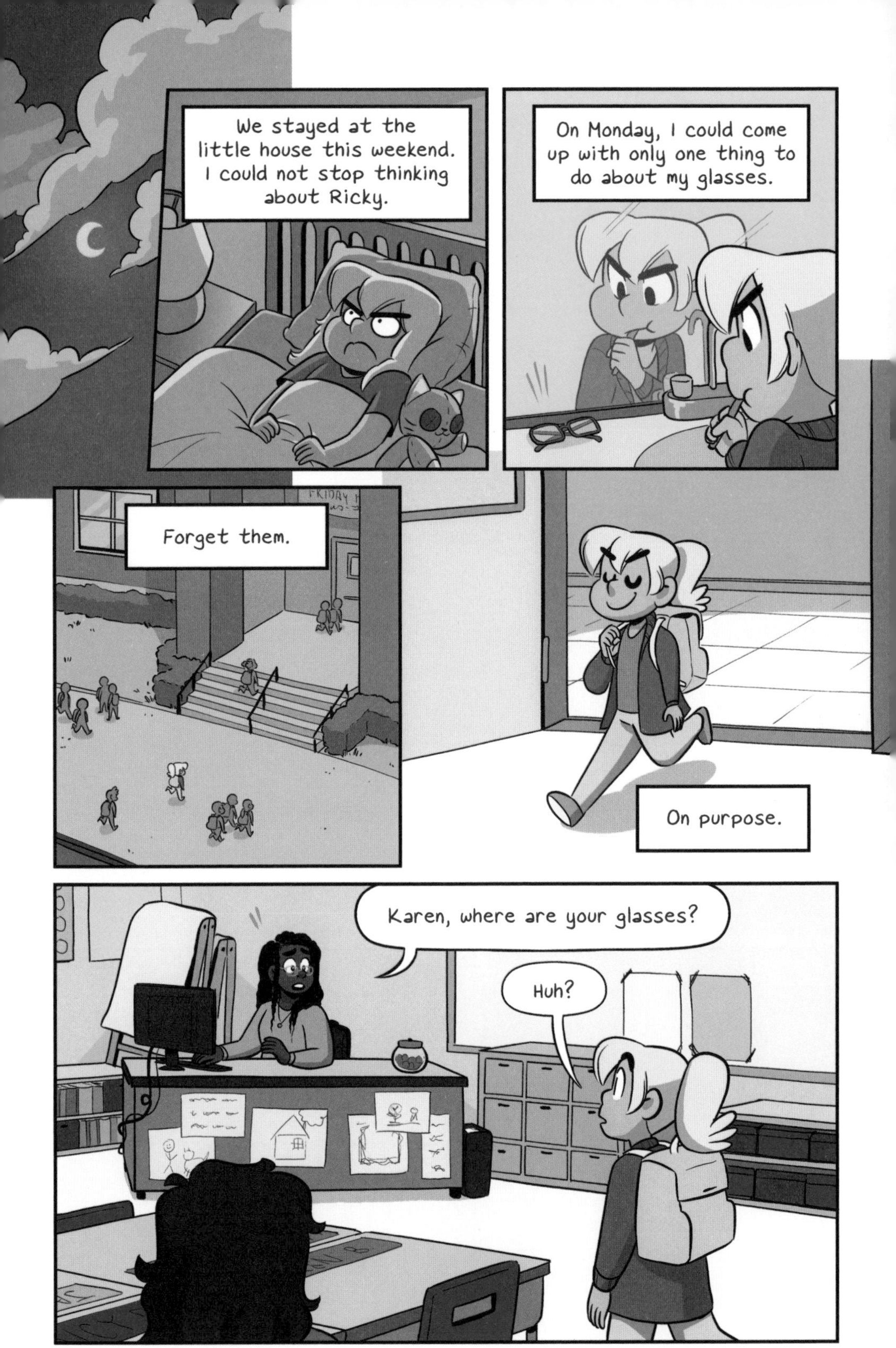
We stayed at the little house this weekend. I could not stop thinking about Ricky.
On Monday, I could come up with only one thing to do about my glasses.
Forget them.
On purpose.
Karen, where are your glasses?
Huh?

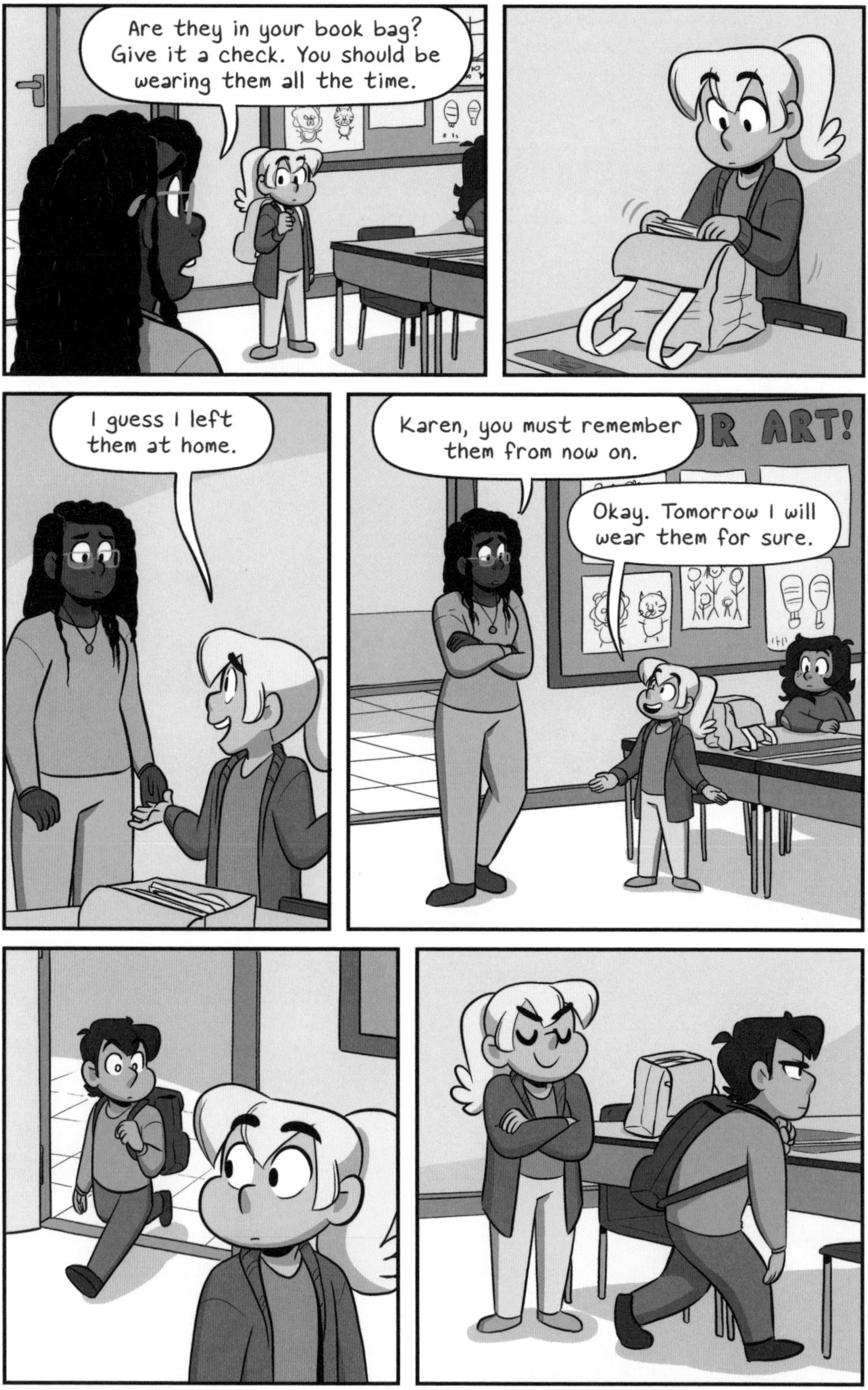
Are they in your book bag? Give it a check. You should be wearing them all the time.
I guess I left them at home.
Karen, you must remember them from now on.
Okay. Tomorrow I will wear them for sure.
UR ART!

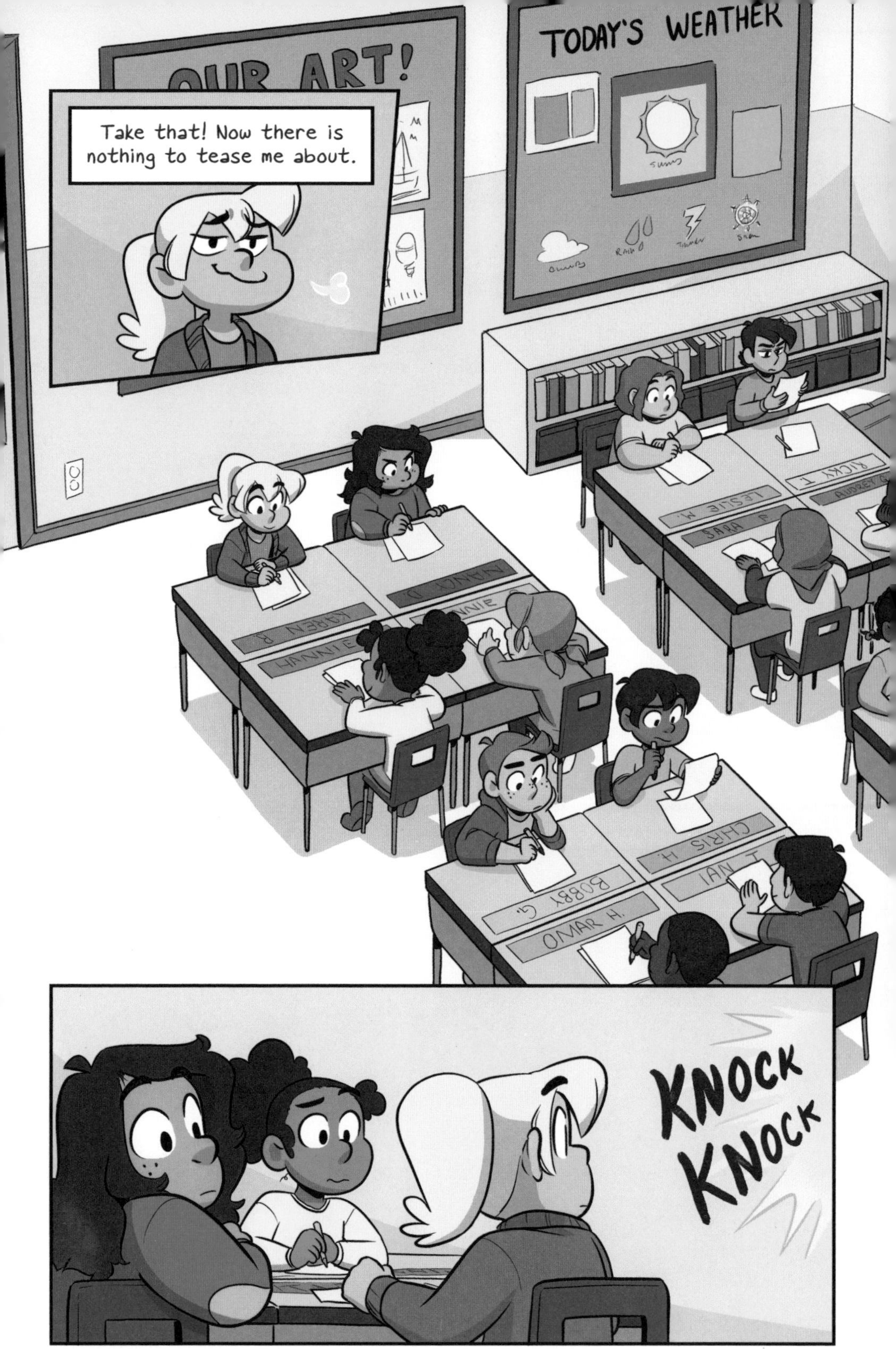

TODAY'S WEATHER
OUR ART!
Take that! Now there is nothing to tease me about.
KAREN B.
NANCY D.
HANNIE
LESLIE M.
RICKY T.
SARA F.
CHRIS H.
BOBBY G.
IAN T.
OMAR H.
KNOCK KNOCK

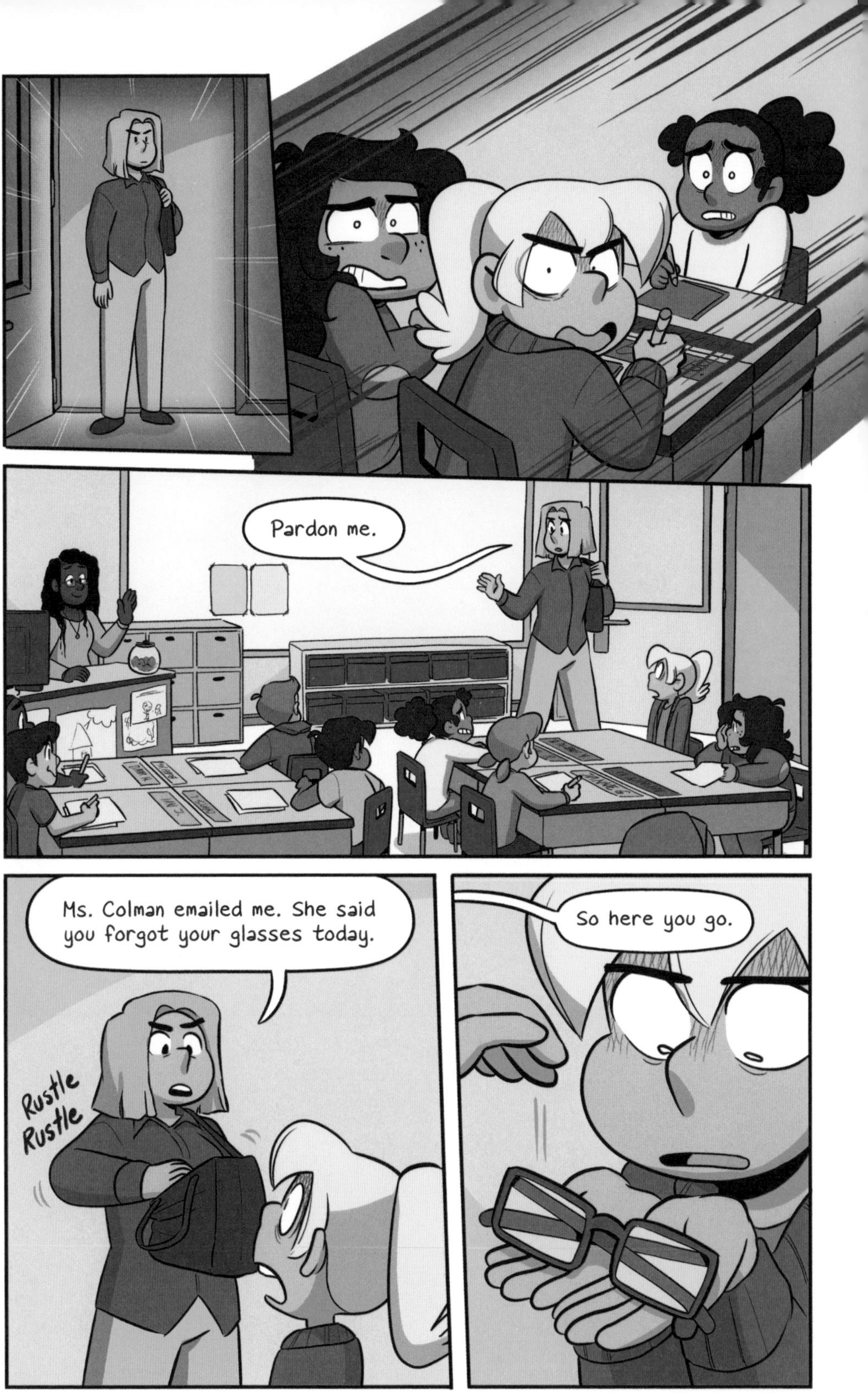
Pardon me.
Ms. Colman emailed me. She said you forgot your glasses today.
Rustle Rustle
So here you go.

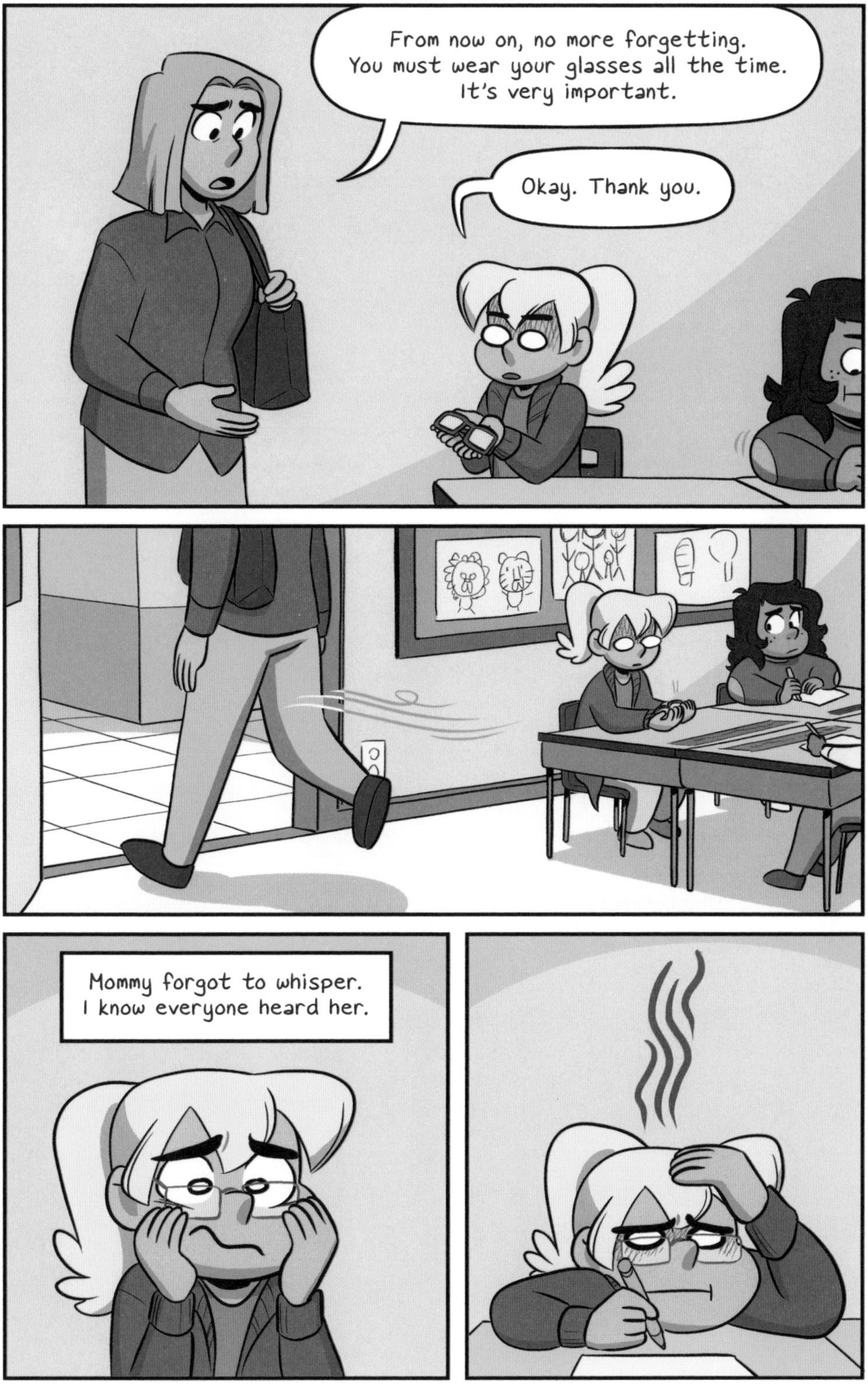
From now on, no more forgetting. You must wear your glasses all the time. It's very important.
Okay. Thank you.
Mommy forgot to whisper. I know everyone heard her.

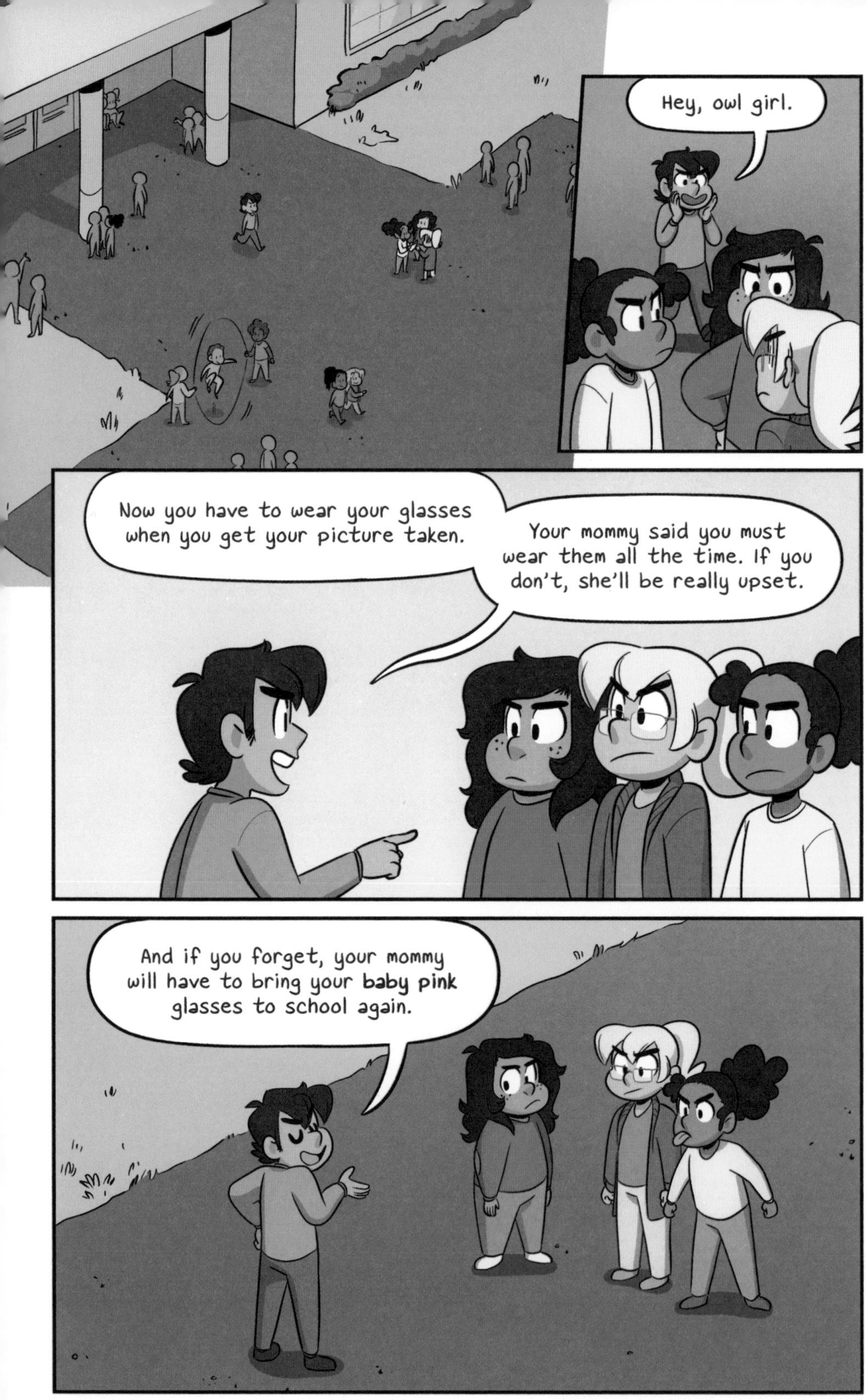
Hey, owl girl.
Now you have to wear your glasses when you get your picture taken.
Your mommy said you must wear them all the time. If you don't, she'll be really upset.
And if you forget, your mommy will have to bring your **baby pink** glasses to school again.

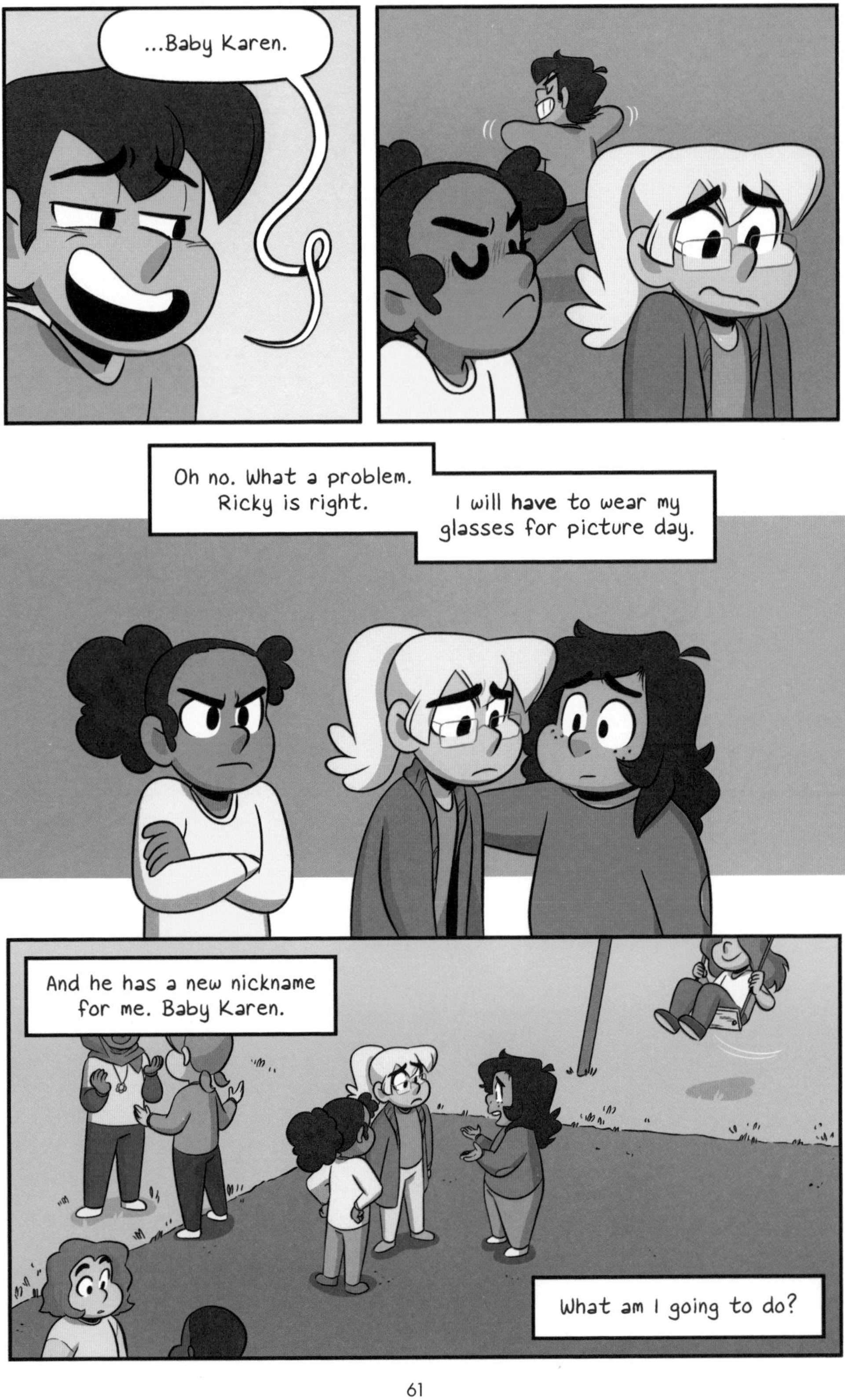
...Baby Karen.
Oh no. What a problem. Ricky is right.
I will **have** to wear my glasses for picture day.
And he has a new nickname for me. Baby Karen.
What am I going to do?

CHAPTER 6

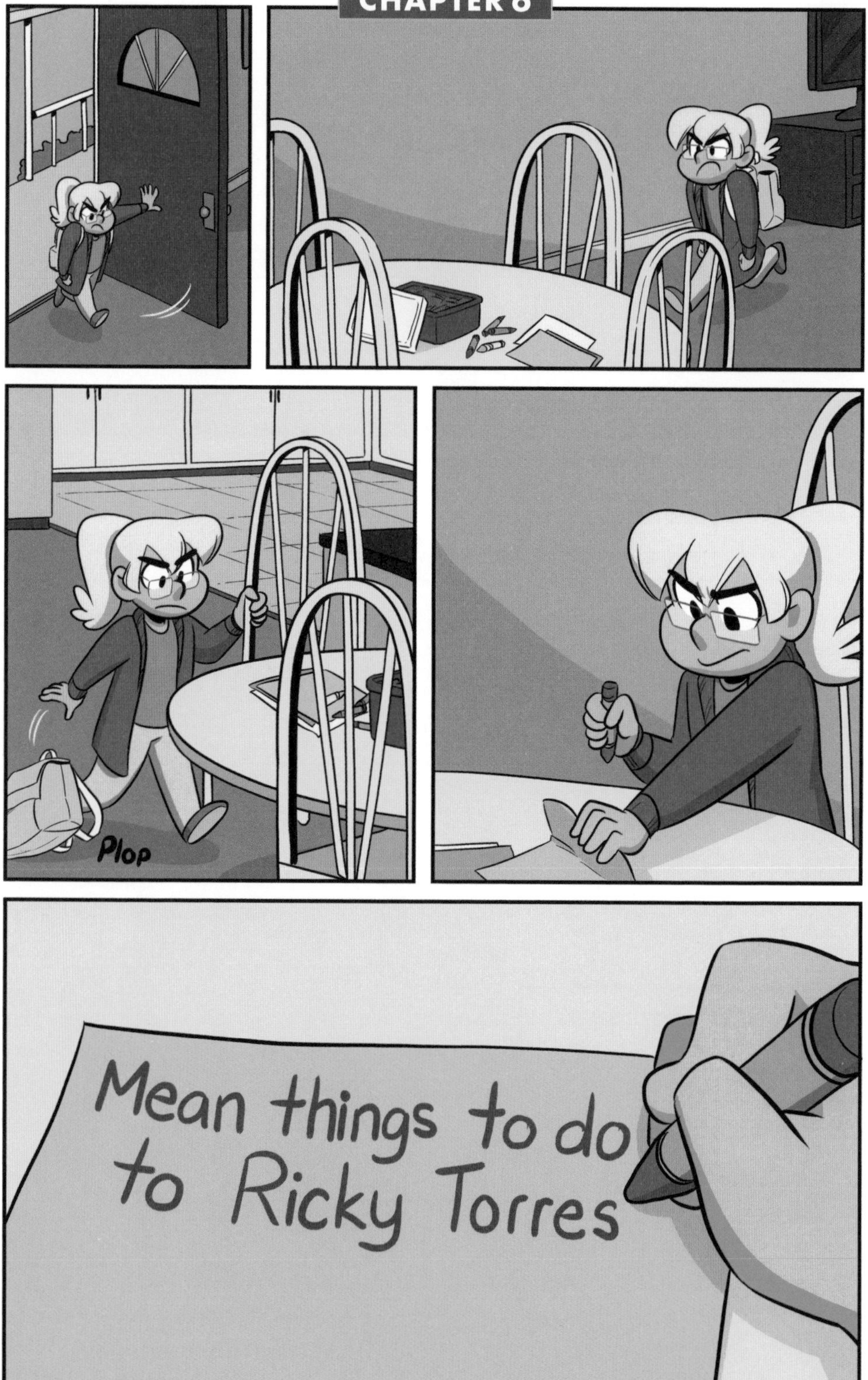

Plop
Mean things to do
to Ricky Torres

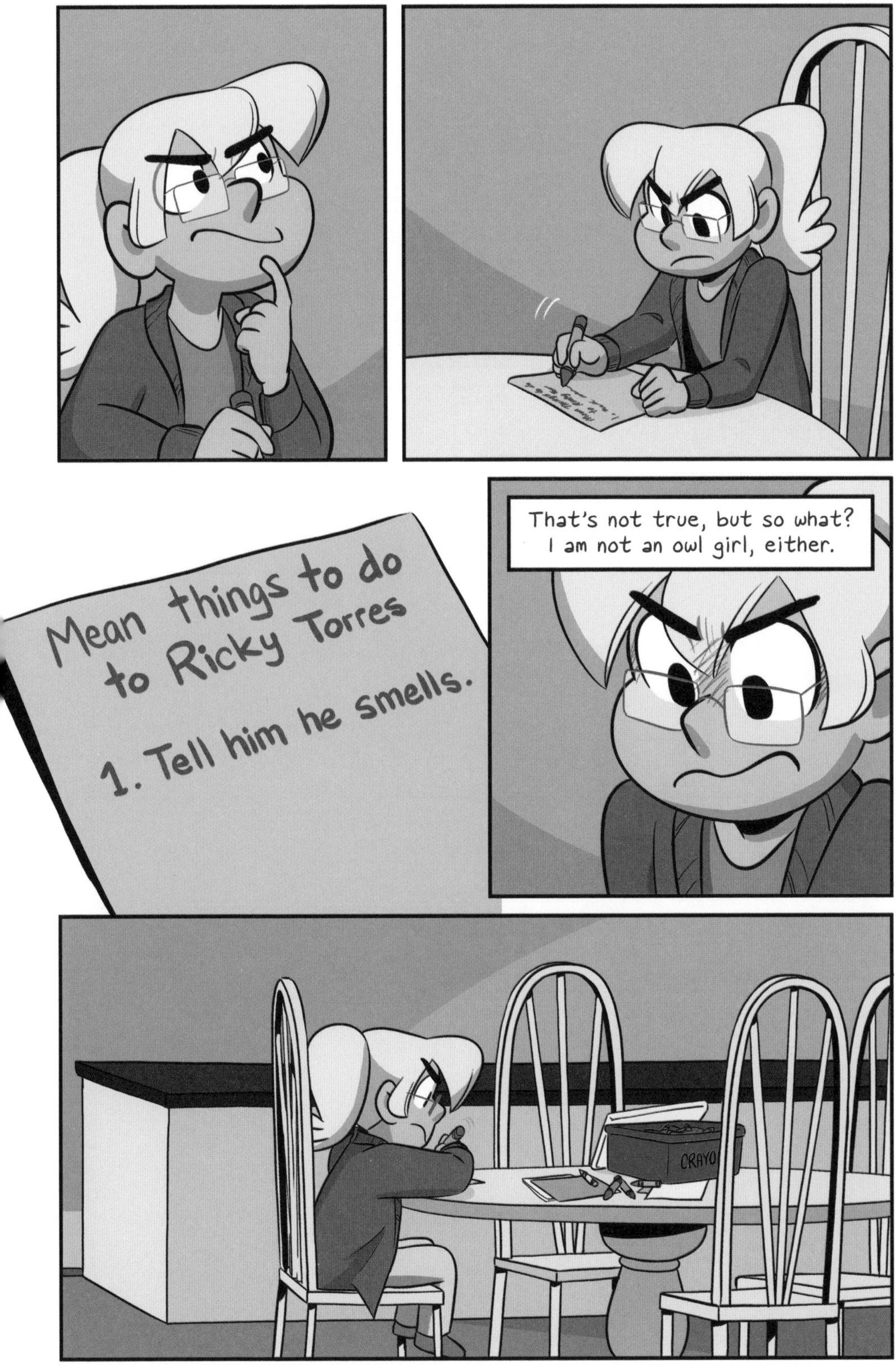
Mean things to do
to Ricky Torres
1. Tell him he smells.
That's not true, but so what?
I am not an owl girl, either.
CRAYO

1. Tell him he st[...]

2. Put my favorite pencil in his desk and tell Ms. Colman he stole it.

That is really mean, plus it would be lying. I would never do it, really.

But writing it down makes me feel better.

What else...

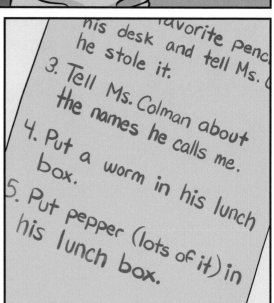

his desk and tell Ms. [...]
he stole it.

3. Tell Ms. Colman about the names he calls me.

4. Put a worm in his lunch box.

5. Put pepper (lots of it) in his lunch box.

I think I need ten things. Ten is a nice number.

Put pepper his lunch box.

6. Hide his reading book.

Hide his reading book.

7. Tell him his eyes turned orange. Have Nancy and Hannie also say his eyes are orange.

also say his eyes are orange.

8. Find lots of bugs at recess and then put them in his backpack.

recess and th Put them in his backpack.

9. Pretend he is invisible for a whole day.

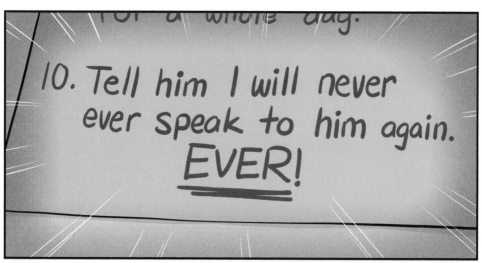

10. Tell him I will never ever speak to him again. EVER!

I am ready to get back at Ricky Torres.

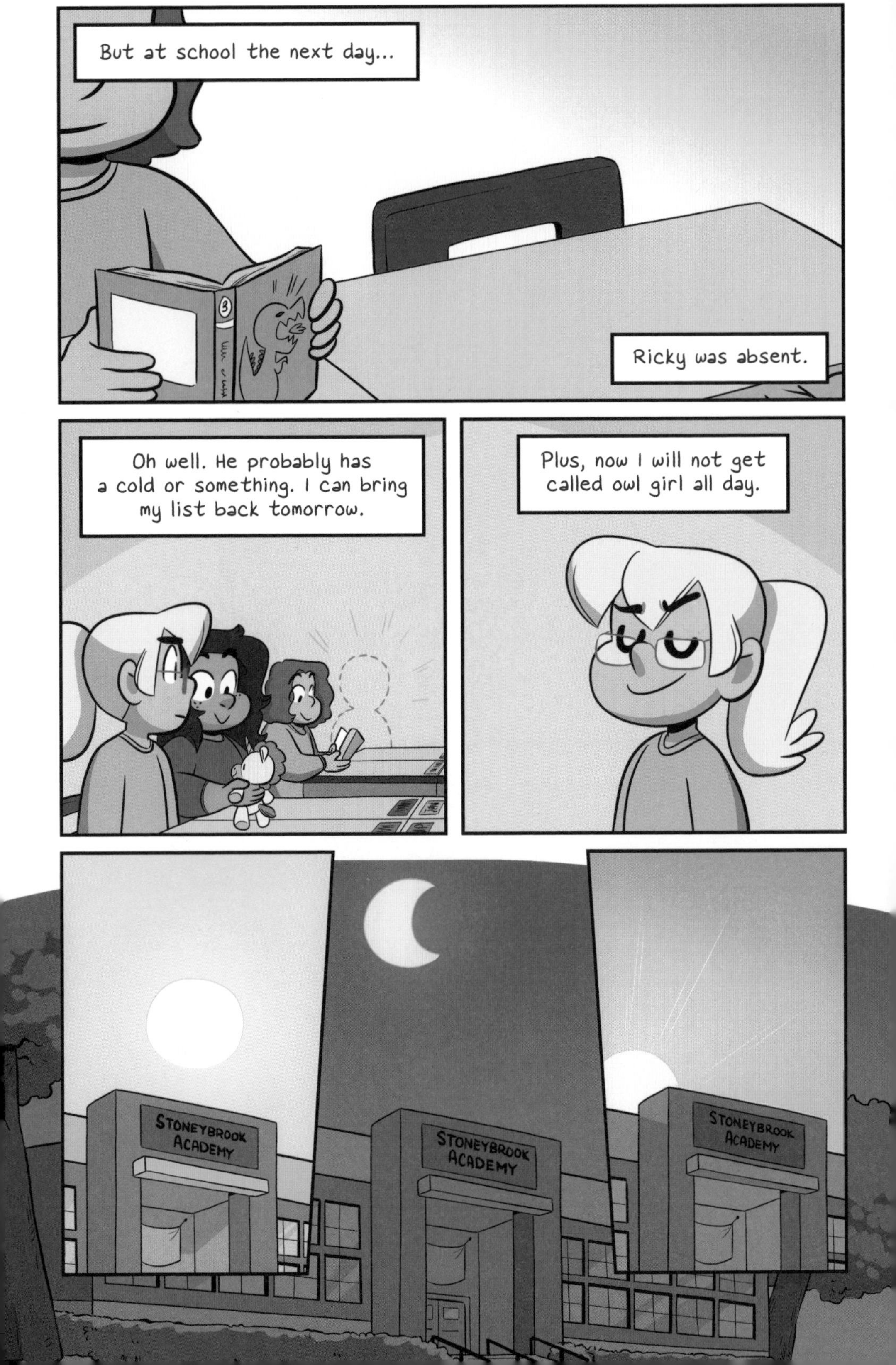
But at school the next day...
Ricky was absent.
Oh well. He probably has a cold or something. I can bring my list back tomorrow.
Plus, now I will not get called owl girl all day.
STONEYBROOK ACADEMY
STONEYBROOK ACADEMY
STONEYBROOK ACADEMY

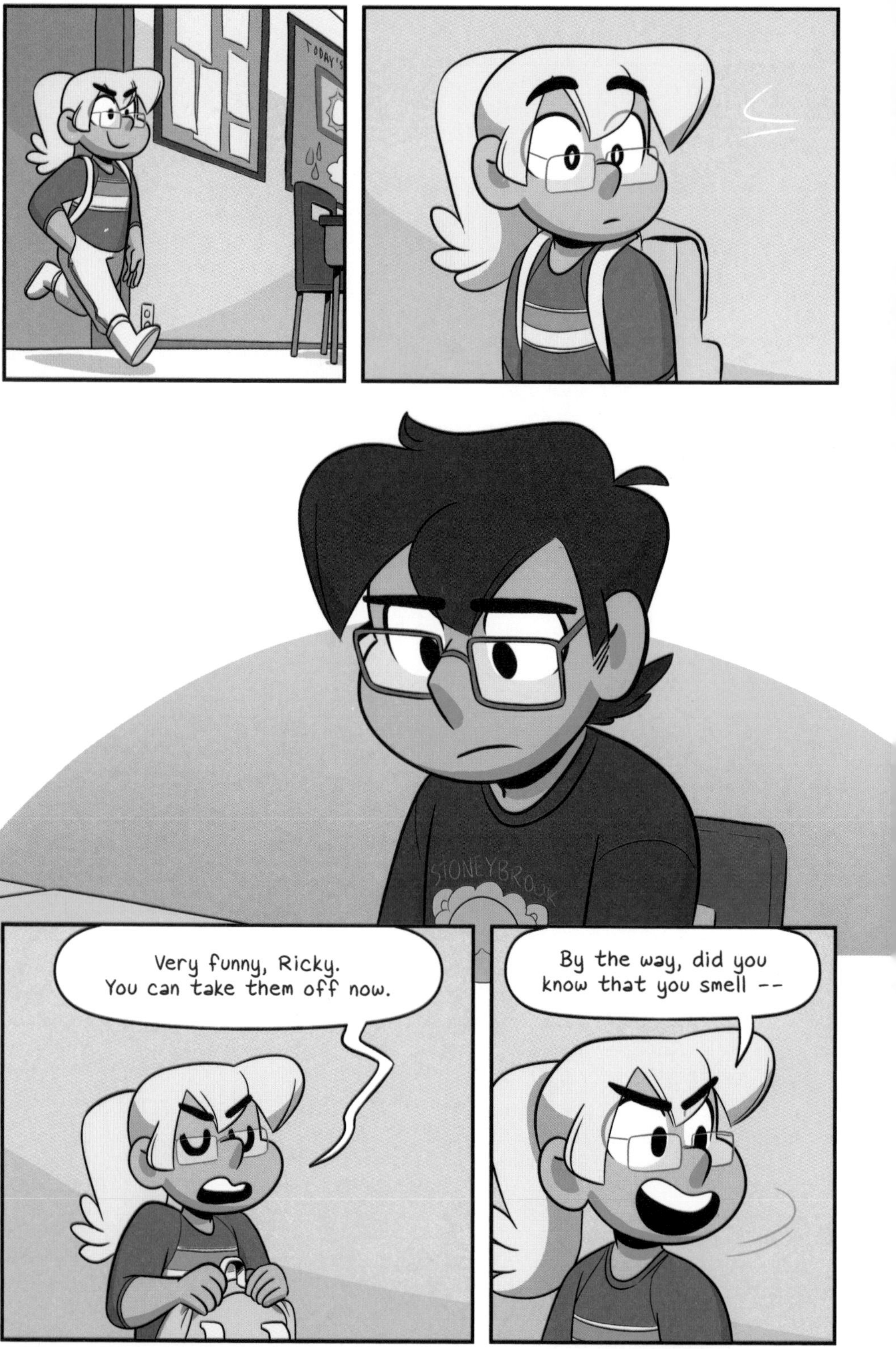
TODAY'S
STONEYBROOK
Very funny, Ricky. You can take them off now.
By the way, did you know that you smell --

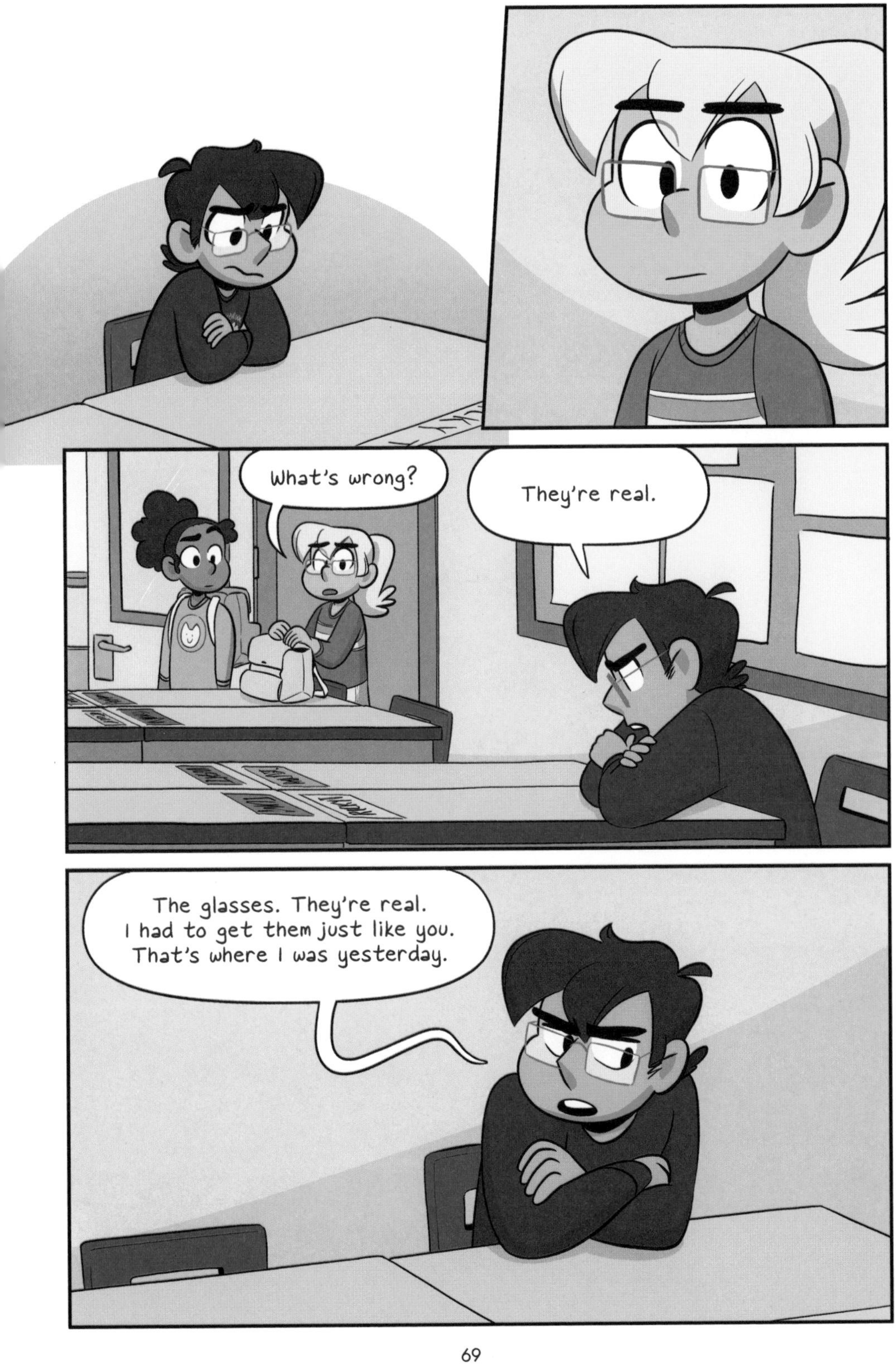
What's wrong?
They're real.
The glasses. They're real.
I had to get them just like you.
That's where I was yesterday.

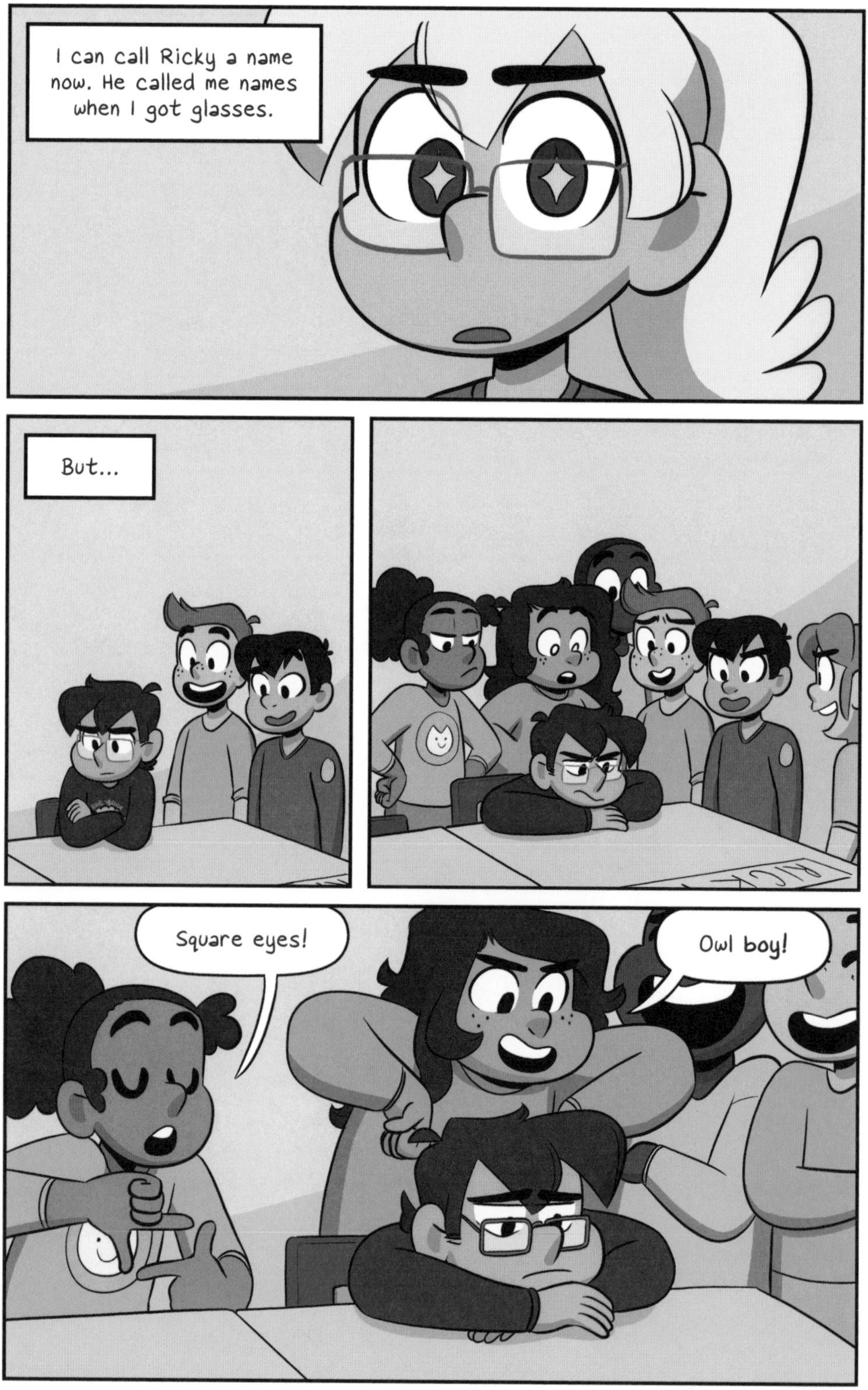

I can call Ricky a name now. He called me names when I got glasses.
But...
Square eyes!
Owl boy!

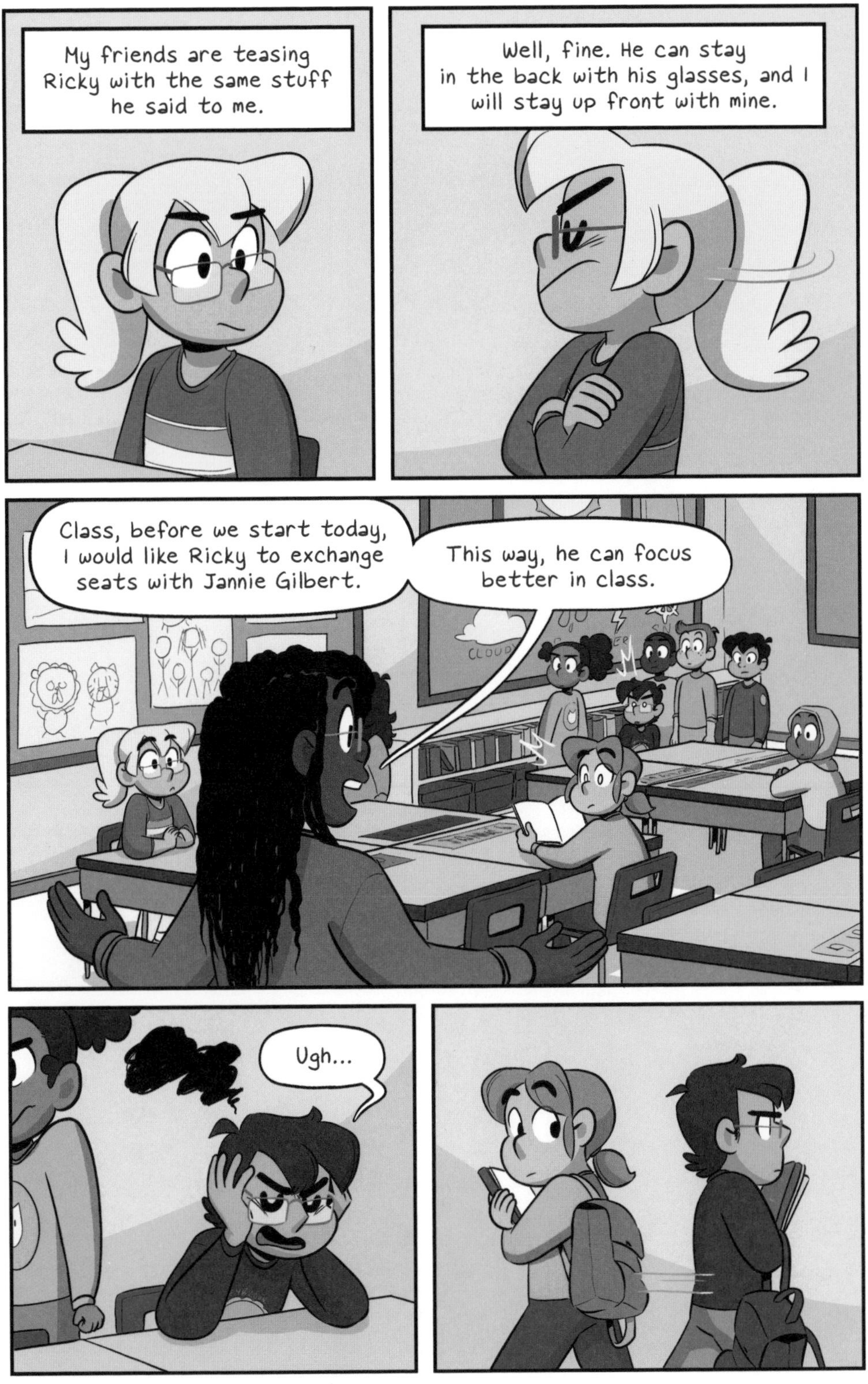
My friends are teasing Ricky with the same stuff he said to me.
Well, fine. He can stay in the back with his glasses, and I will stay up front with mine.
Class, before we start today, I would like Ricky to exchange seats with Jannie Gilbert.
This way, he can focus better in class.
Ugh...

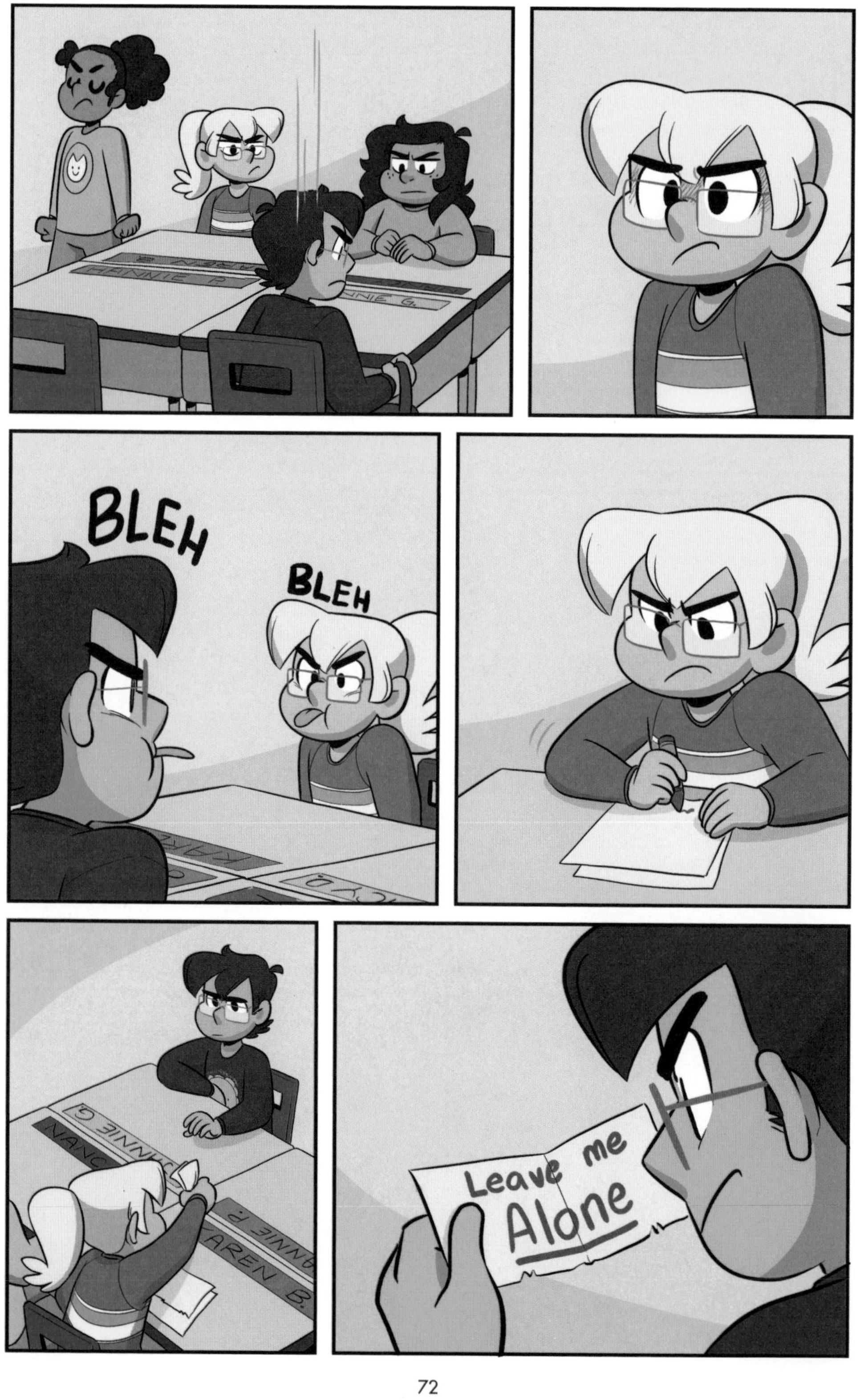
HANNIE P.
BLEH
BLEH
Leave me
Alone

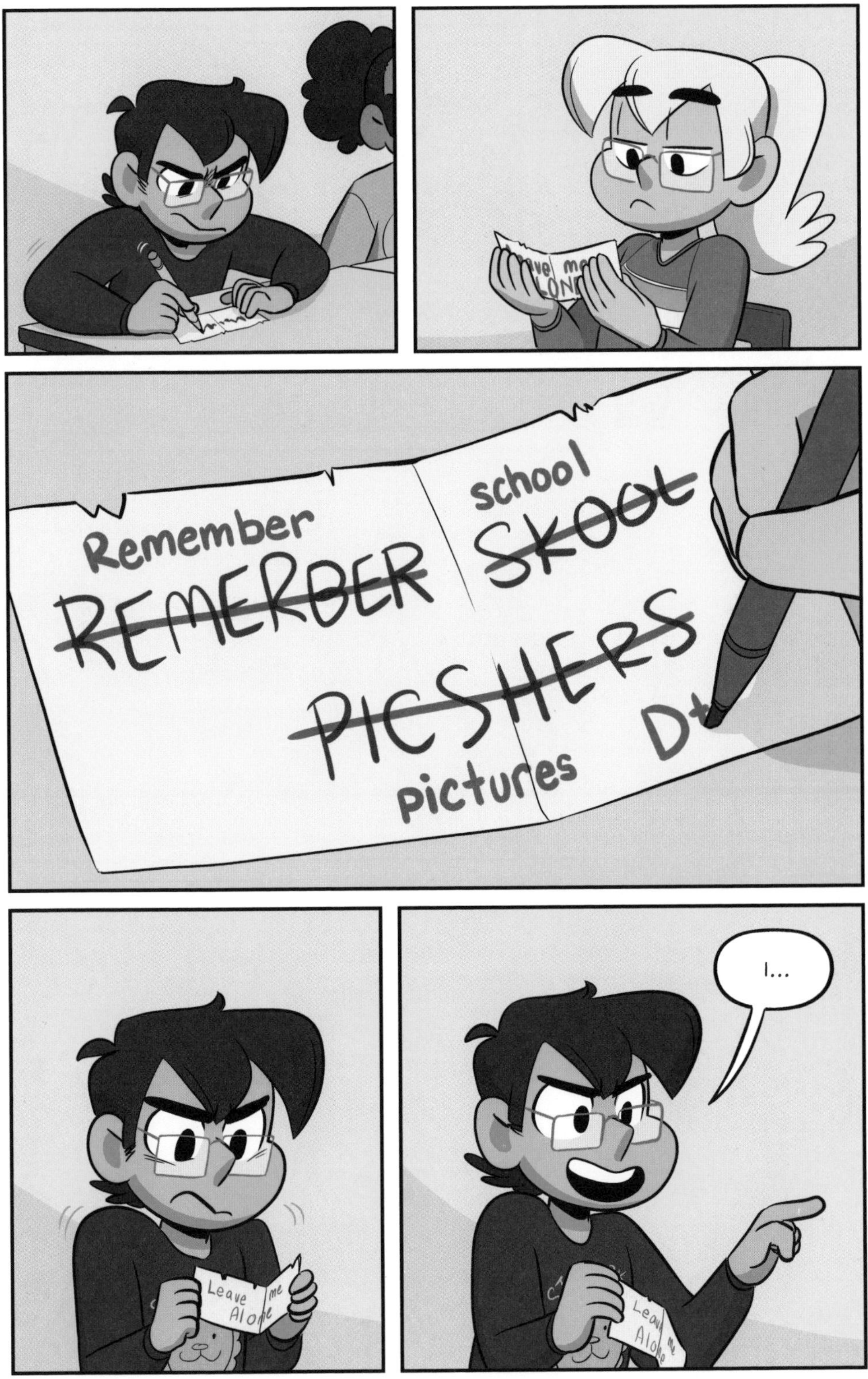
Remember
REMERBER
school
SKOOL
PICSHERS
pictures
D+
Leave me Alone
I...

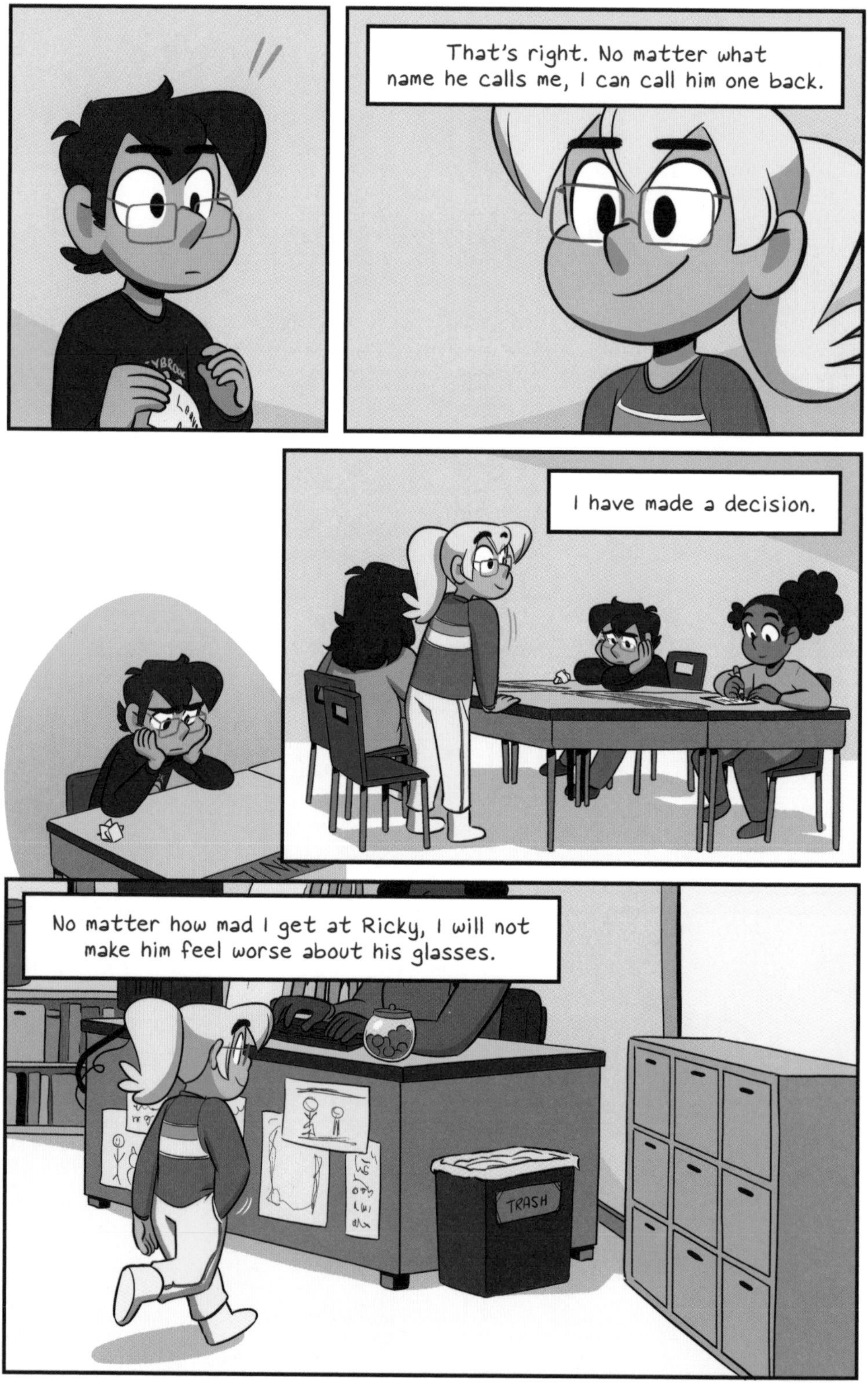
That's right. No matter what name he calls me, I can call him one back.
I have made a decision.
No matter how mad I get at Ricky, I will not make him feel worse about his glasses.
TRASH

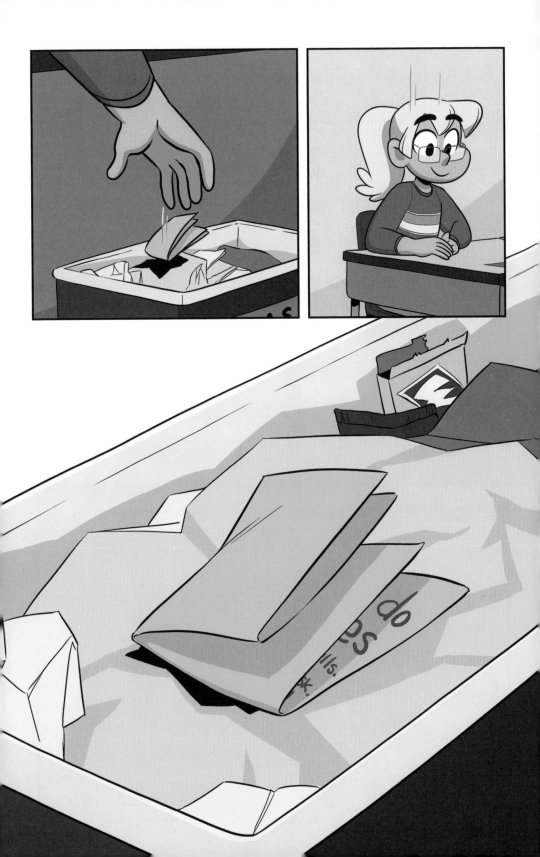

CHAPTER 7

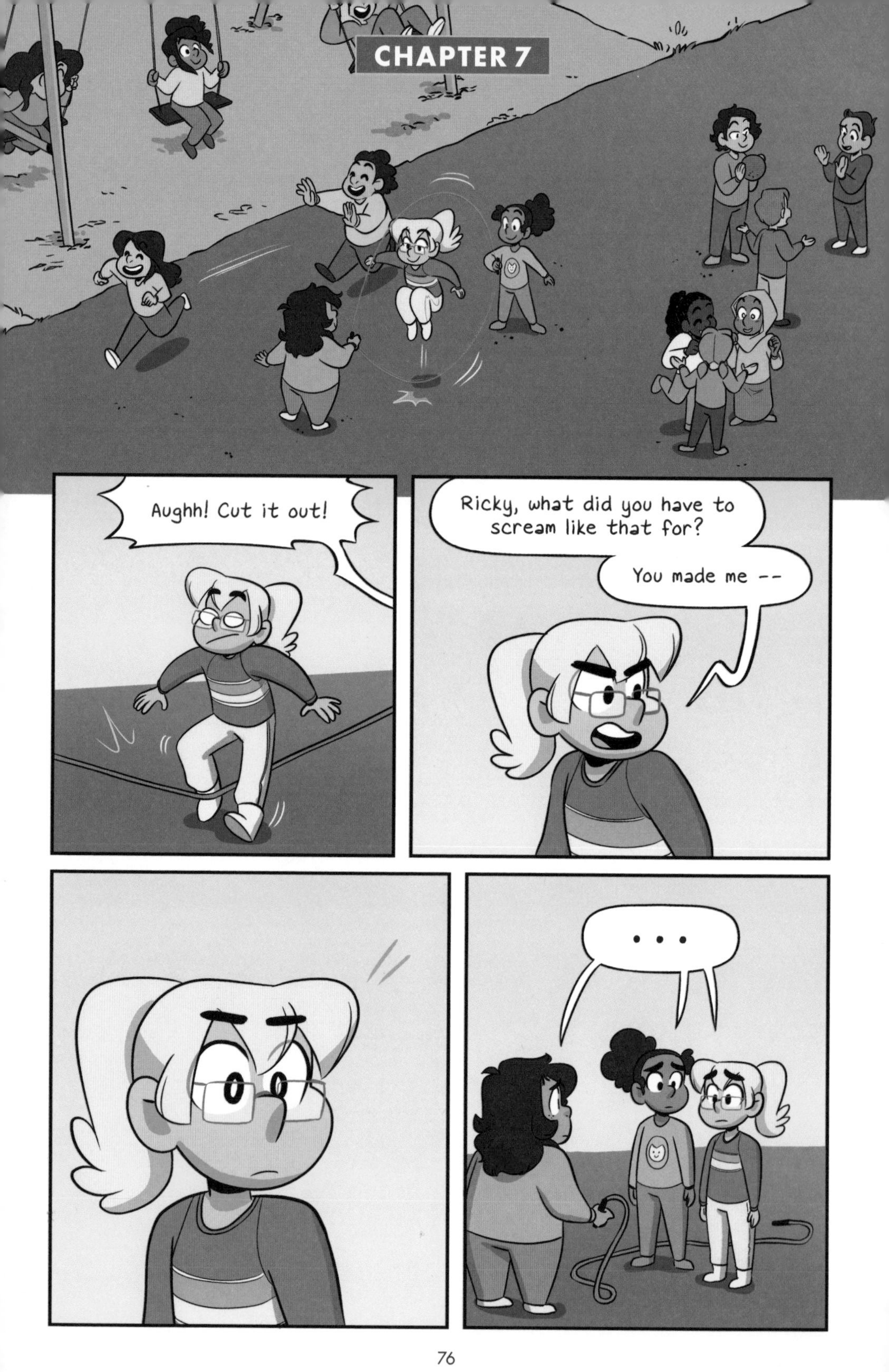

Aughh! Cut it out!
Ricky, what did you have to scream like that for?
You made me --
. . .

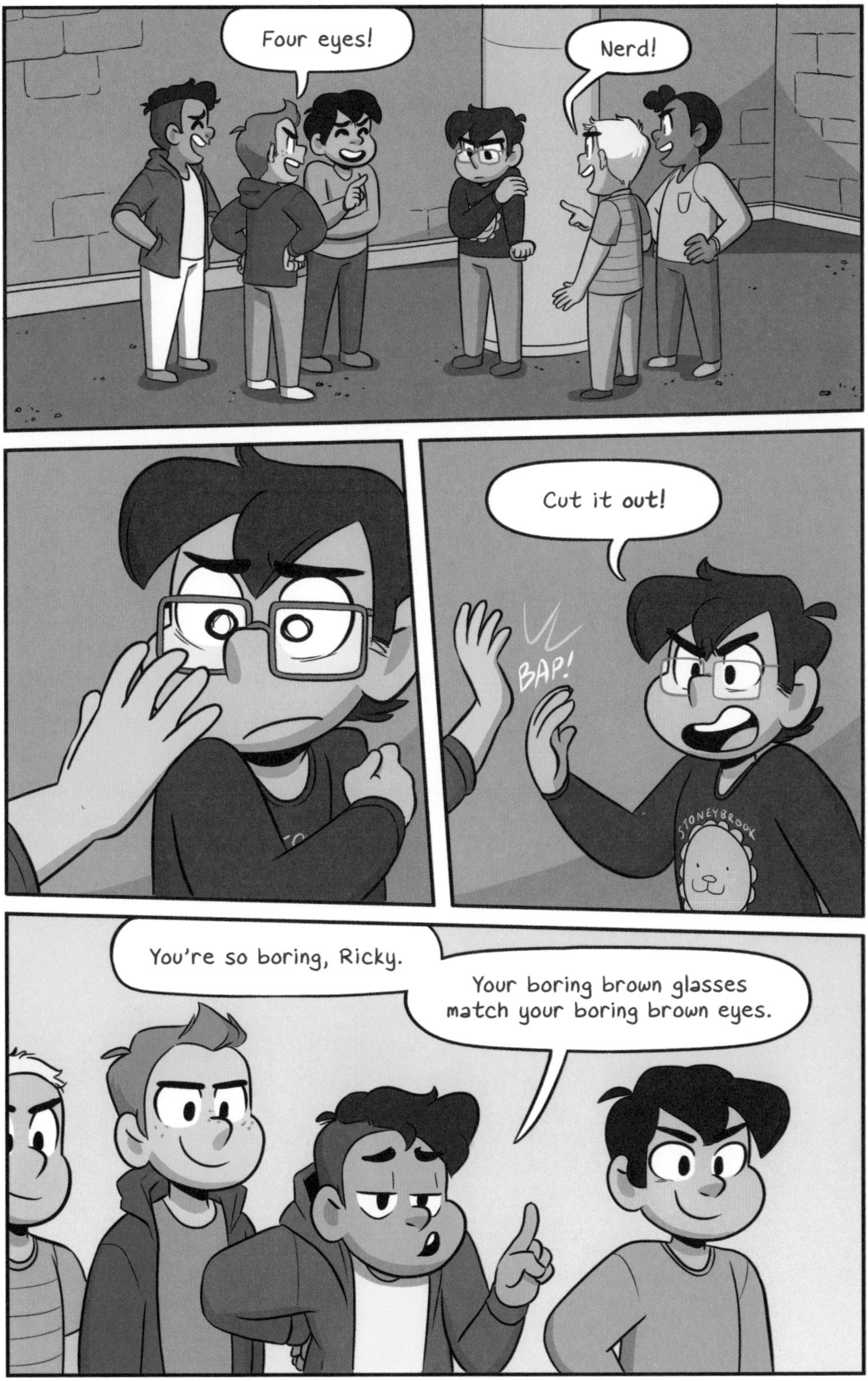
Four eyes!
Nerd!
Cut it out!
BAP!
STONEYBROOK
You're so boring, Ricky.
Your boring brown glasses match your boring brown eyes.

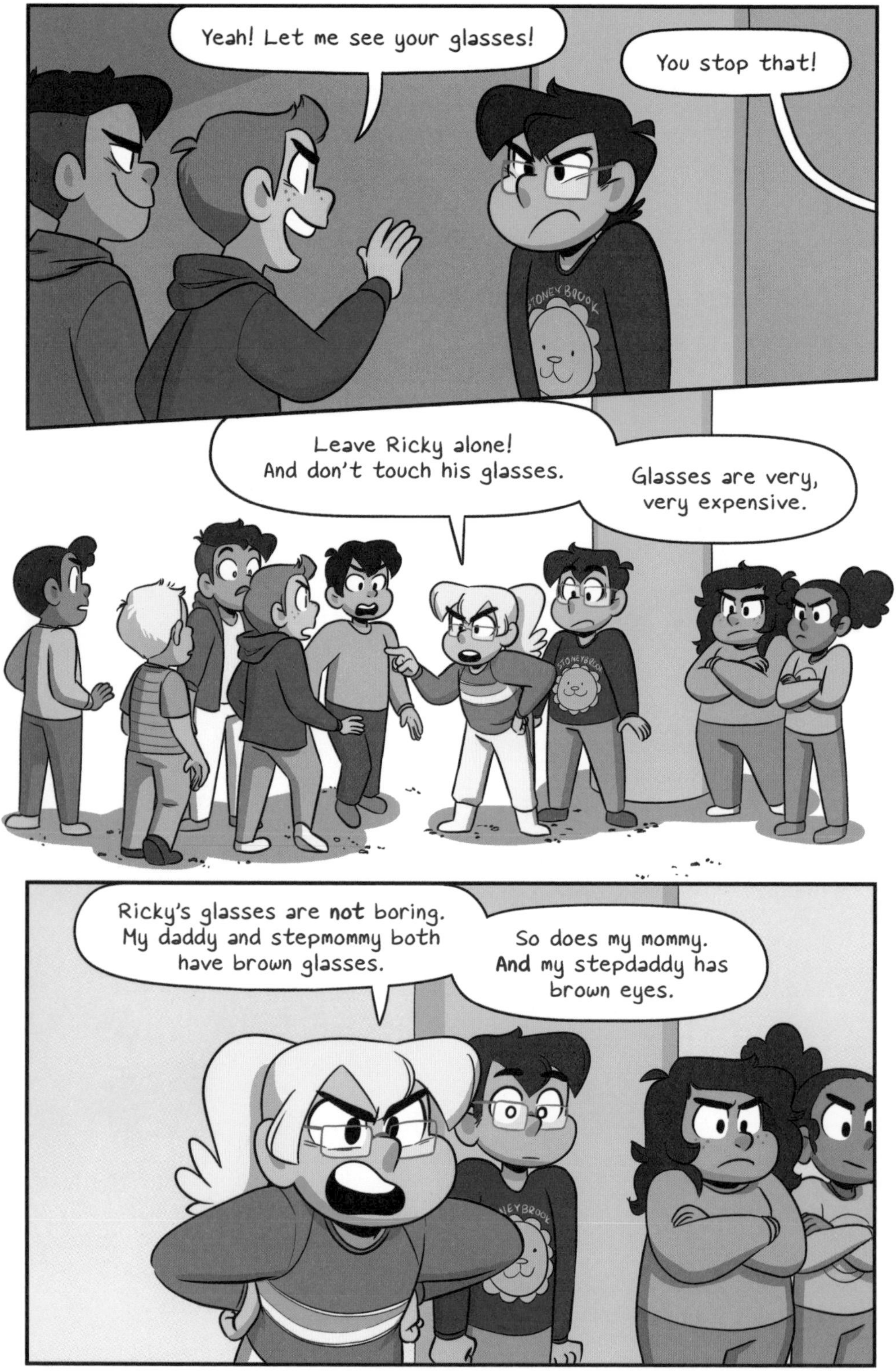
Yeah! Let me see your glasses!
You stop that!
Leave Ricky alone! And don't touch his glasses.
Glasses are very, very expensive.
STONEYBROOK
Ricky's glasses are not boring. My daddy and stepmommy both have brown glasses.
So does my mommy. And my stepdaddy has brown eyes.

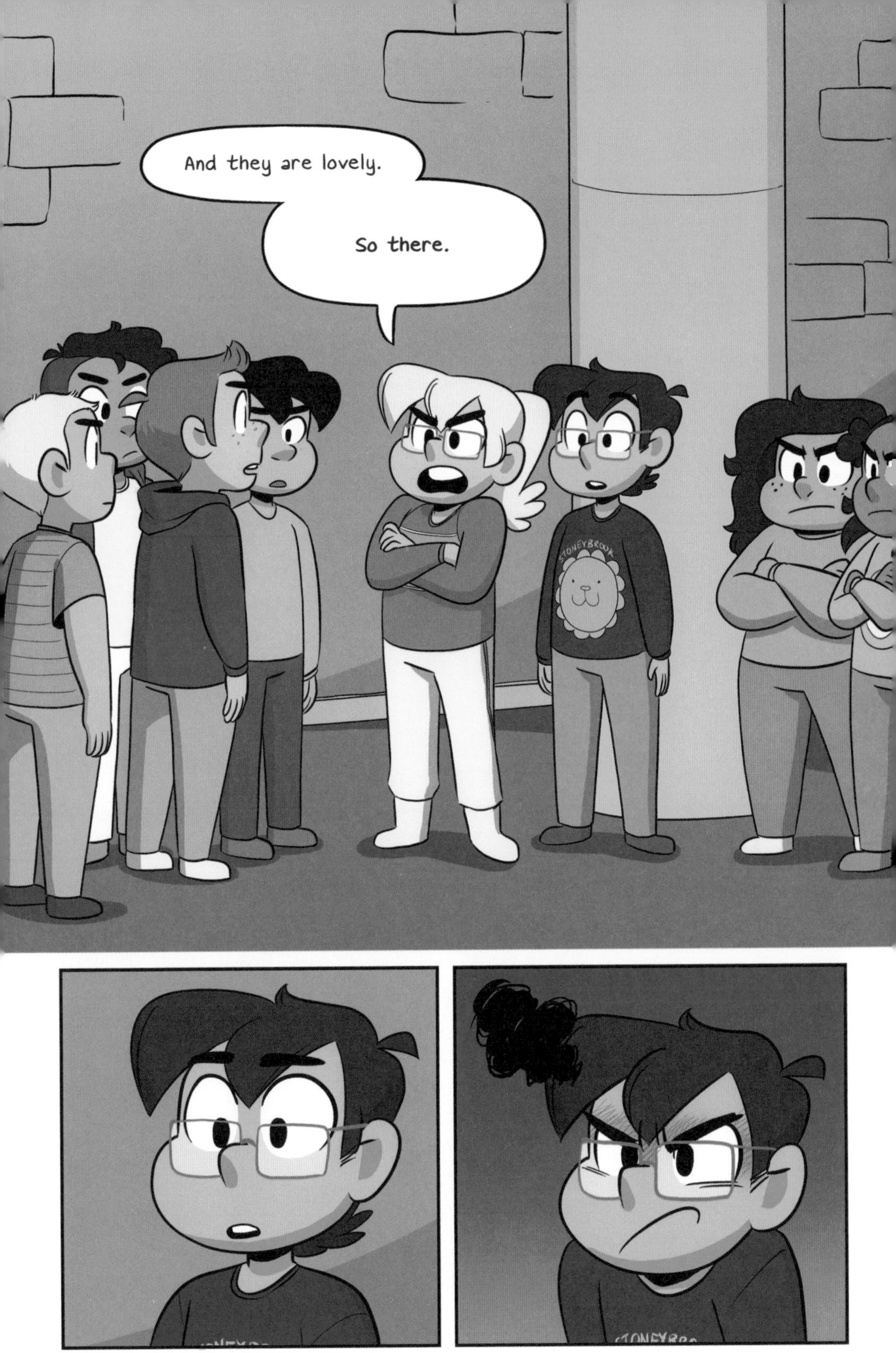
And they are lovely.
So there.
STONEYBROOK

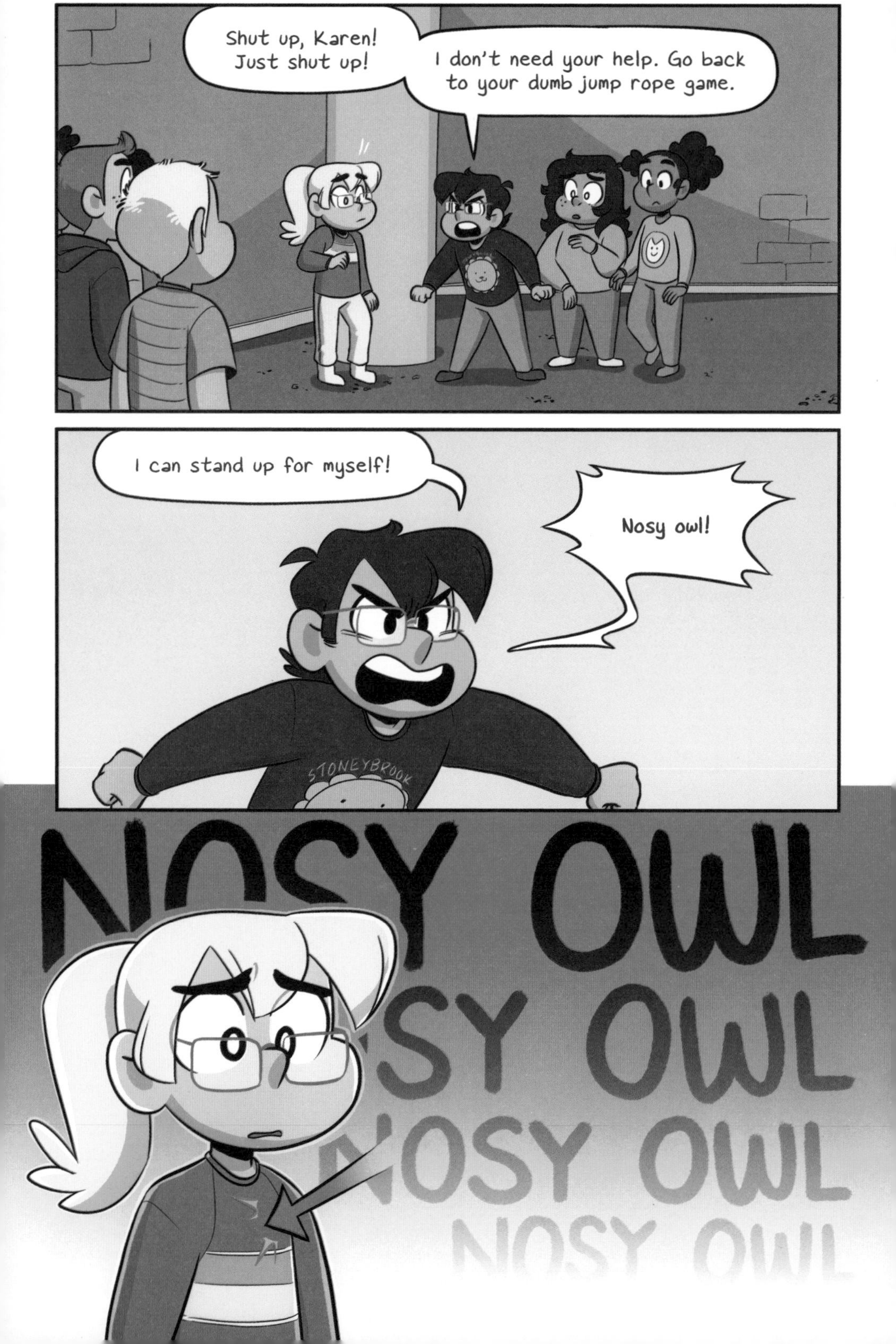
Shut up, Karen! Just shut up!
I don't need your help. Go back to your dumb jump rope game.
I can stand up for myself!
Nosy owl!
STONEYBROOK
NOSY OWL
NOSY OWL
NOSY OWL
NOSY OWL

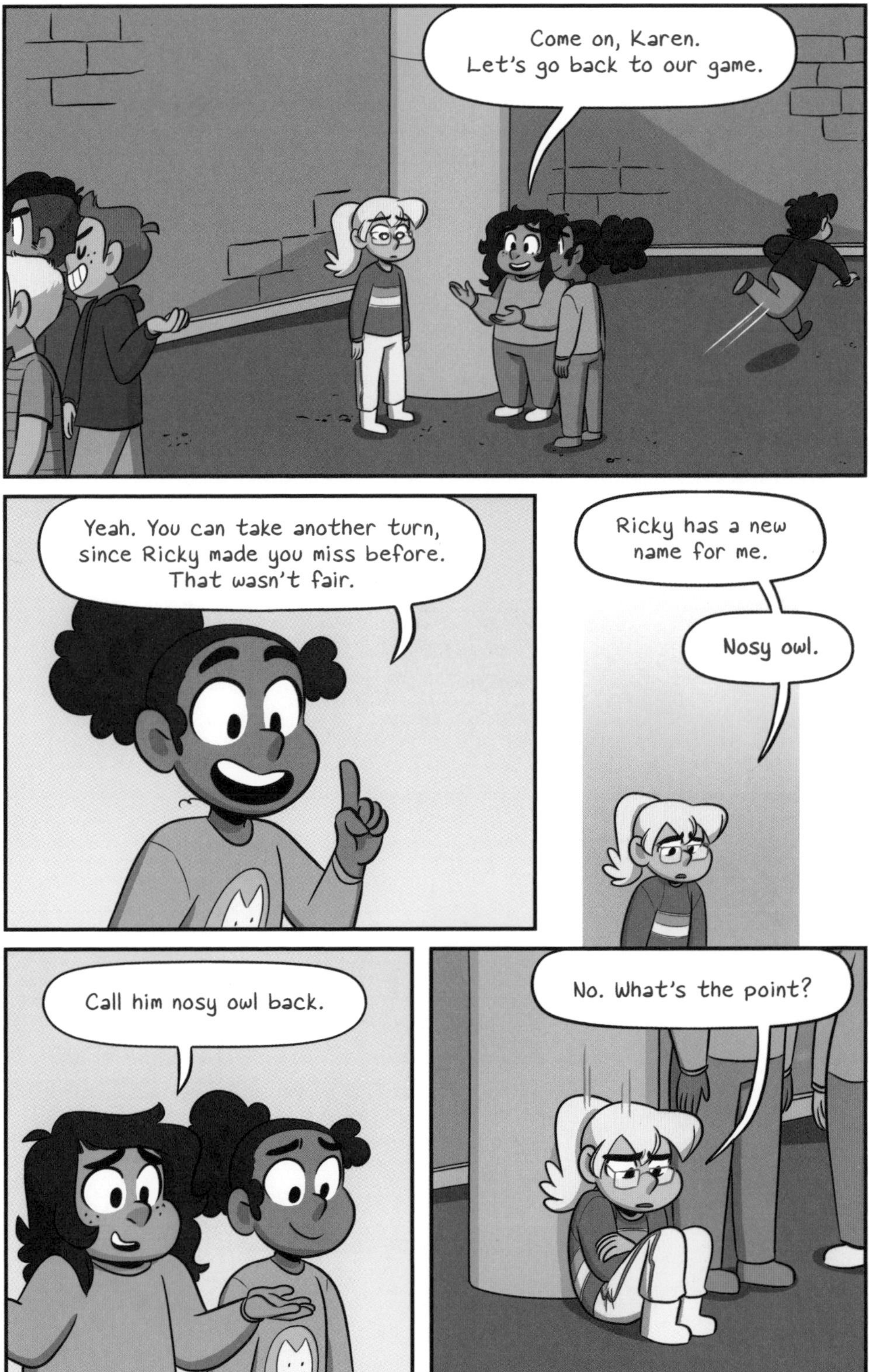
Come on, Karen.
Let's go back to our game.
Yeah. You can take another turn, since Ricky made you miss before. That wasn't fair.
Ricky has a new name for me.
Nosy owl.
Call him nosy owl back.
No. What's the point?

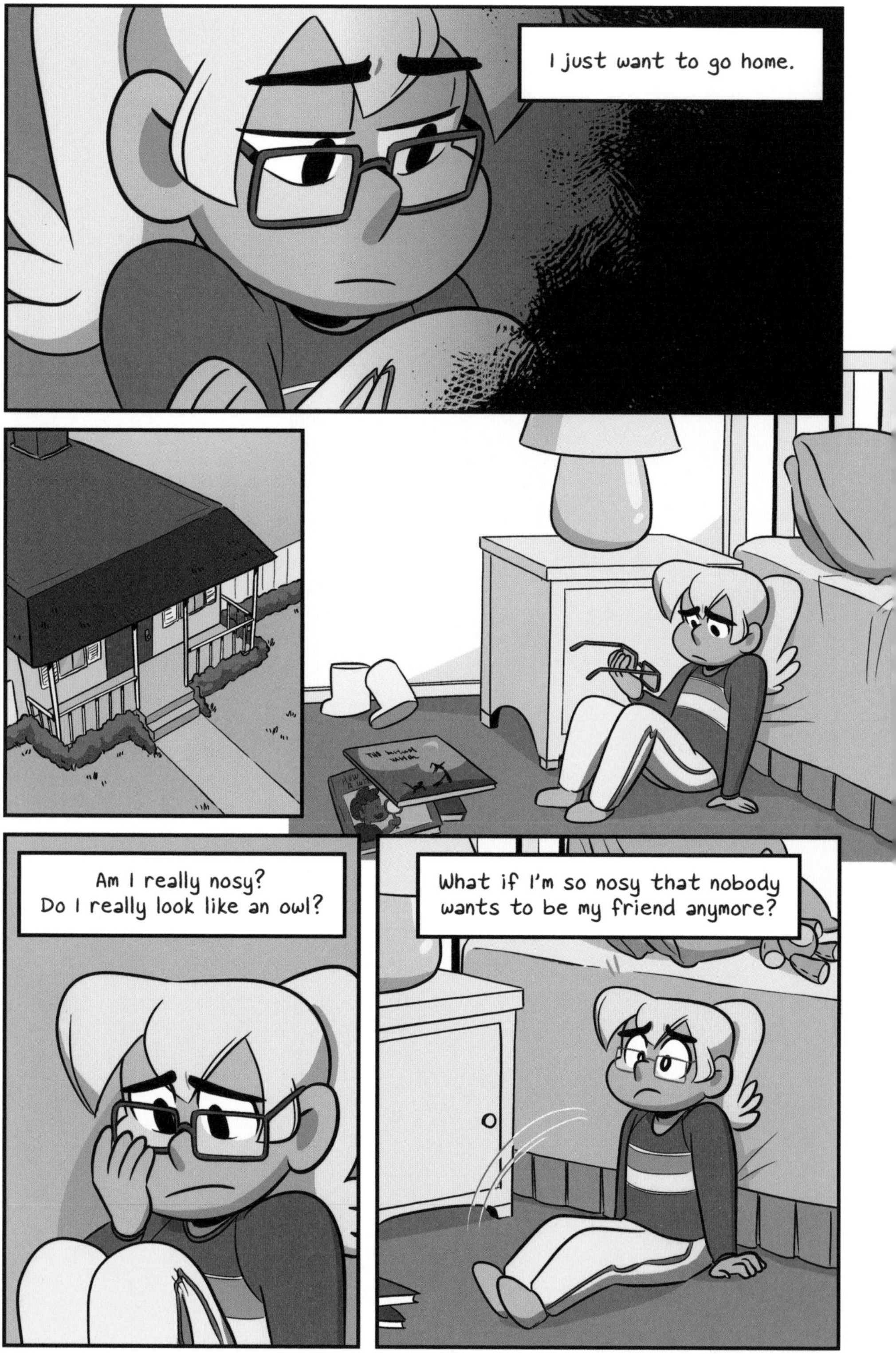
I just want to go home.
Am I really nosy?
Do I really look like an owl?
What if I'm so nosy that nobody wants to be my friend anymore?

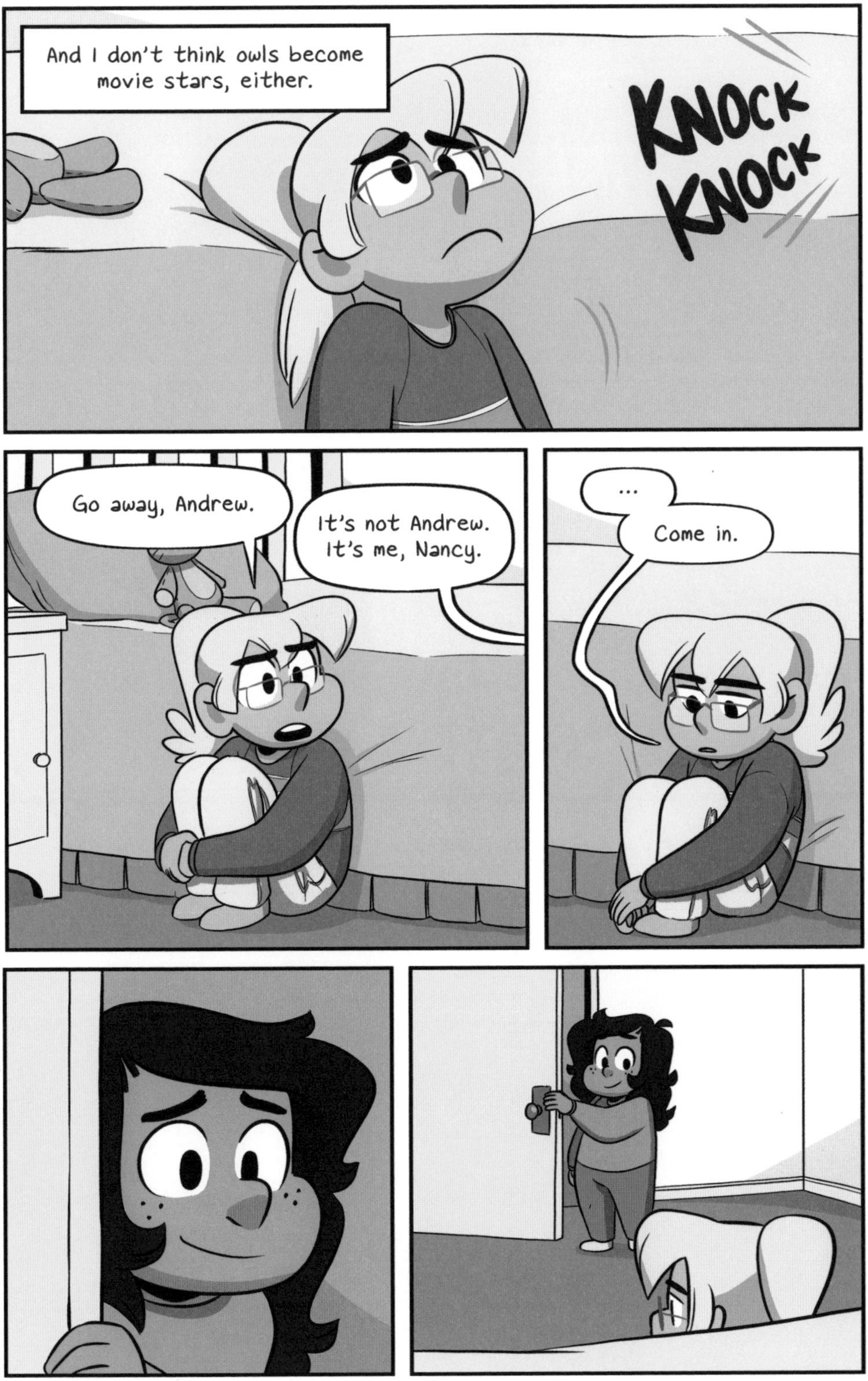
And I don't think owls become movie stars, either.
KNOCK KNOCK
Go away, Andrew.
It's not Andrew. It's me, Nancy.
...
Come in.

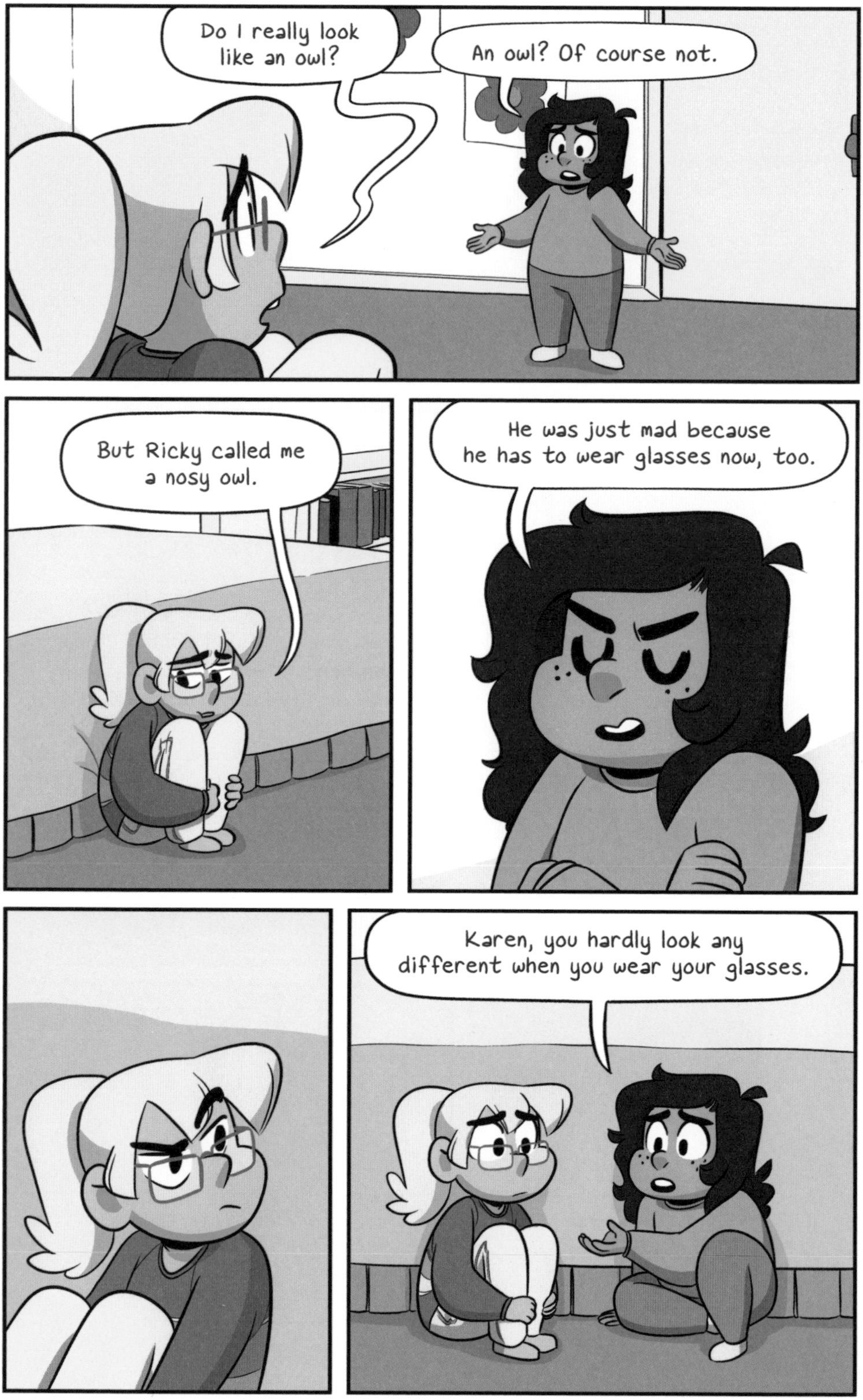
Do I really look like an owl?
An owl? Of course not.
But Ricky called me a nosy owl.
He was just mad because he has to wear glasses now, too.
Karen, you hardly look any different when you wear your glasses.

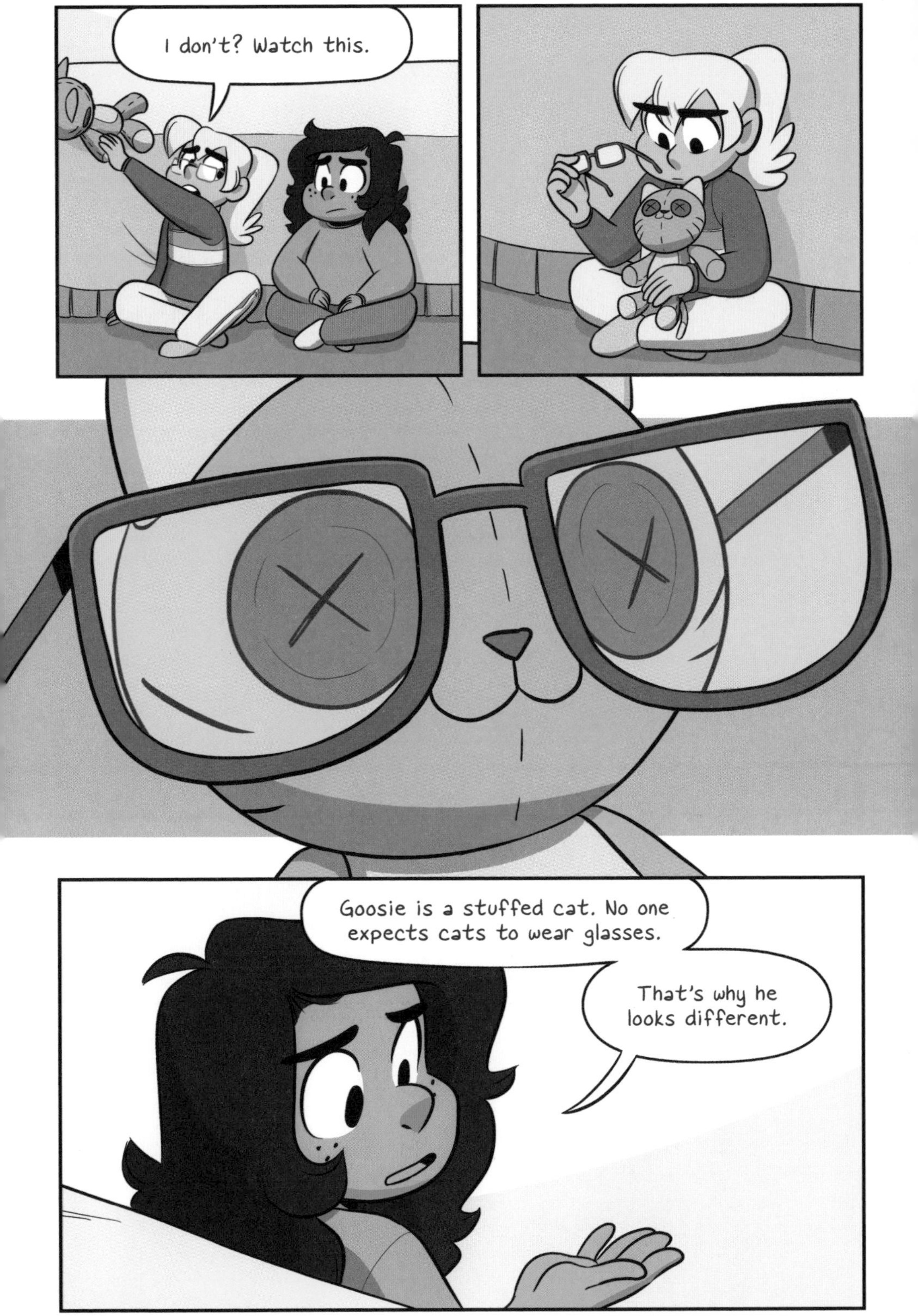
I don't? Watch this.
Goosie is a stuffed cat. No one expects cats to wear glasses.
That's why he looks different.

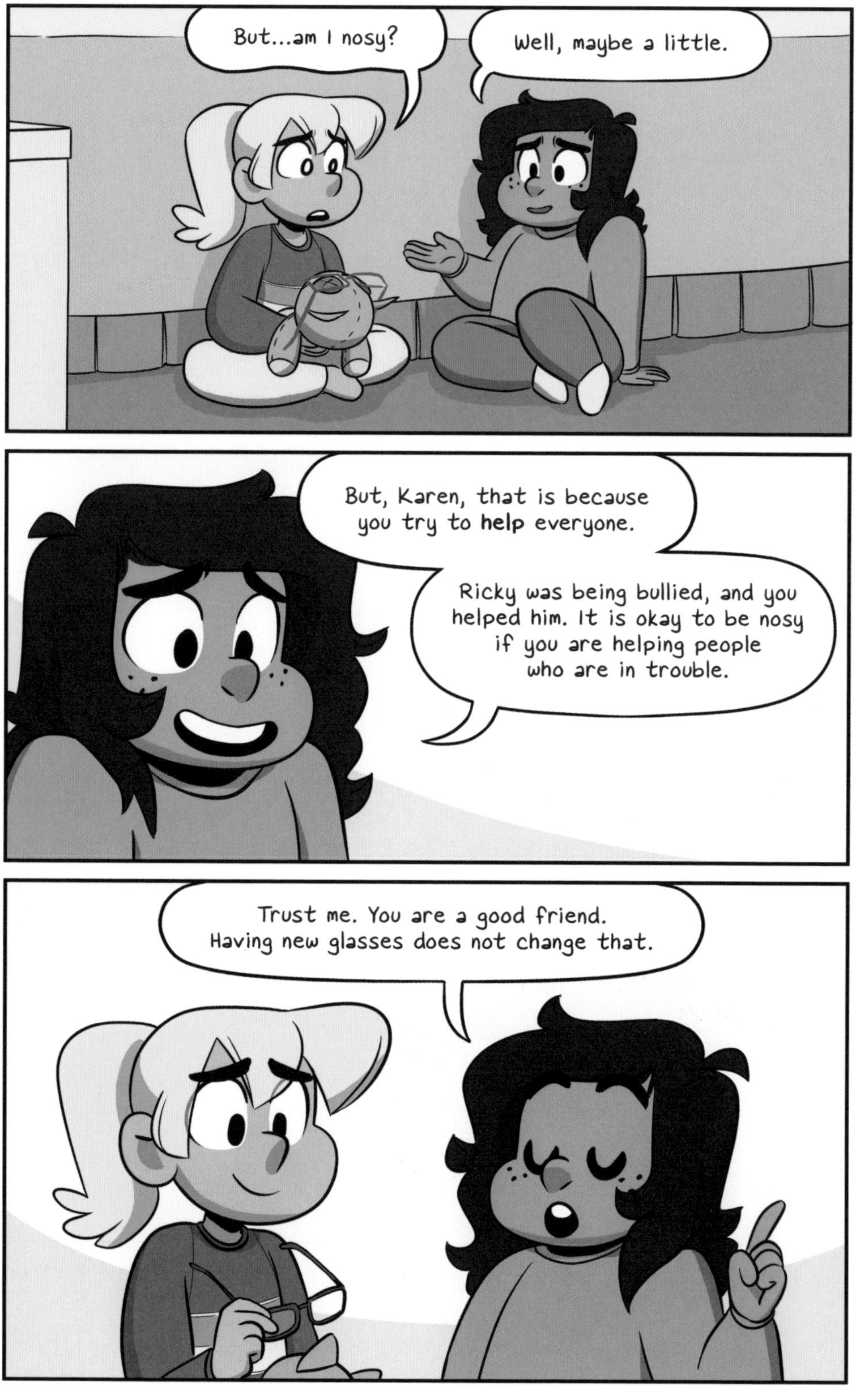
But...am I nosy?
Well, maybe a little.
But, Karen, that is because you try to **help** everyone.
Ricky was being bullied, and you helped him. It is okay to be nosy if you are helping people who are in trouble.
Trust me. You are a good friend. Having new glasses does not change that.

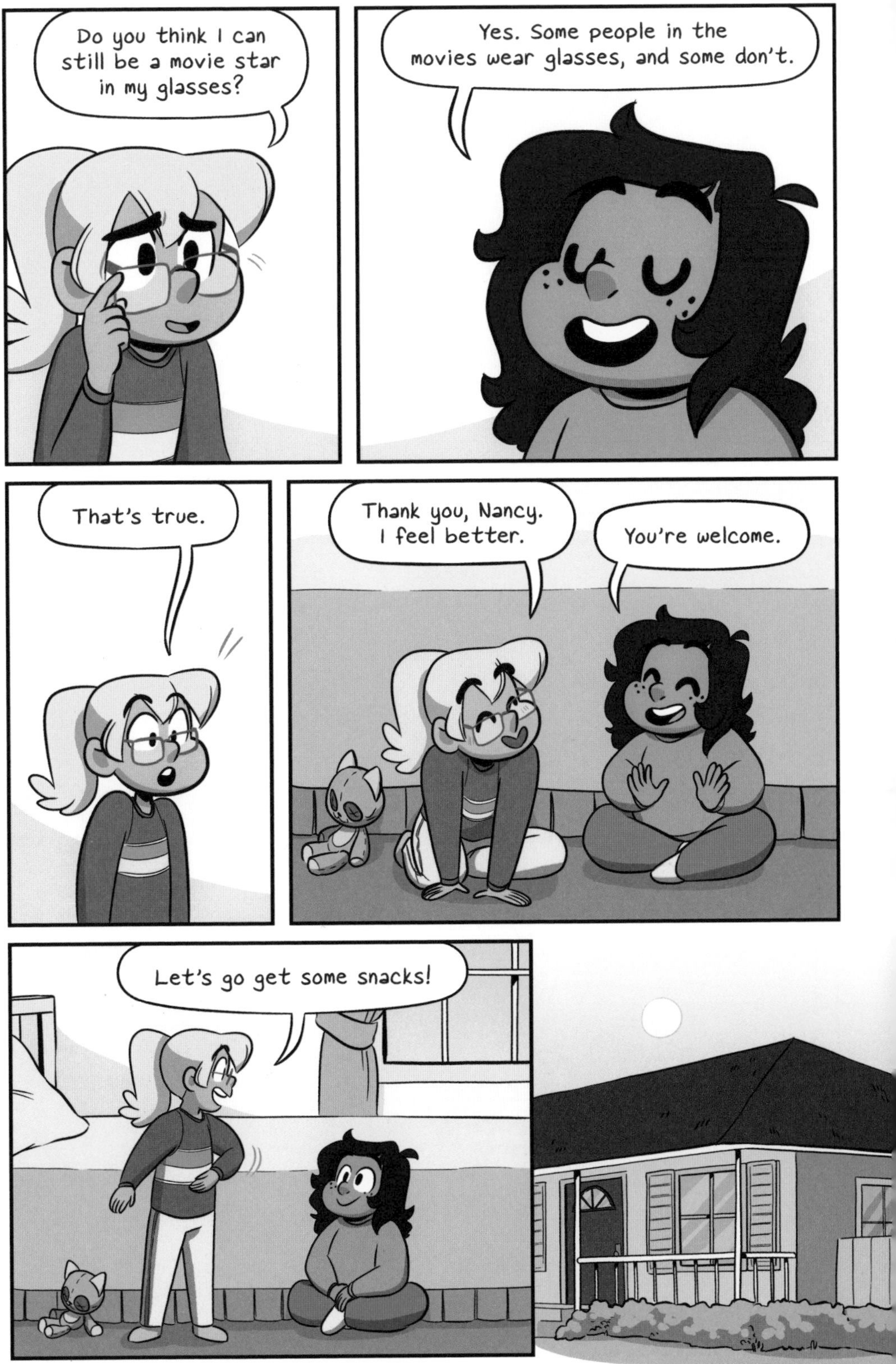
Do you think I can still be a movie star in my glasses?
Yes. Some people in the movies wear glasses, and some don't.
That's true.
Thank you, Nancy. I feel better.
You're welcome.
Let's go get some snacks!

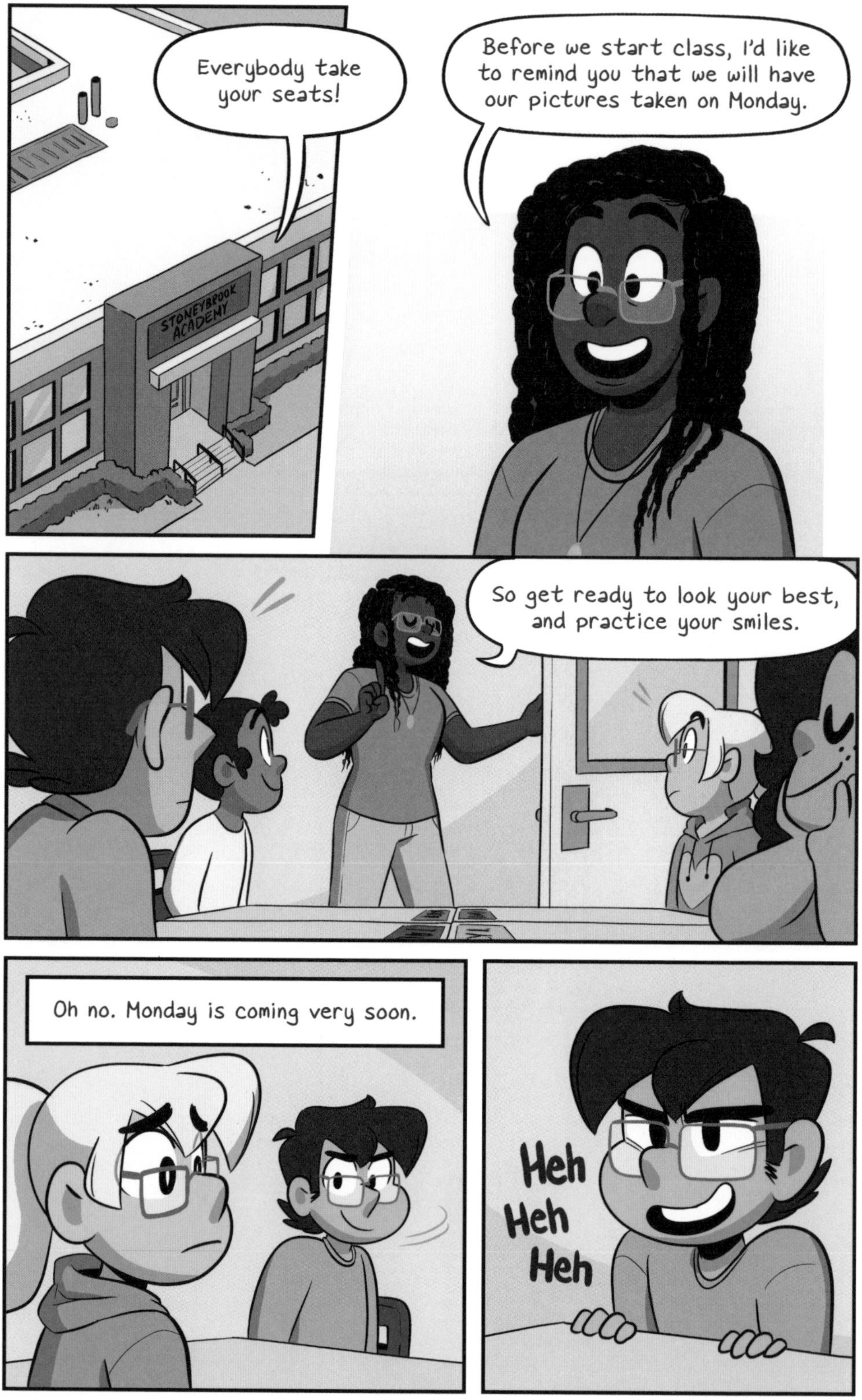
Everybody take your seats!
STONEYBROOK ACADEMY
Before we start class, I'd like to remind you that we will have our pictures taken on Monday.
So get ready to look your best, and practice your smiles.
Oh no. Monday is coming very soon.
Heh Heh Heh

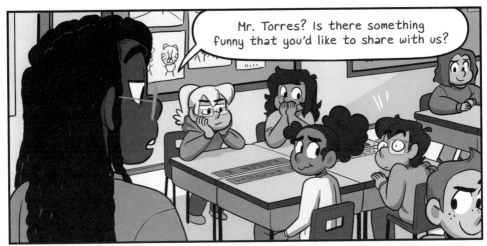

Mr. Torres? Is there something funny that you'd like to share with us?

No.

Good.

But what am I going to do about Monday?

CHAPTER 8

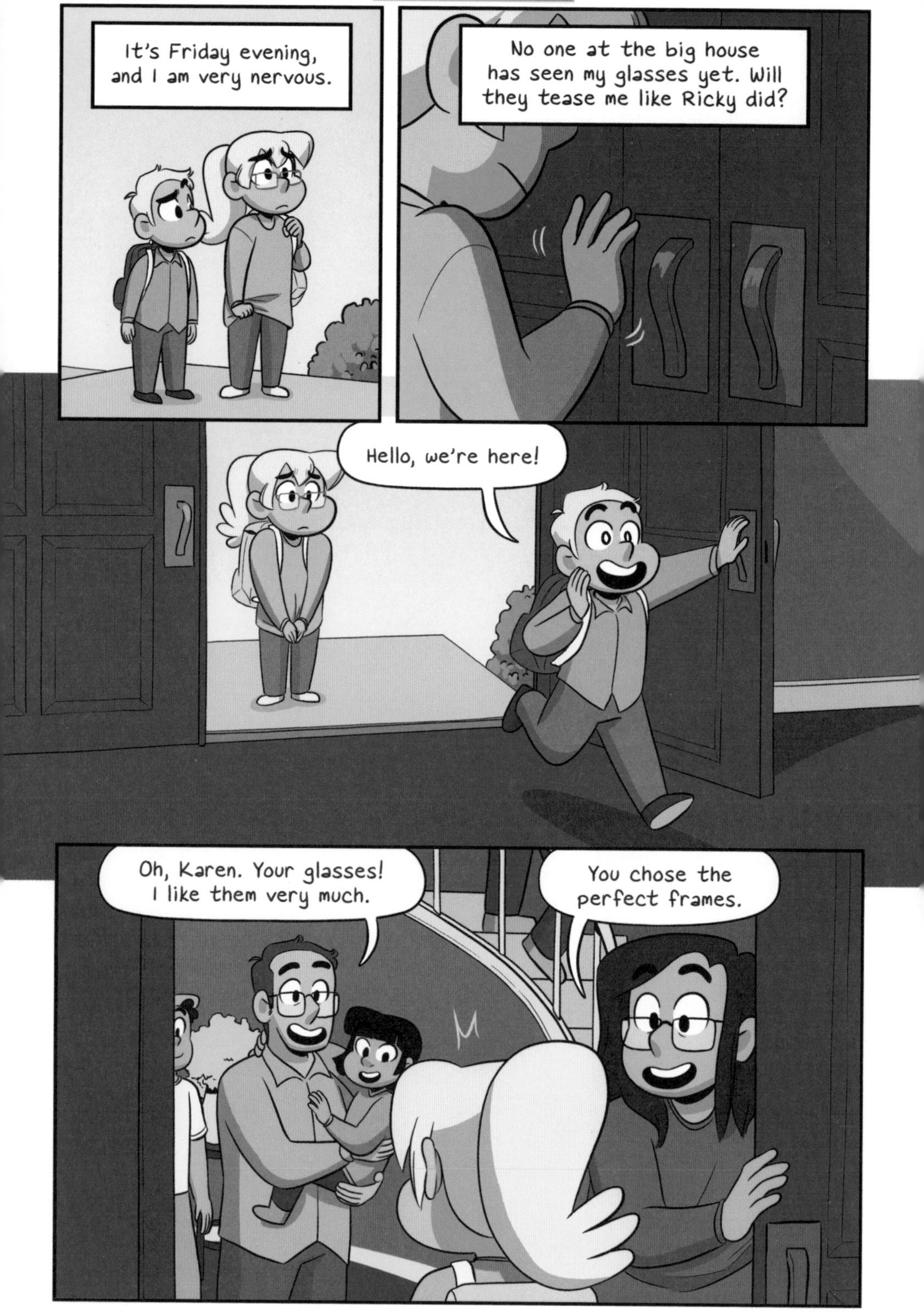

It's Friday evening, and I am very nervous.
No one at the big house has seen my glasses yet. Will they tease me like Ricky did?
Hello, we're here!
Oh, Karen. Your glasses! I like them very much.
You chose the perfect frames.

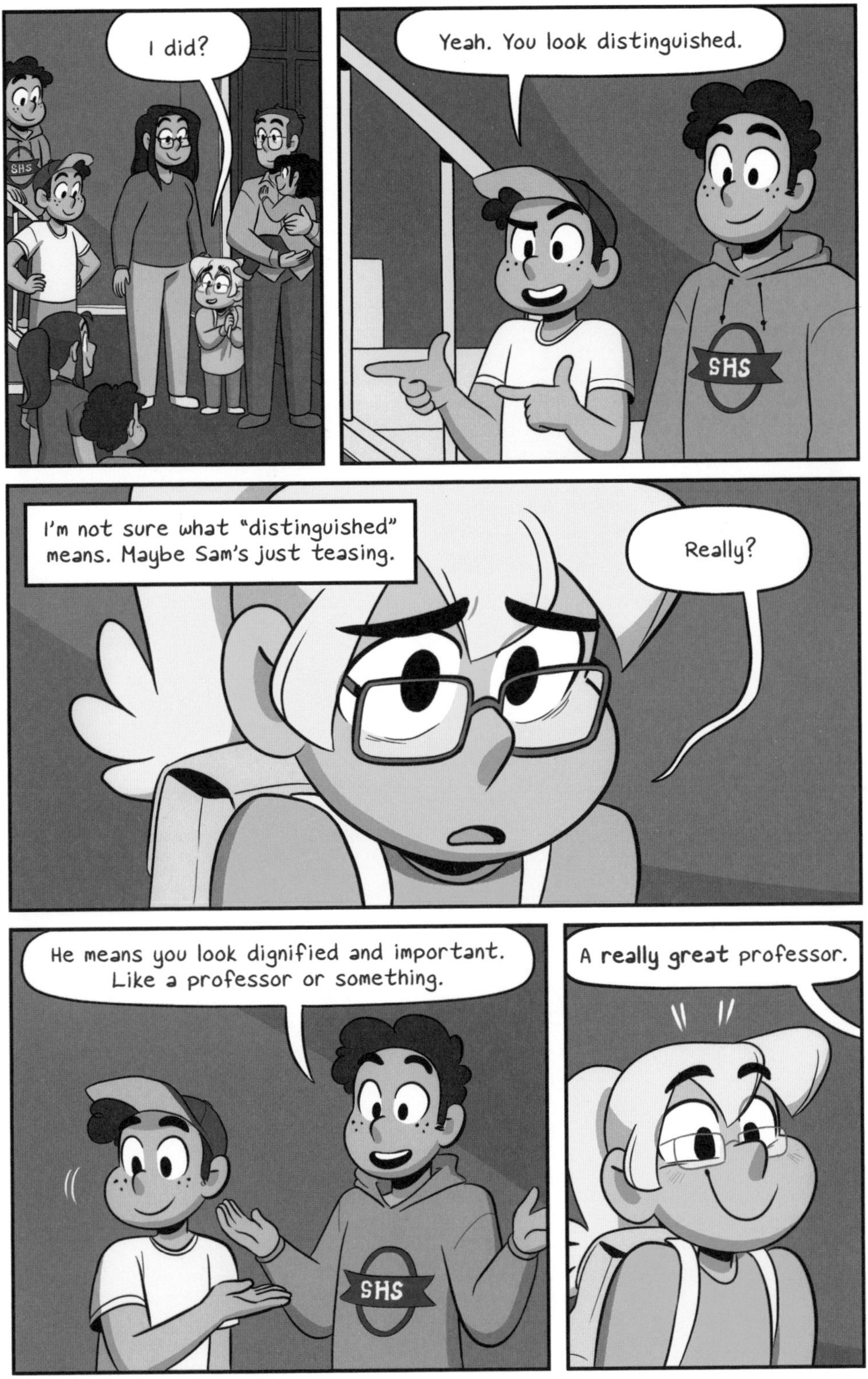
I did?
Yeah. You look distinguished.
I'm not sure what "distinguished" means. Maybe Sam's just teasing.
Really?
He means you look dignified and important. Like a professor or something.
A really great professor.

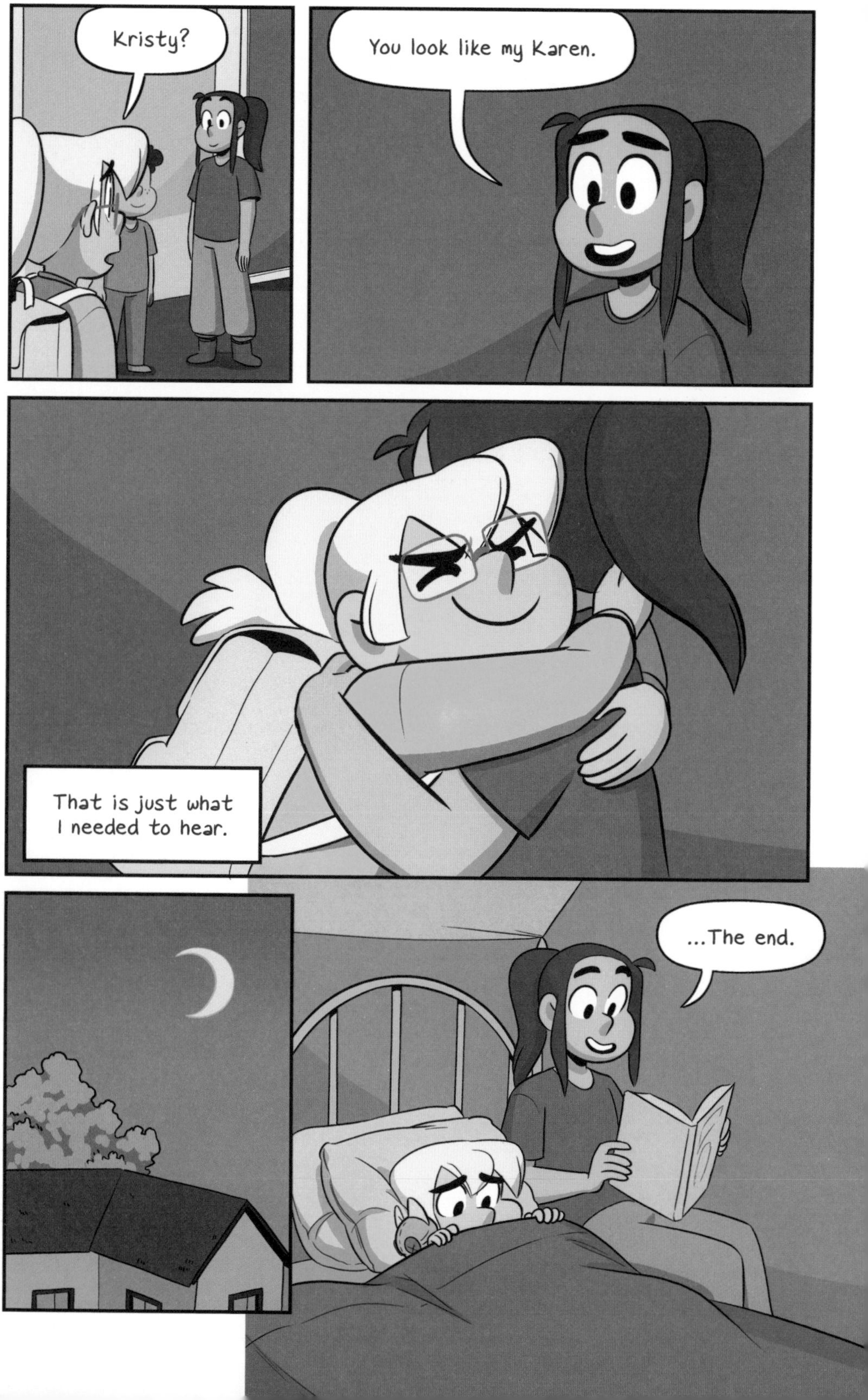
Kristy?
You look like my Karen.
That is just what I needed to hear.
...The end.

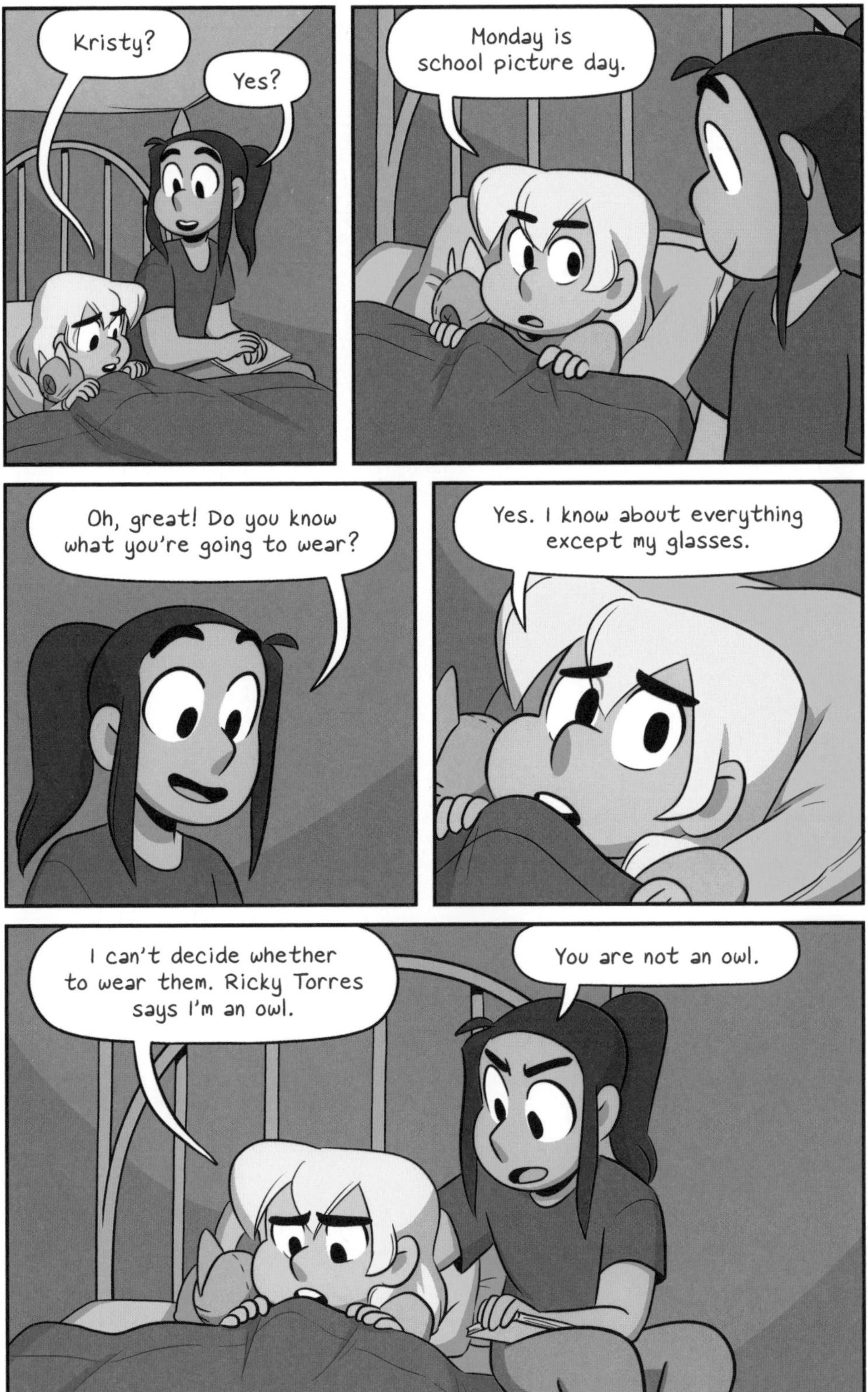
Kristy?
Yes?
Monday is school picture day.
Oh, great! Do you know what you're going to wear?
Yes. I know about everything except my glasses.
I can't decide whether to wear them. Ricky Torres says I'm an owl.
You are not an owl.

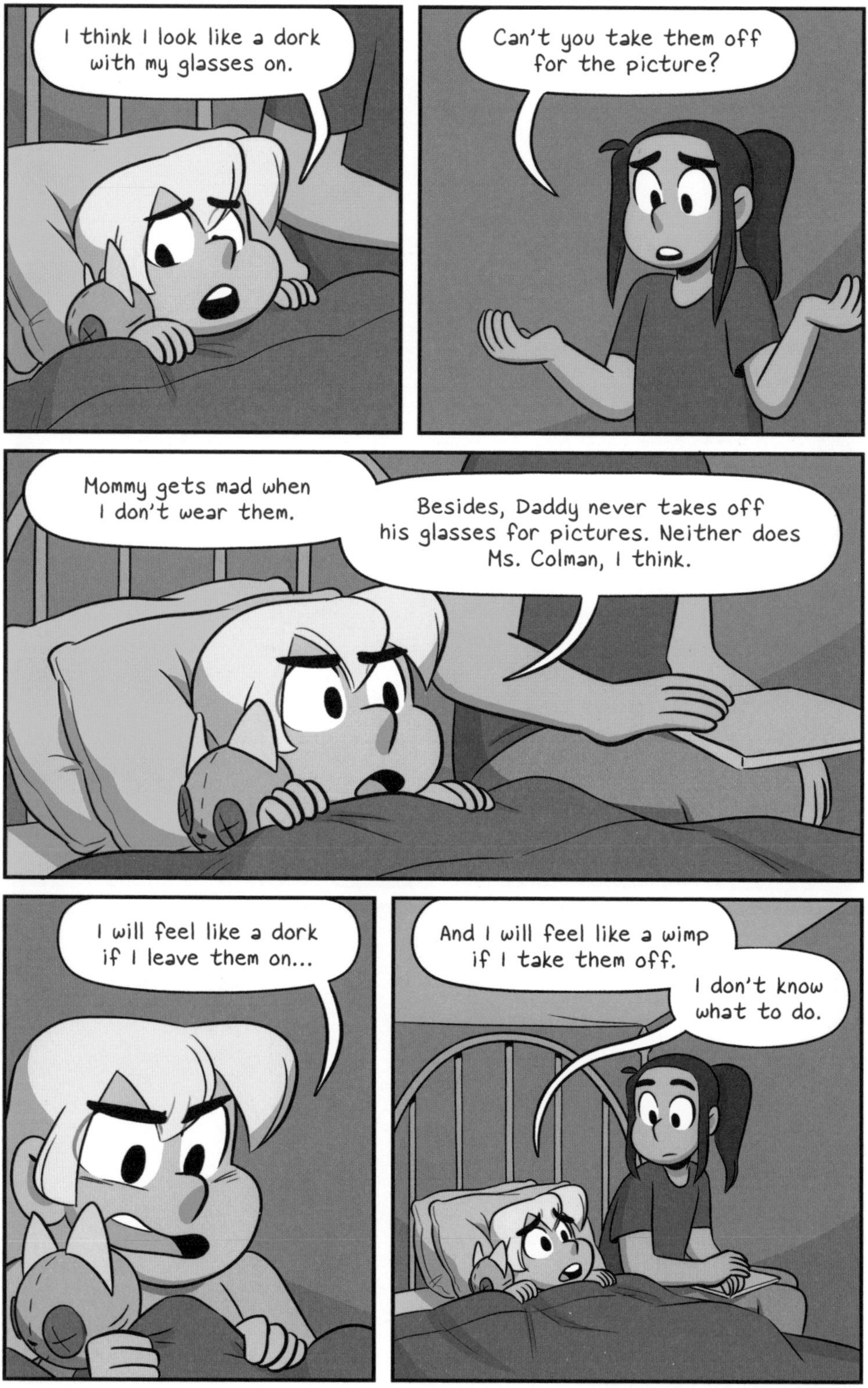
I think I look like a dork with my glasses on.
Can't you take them off for the picture?
Mommy gets mad when I don't wear them.
Besides, Daddy never takes off his glasses for pictures. Neither does Ms. Colman, I think.
I will feel like a dork if I leave them on...
And I will feel like a wimp if I take them off.
I don't know what to do.

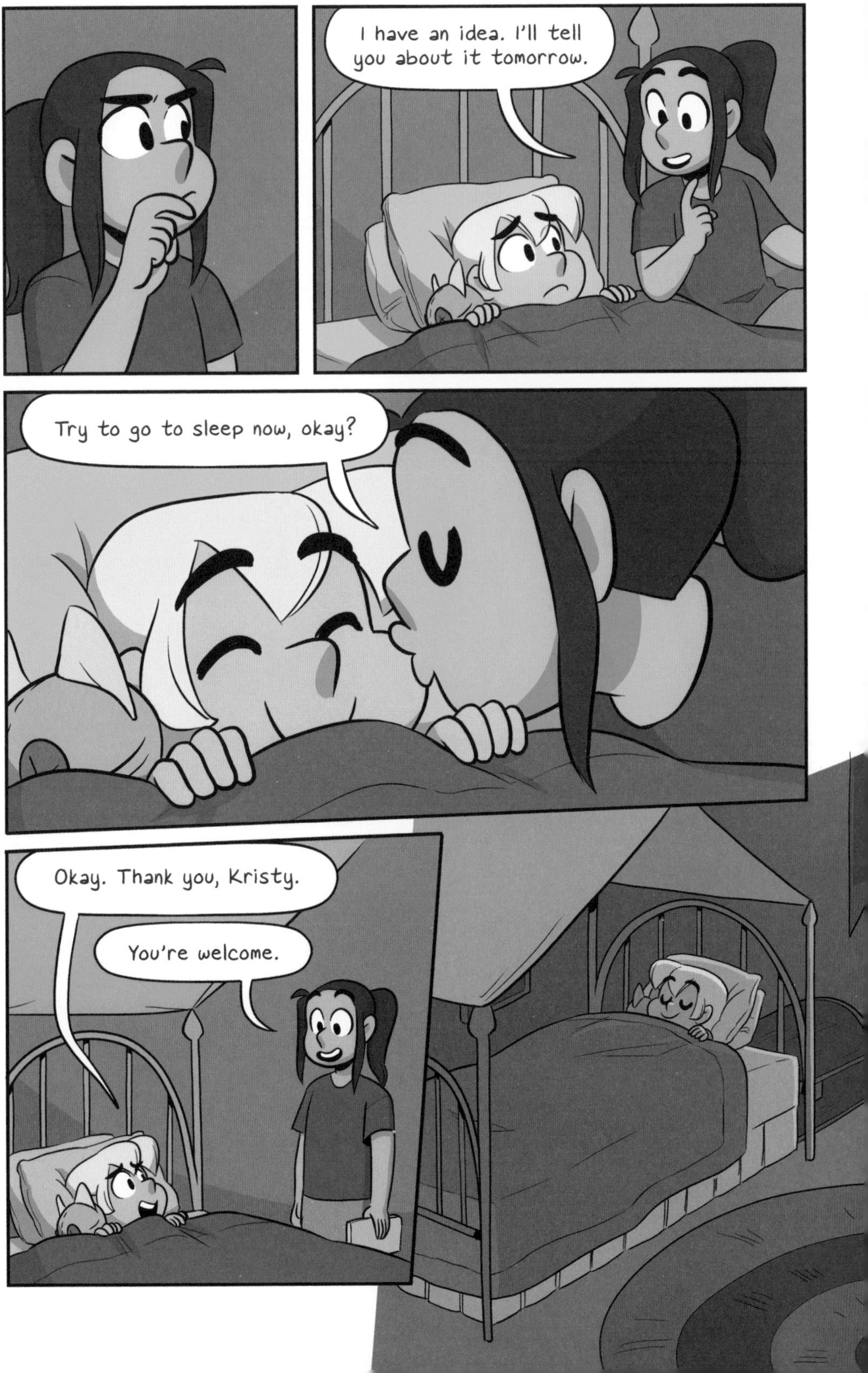
I have an idea. I'll tell you about it tomorrow.
Try to go to sleep now, okay?
Okay. Thank you, Kristy.
You're welcome.

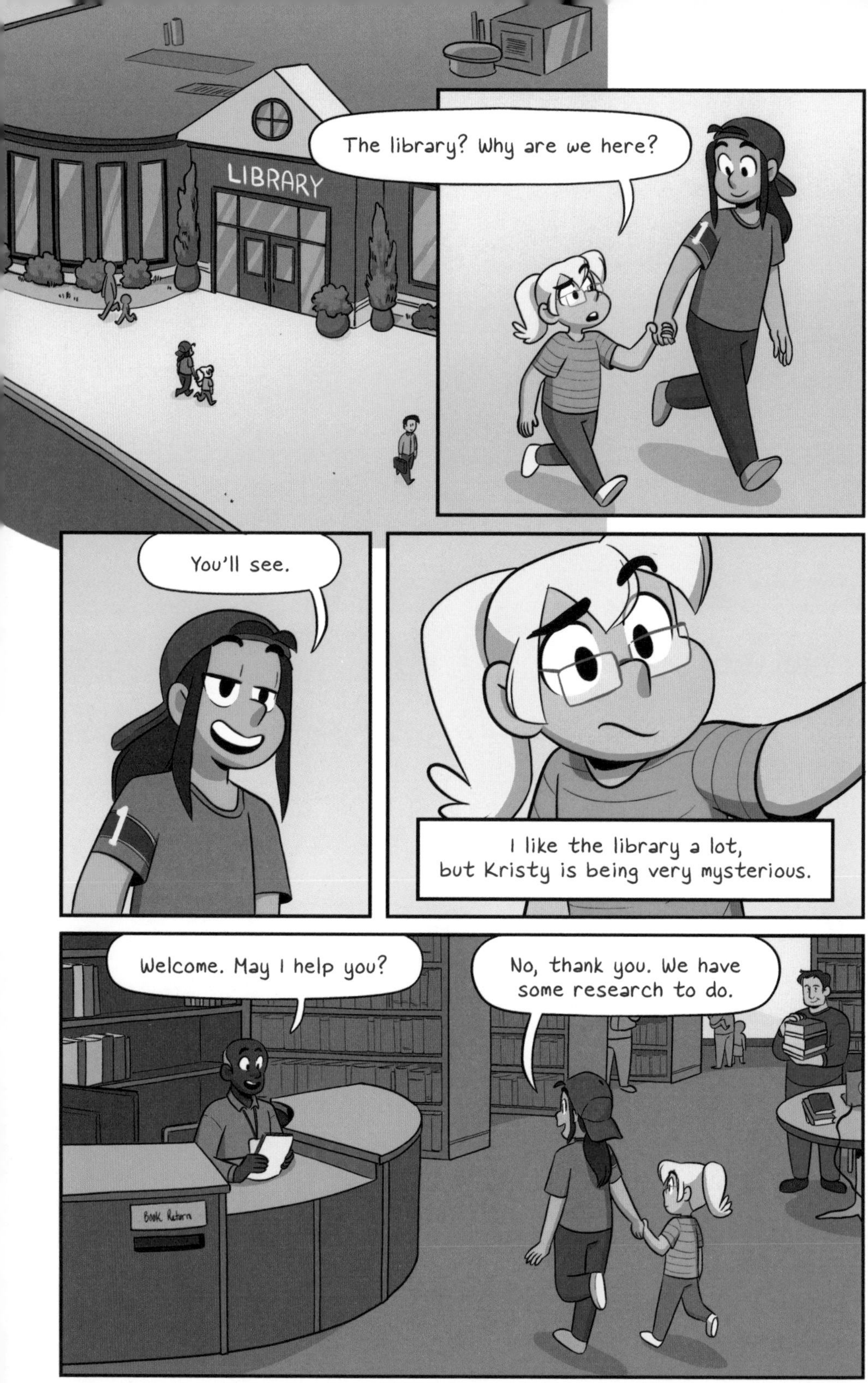

LIBRARY
The library? Why are we here?
You'll see.
I like the library a lot, but Kristy is being very mysterious.
Welcome. May I help you?
No, thank you. We have some research to do.
Book Return

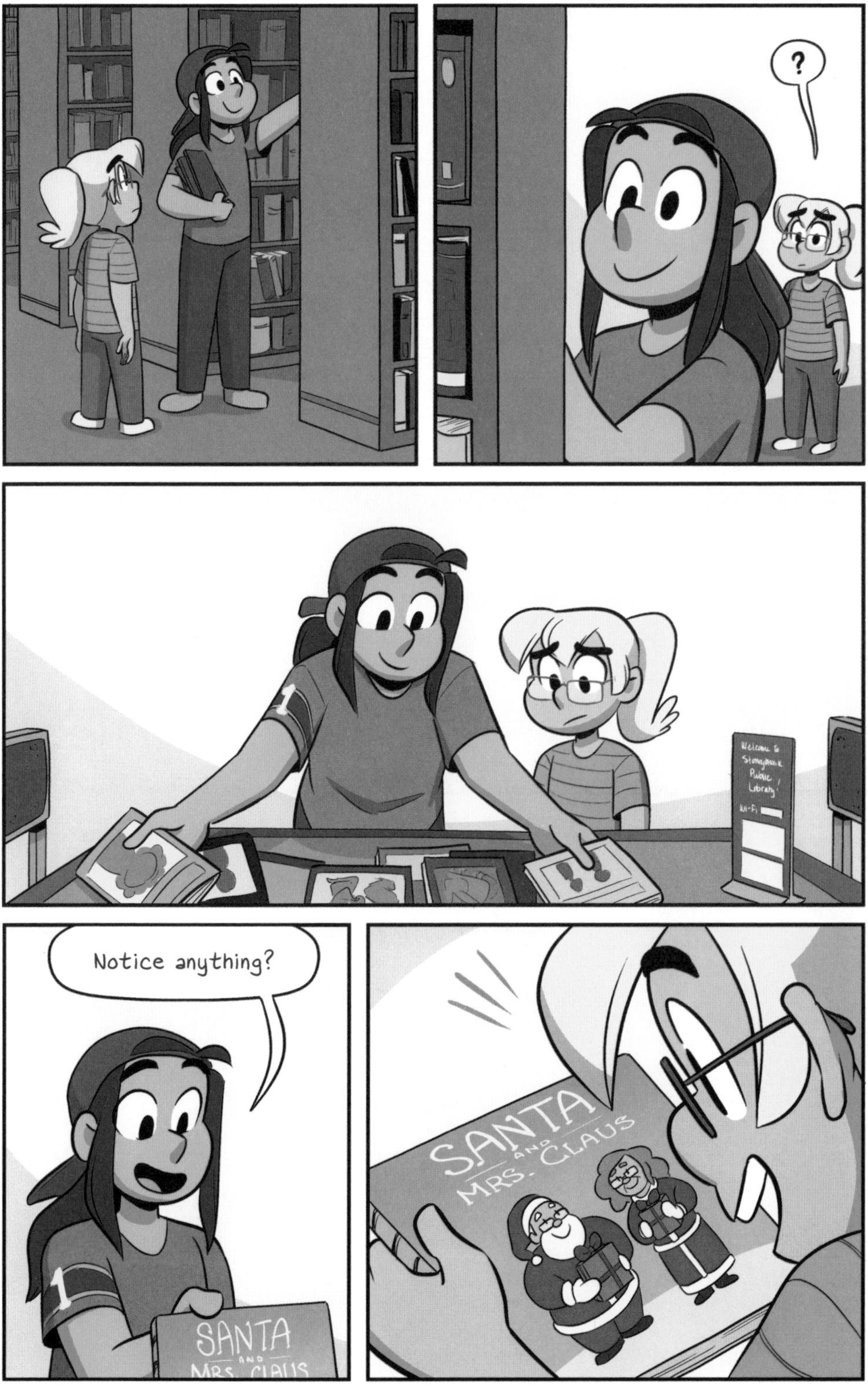
?
Welcome to Stoneybrook Public Library!
Wi-Fi
Notice anything?
SANTA AND MRS. CLAUS
SANTA AND MRS. CLAUS

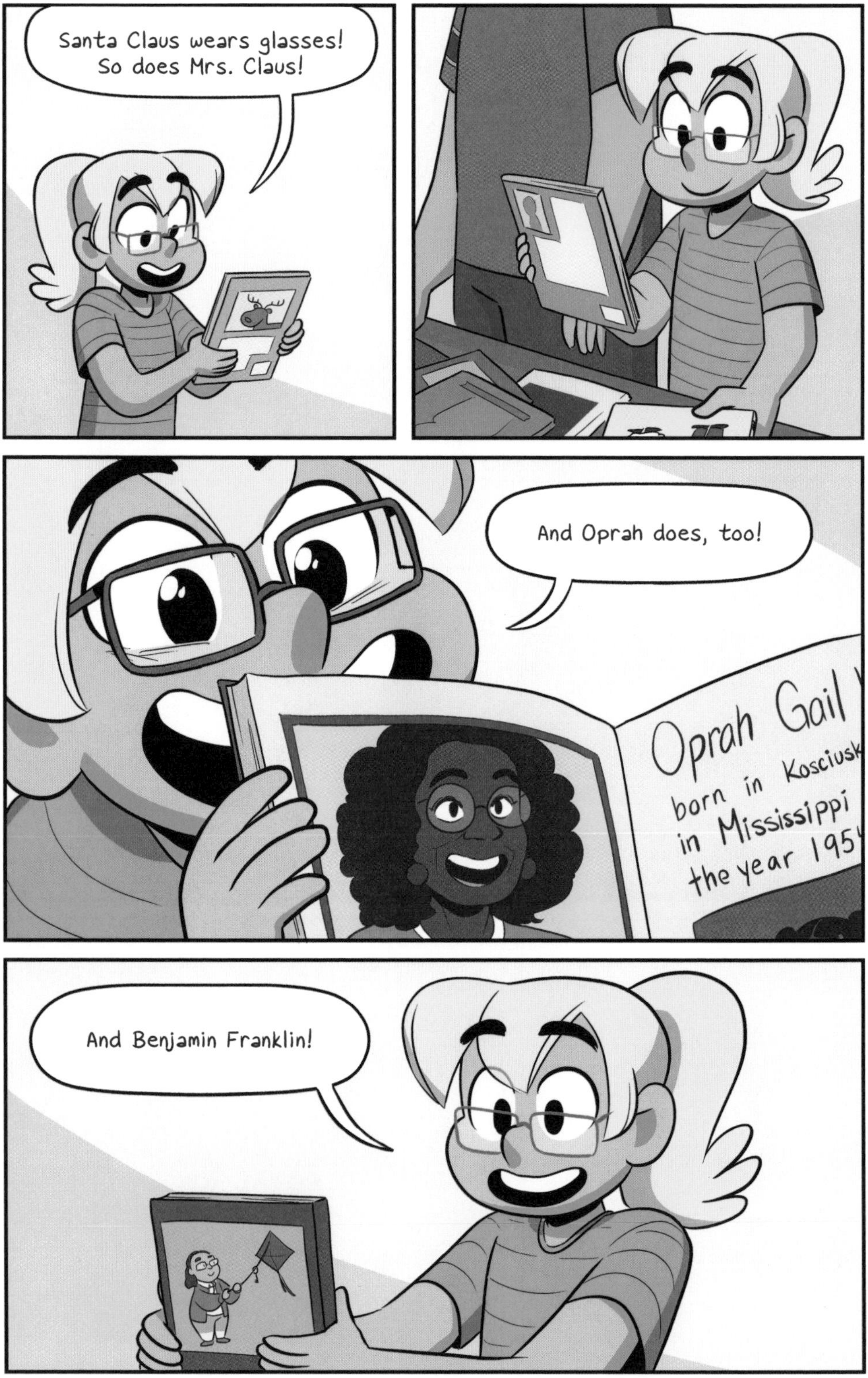
Santa Claus wears glasses! So does Mrs. Claus!
And Oprah does, too!
Oprah Gail
born in
in Mississippi
the year
And Benjamin Franklin!

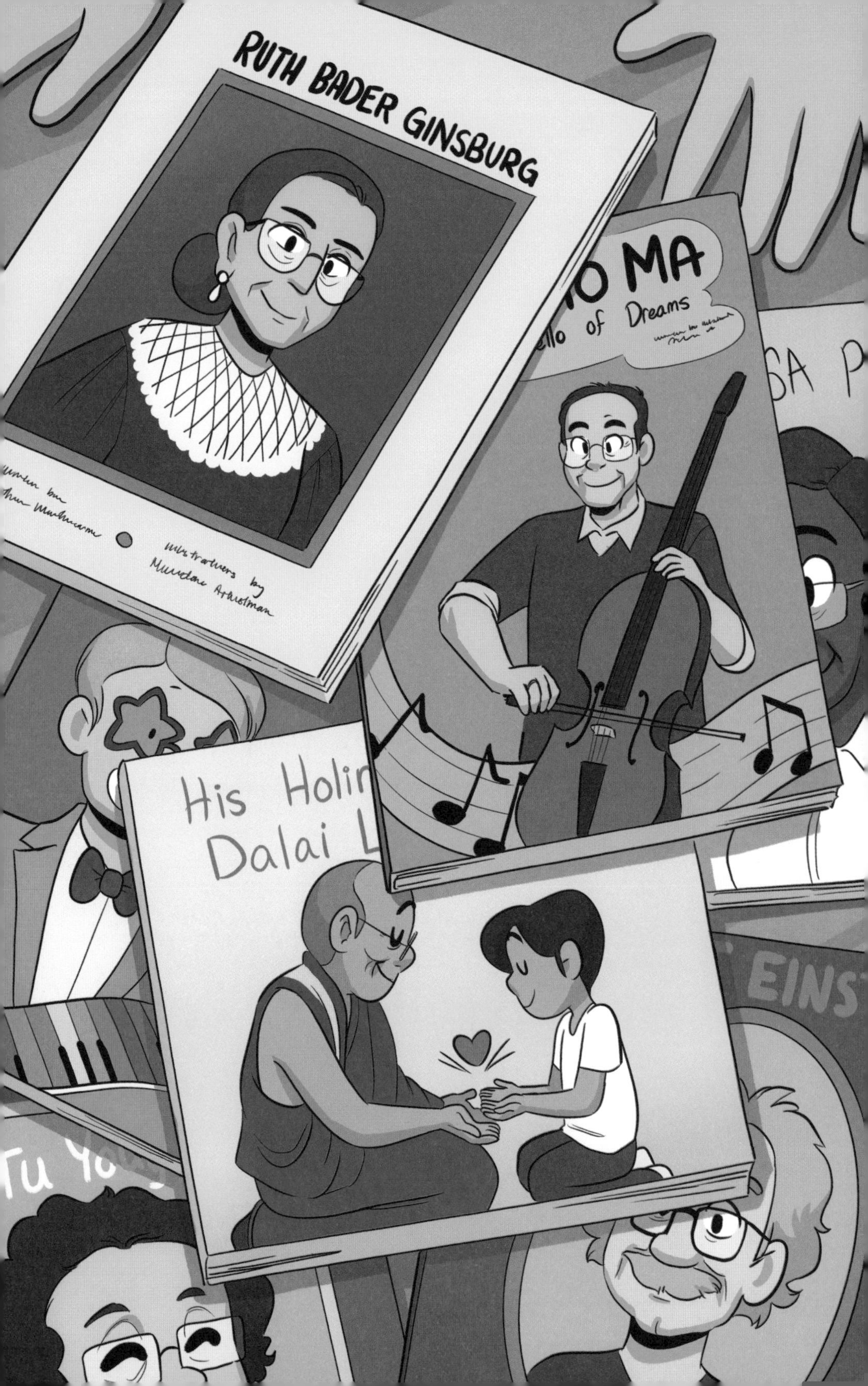

RUTH BADER GINSBURG
MA
ello of Dreams
SA P
His Holin
Dalai L
EINST

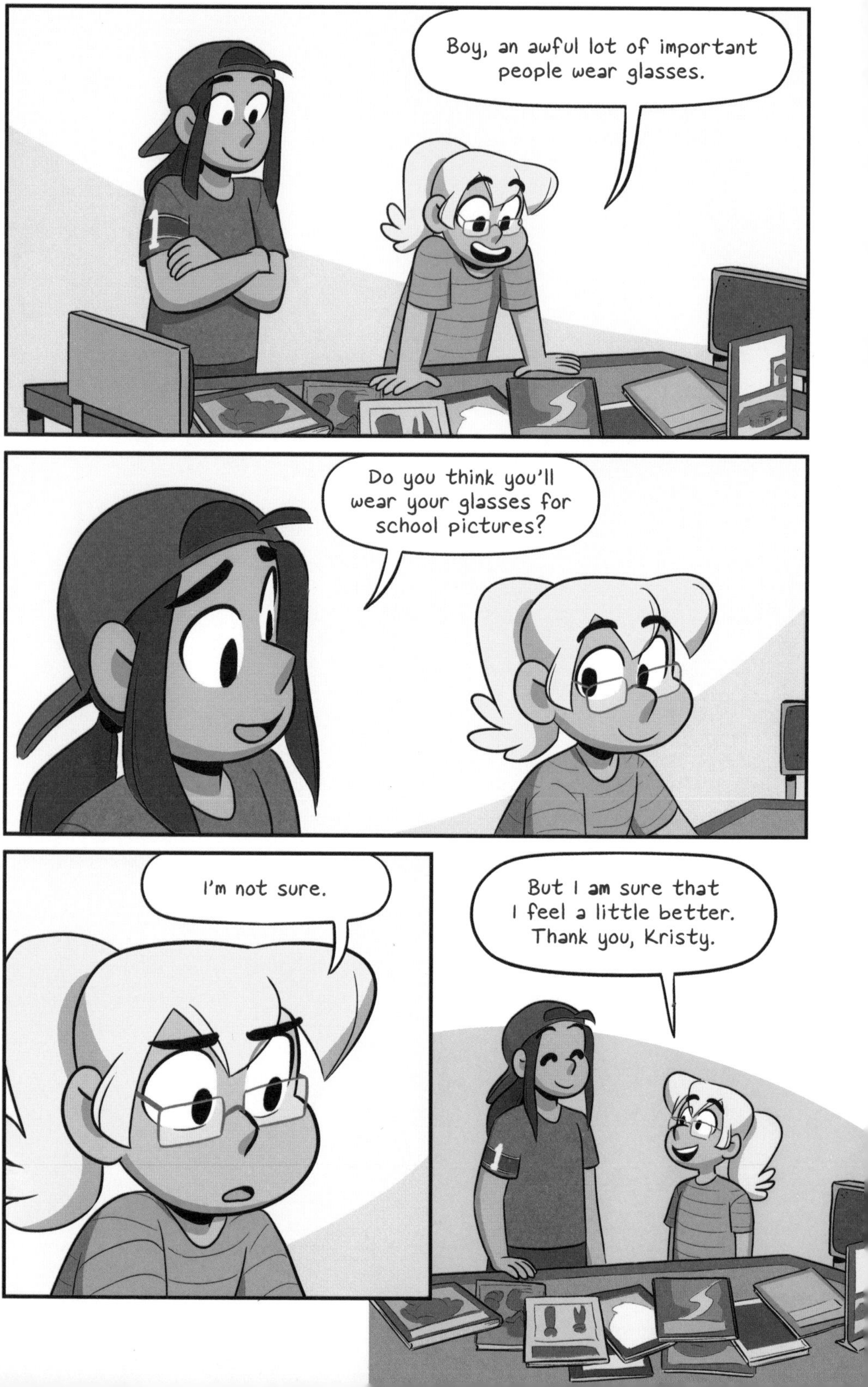
Boy, an awful lot of important people wear glasses.
Do you think you'll wear your glasses for school pictures?
I'm not sure.
But I am sure that I feel a little better. Thank you, Kristy.

CHAPTER 9

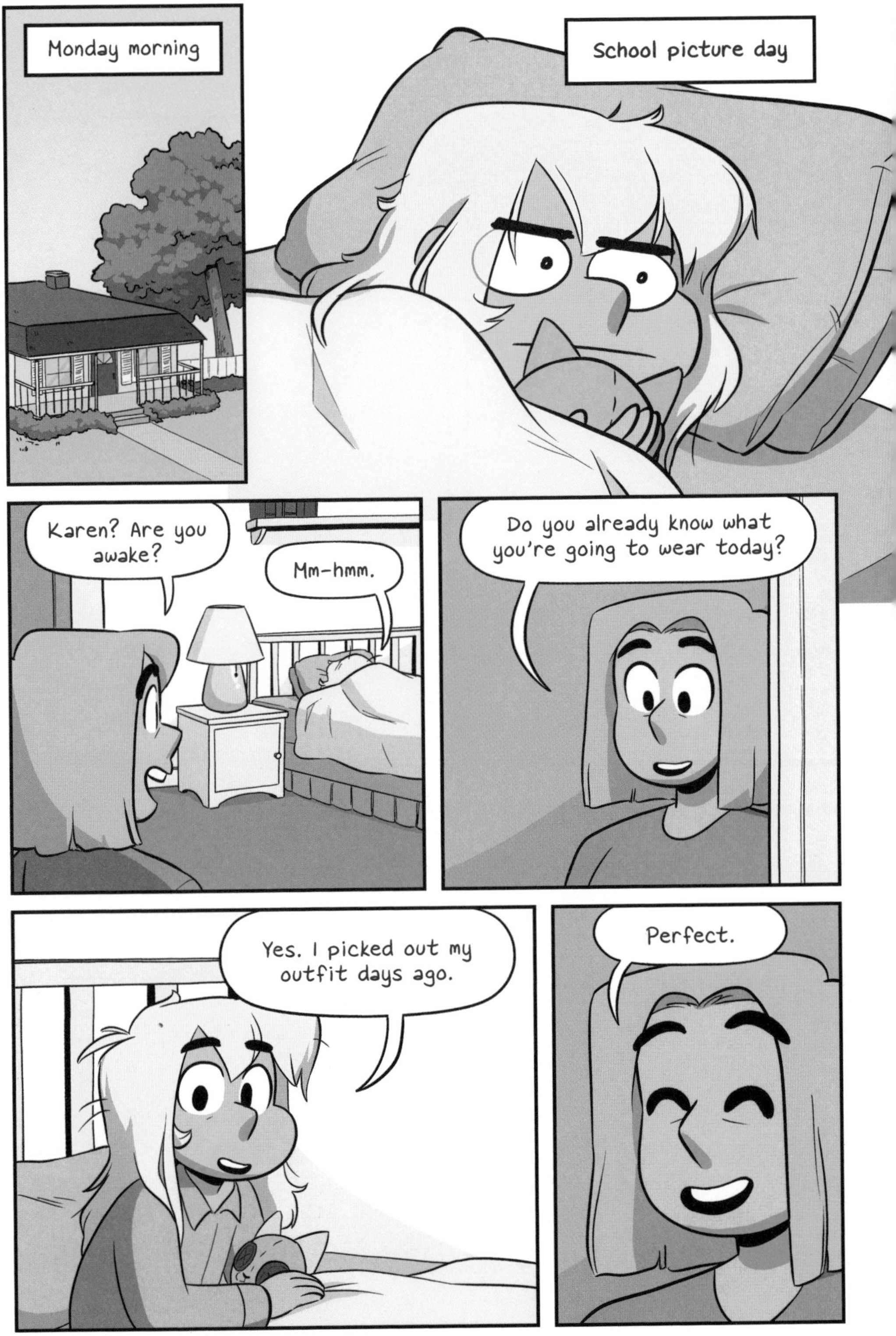
Monday morning
School picture day
Karen? Are you awake?
Mm-hmm.
Do you already know what you're going to wear today?
Yes. I picked out my outfit days ago.
Perfect.

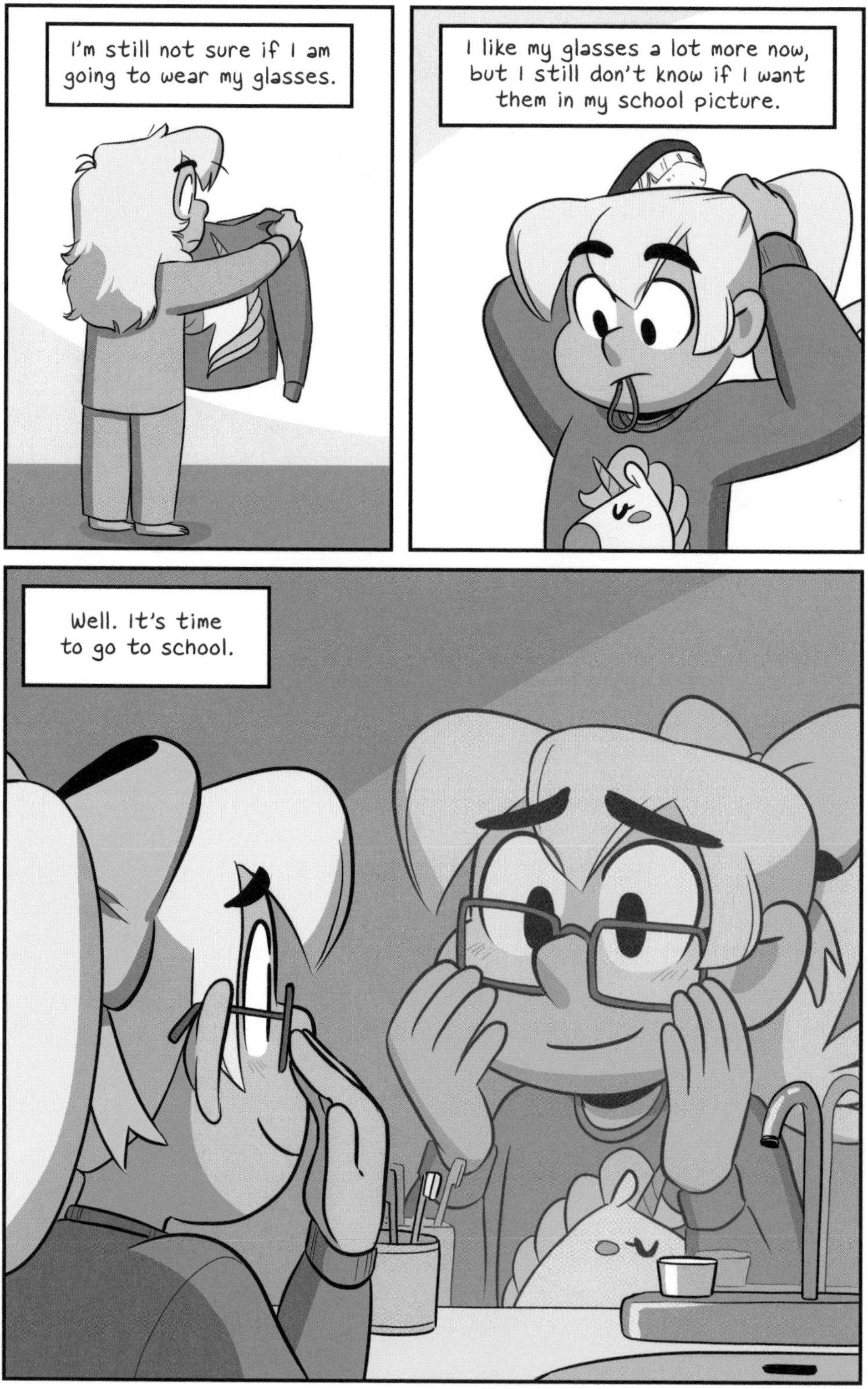
I'm still not sure if I am going to wear my glasses.
I like my glasses a lot more now, but I still don't know if I want them in my school picture.
Well. It's time to go to school.

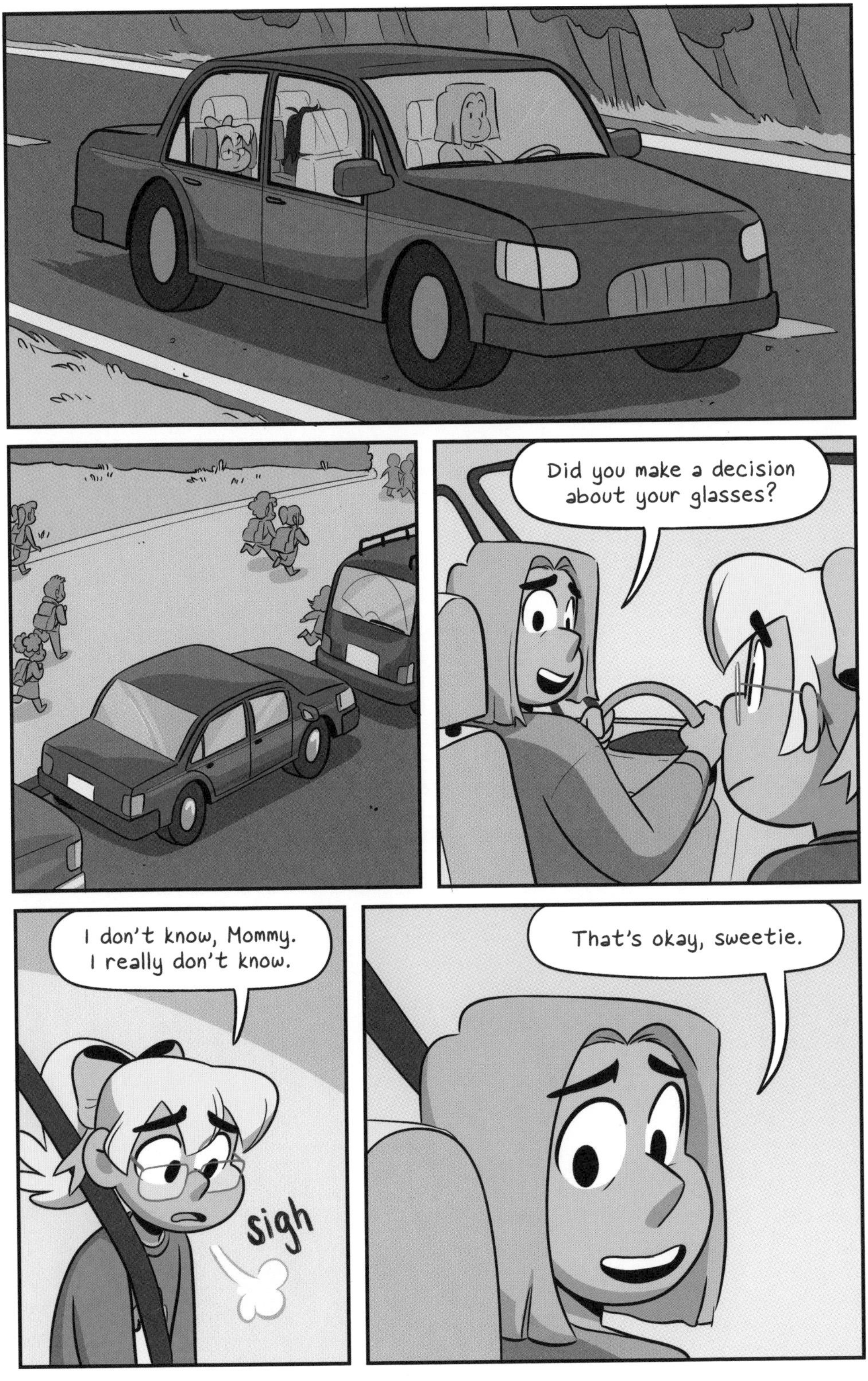
Did you make a decision about your glasses?
I don't know, Mommy. I really don't know.
sigh
That's okay, sweetie.

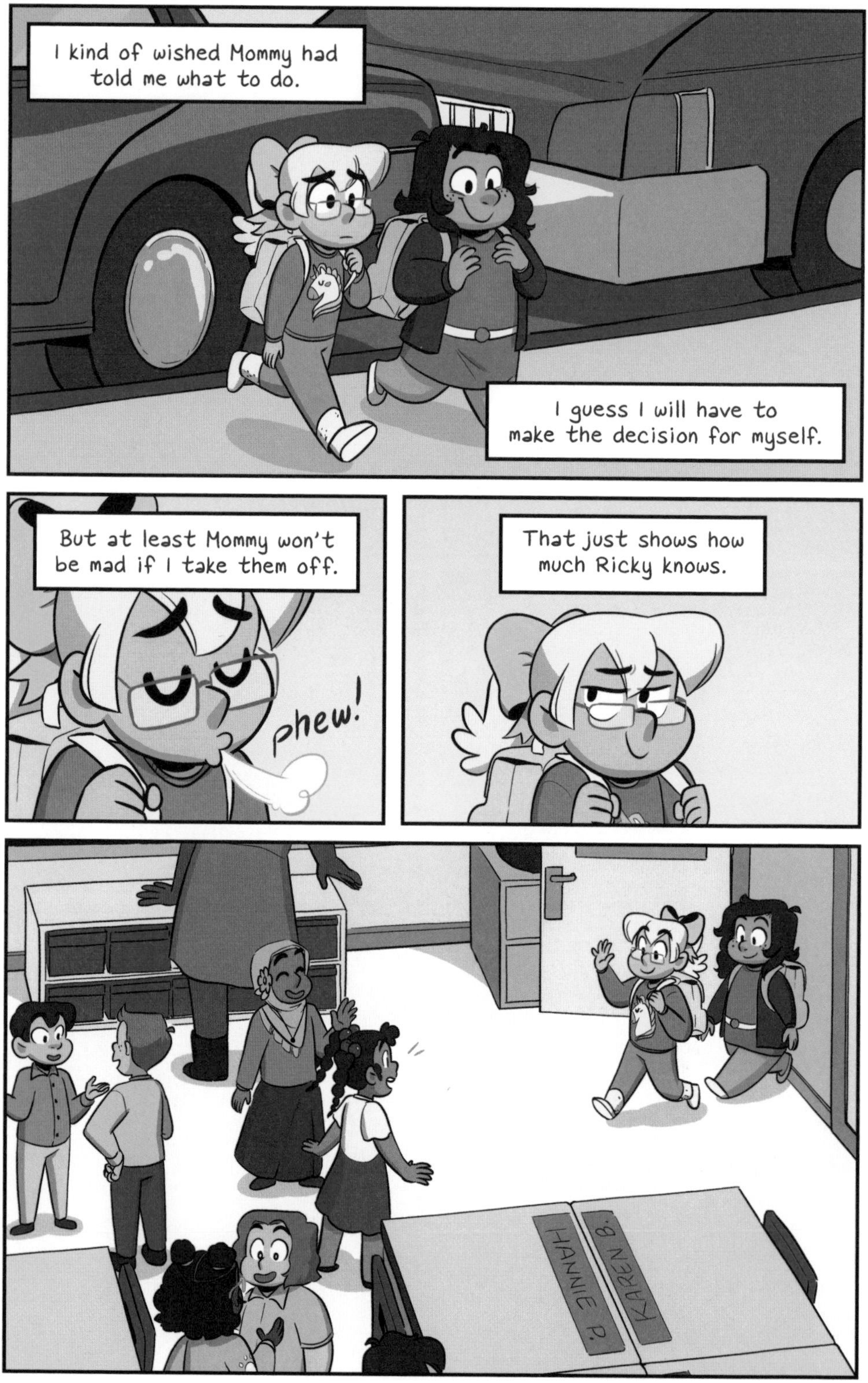
I kind of wished Mommy had told me what to do.
I guess I will have to make the decision for myself.
But at least Mommy won't be mad if I take them off.
phew!
That just shows how much Ricky knows.
HANNIE P.
KAREN B.

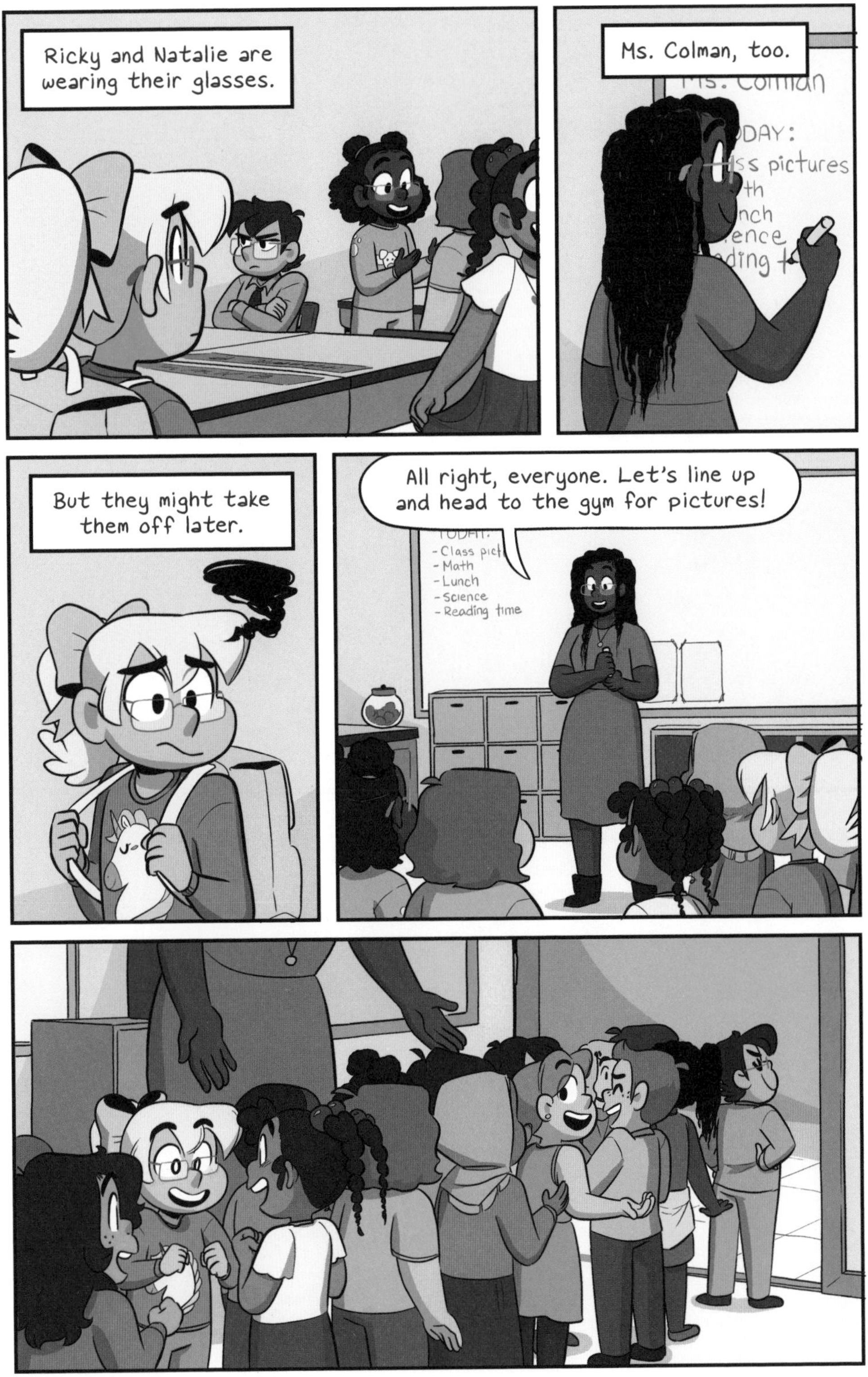
Ricky and Natalie are wearing their glasses.
Ms. Colman, too.
But they might take them off later.
All right, everyone. Let's line up and head to the gym for pictures!
TODAY:
-Class pict
-Math
-Lunch
-Science
-Reading time

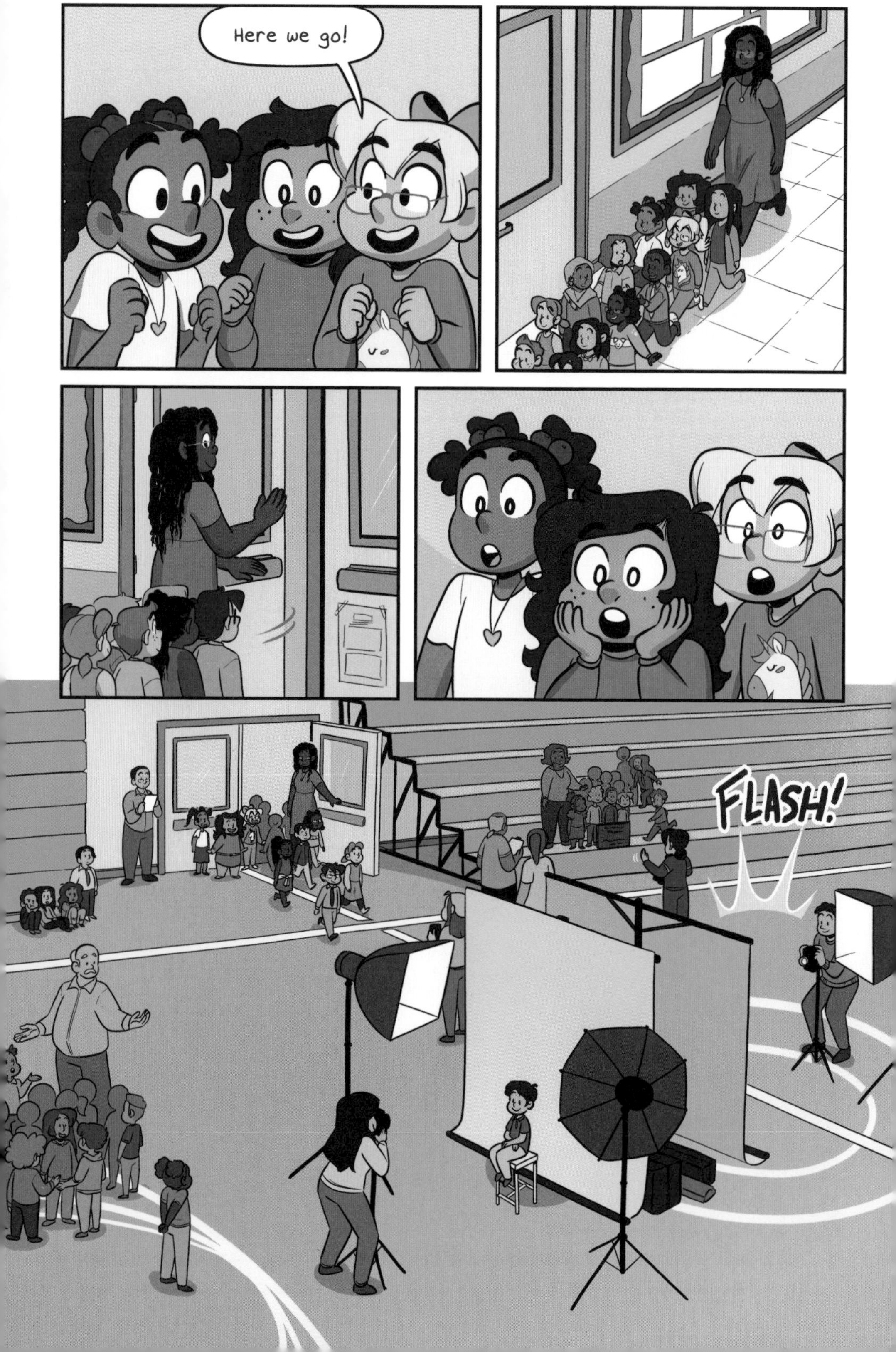
Here we go!
FLASH!

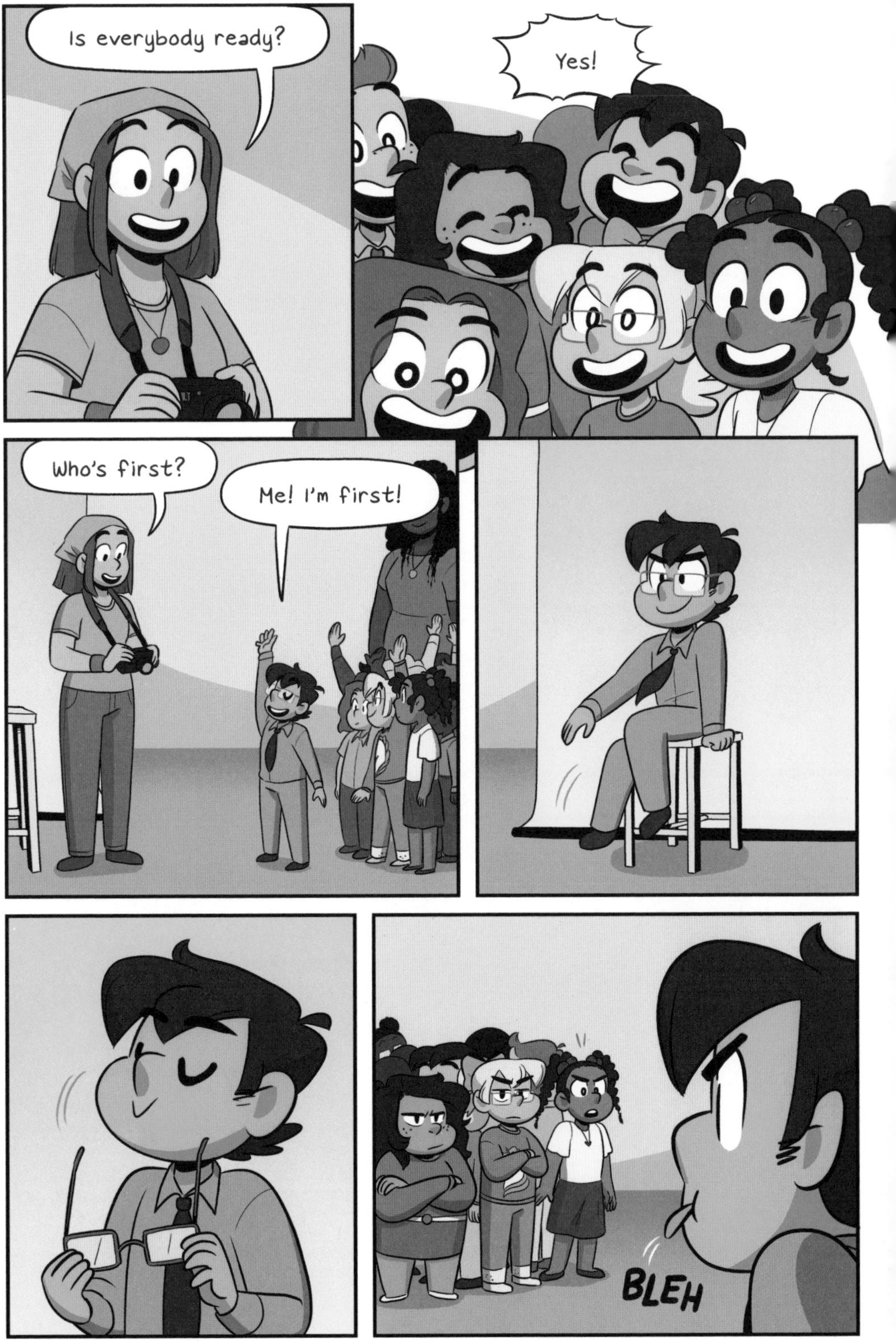
Is everybody ready?
Yes!
Who's first?
Me! I'm first!
BLEH

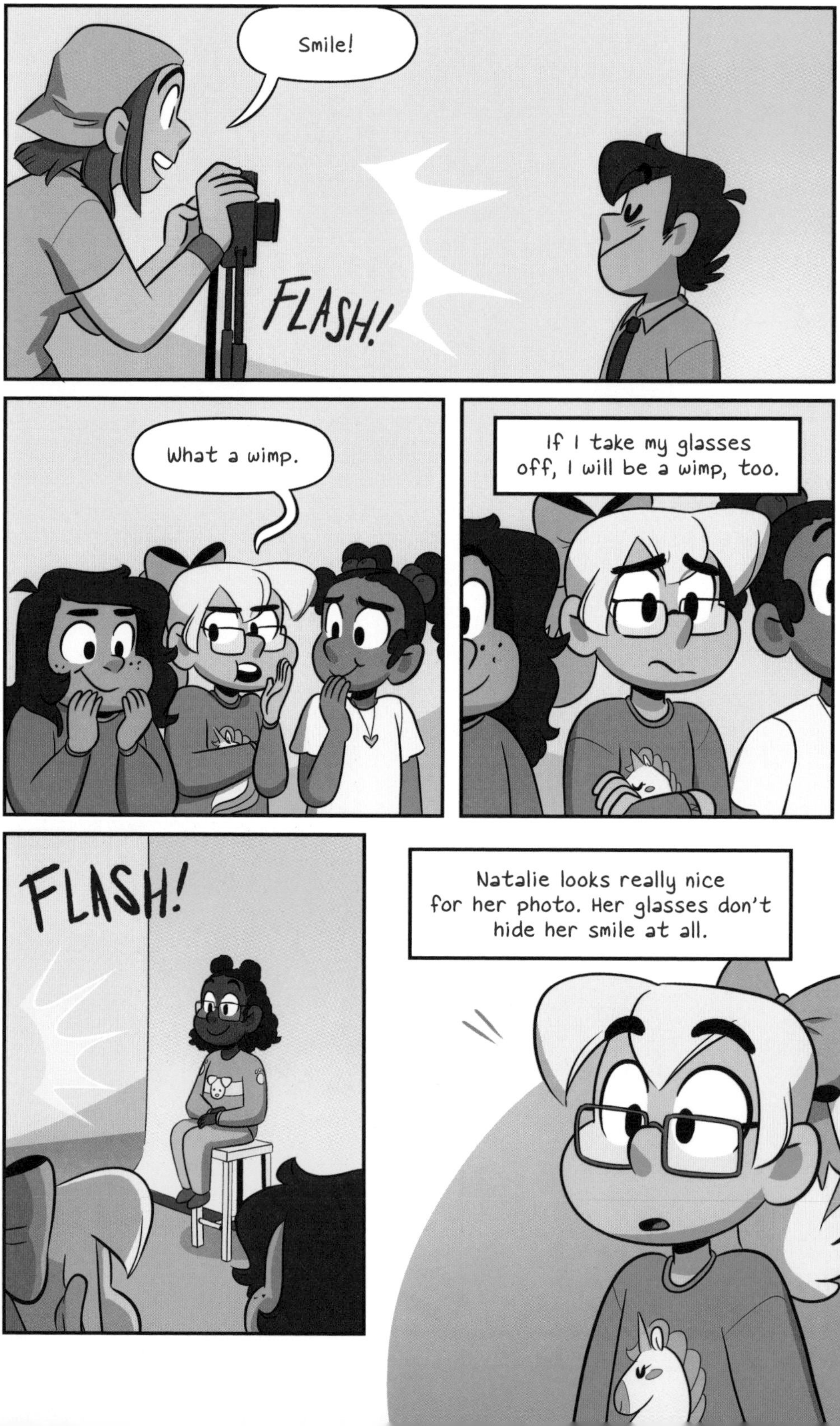
Smile!
FLASH!
What a wimp.
If I take my glasses off, I will be a wimp, too.
FLASH!
Natalie looks really nice for her photo. Her glasses don't hide her smile at all.

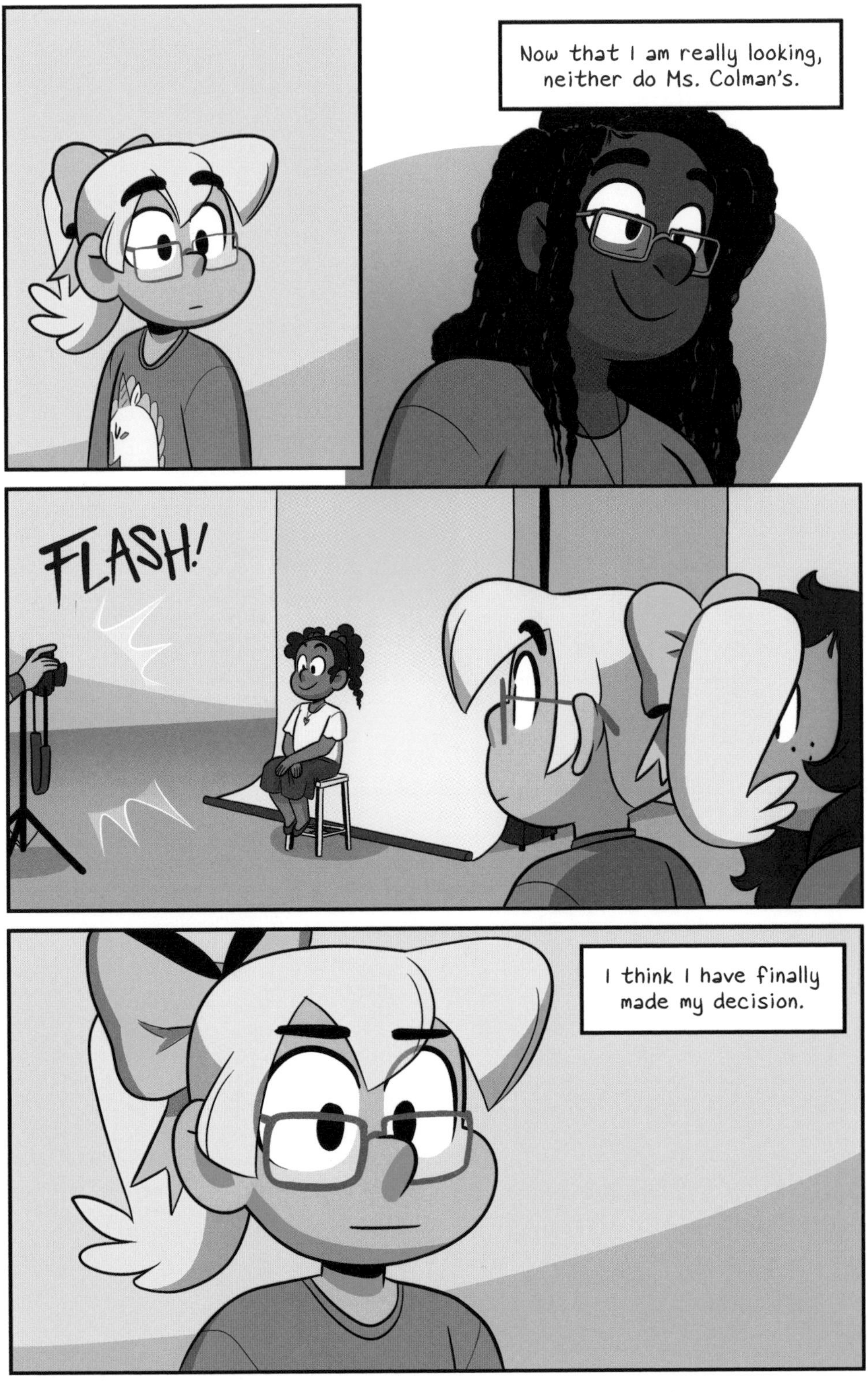
Now that I am really looking, neither do Ms. Colman's.
FLASH!
I think I have finally made my decision.

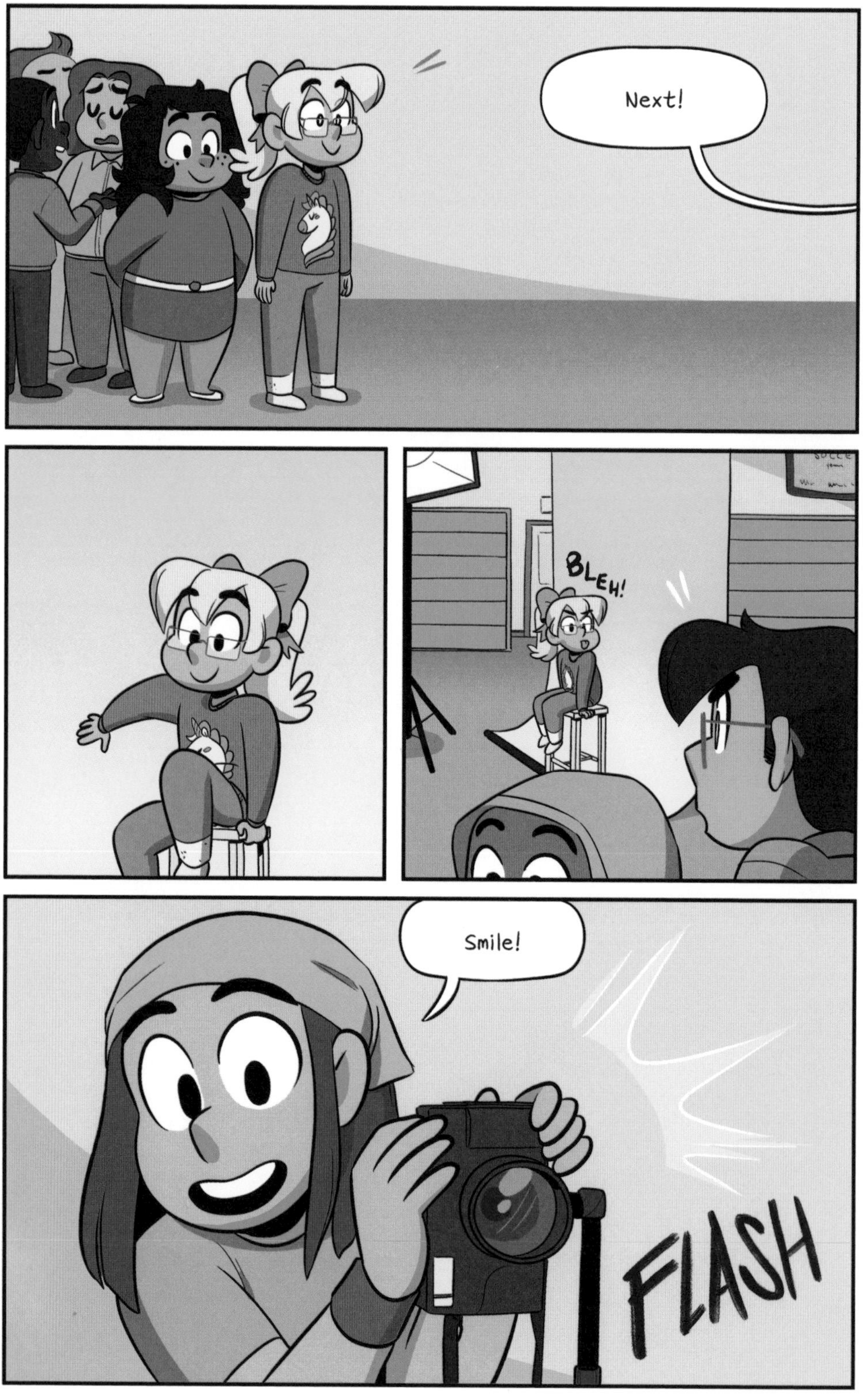
Next!
BLEH!
Smile!
FLASH

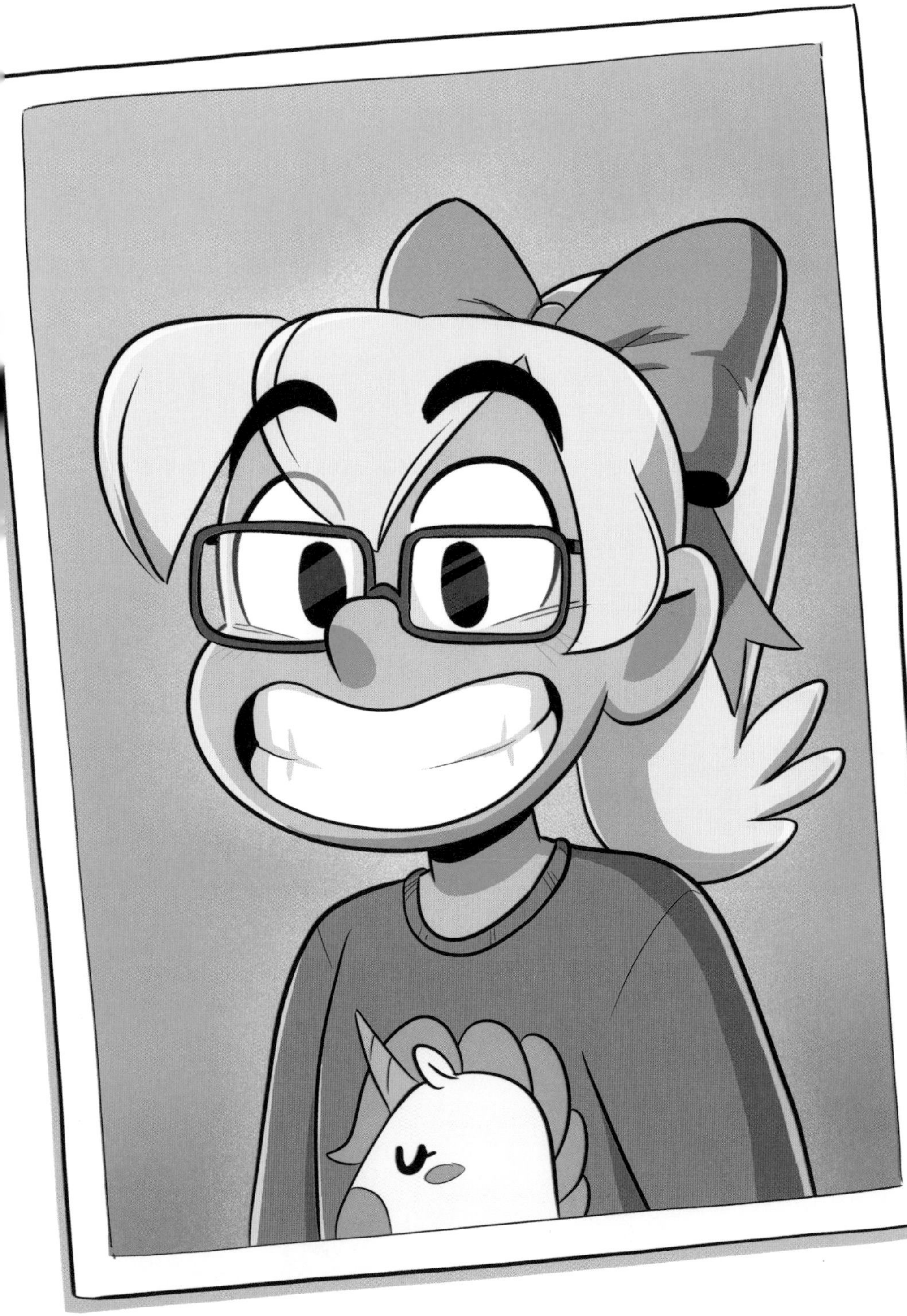

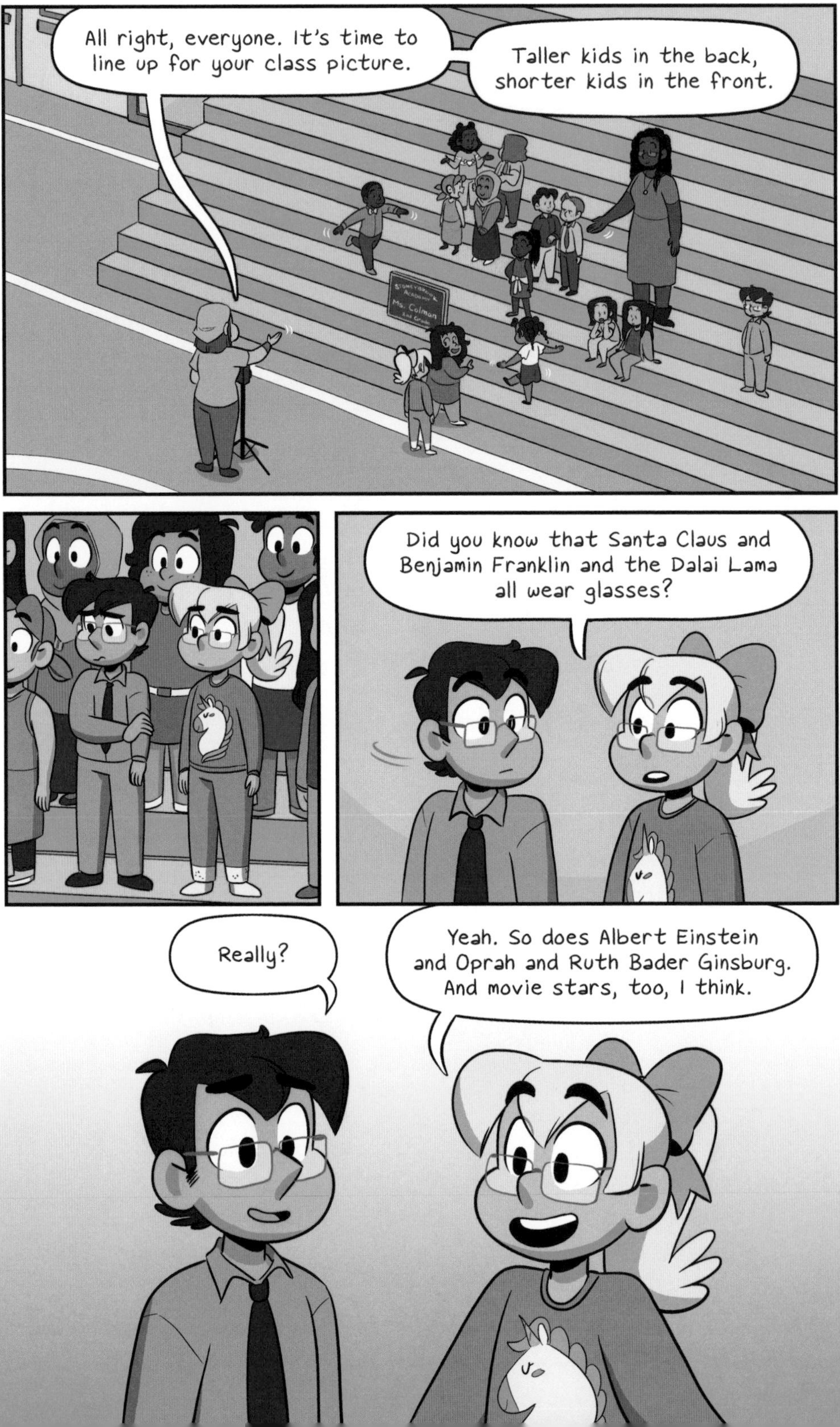
All right, everyone. It's time to line up for your class picture.
Taller kids in the back, shorter kids in the front.
Did you know that Santa Claus and Benjamin Franklin and the Dalai Lama all wear glasses?
Really?
Yeah. So does Albert Einstein and Oprah and Ruth Bader Ginsburg. And movie stars, too, I think.

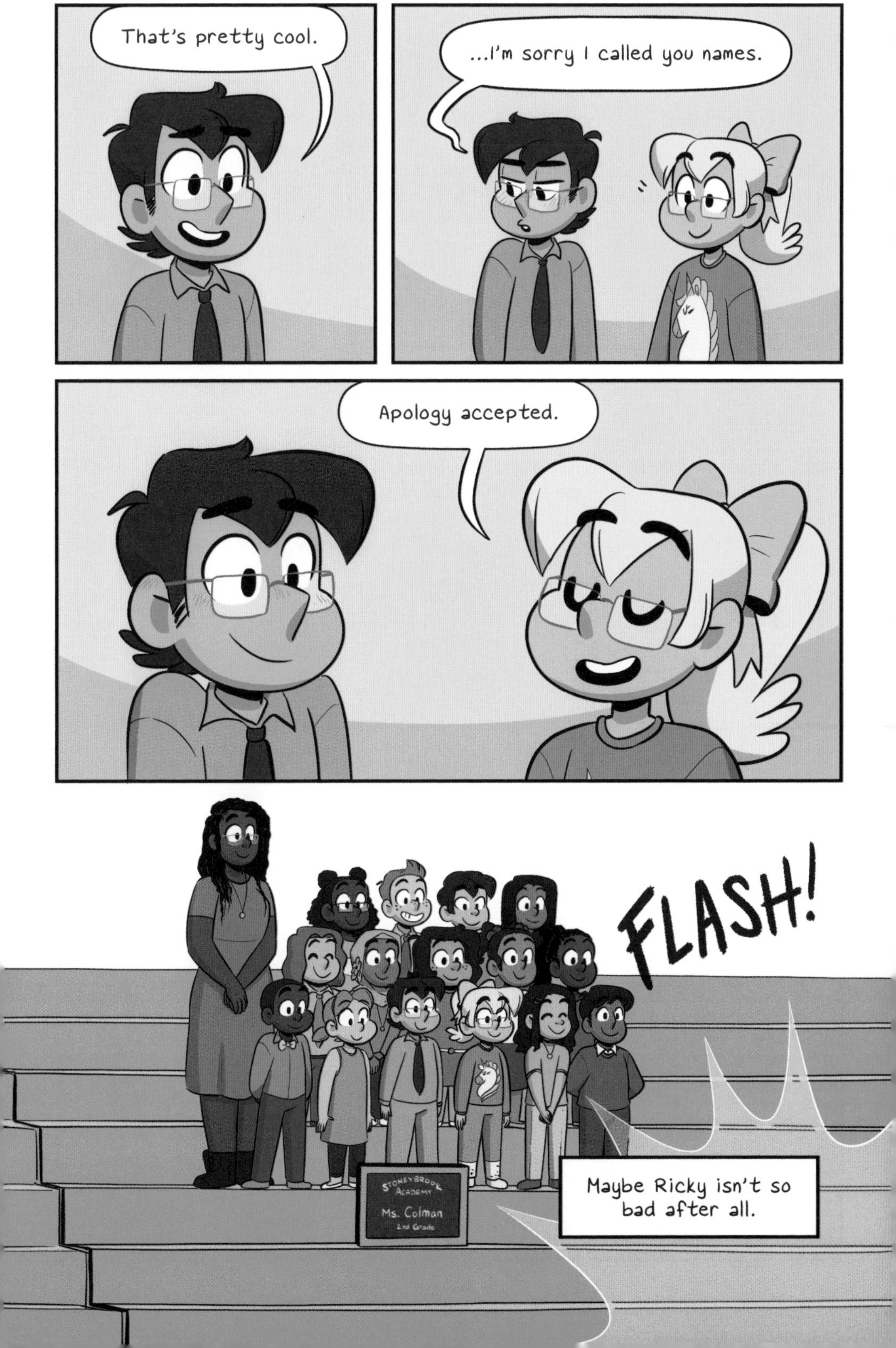
That's pretty cool.
...I'm sorry I called you names.
Apology accepted.
FLASH!
Stoneybrook Academy
Ms. Colman
2nd Grade
Maybe Ricky isn't so bad after all.

CHAPTER 10

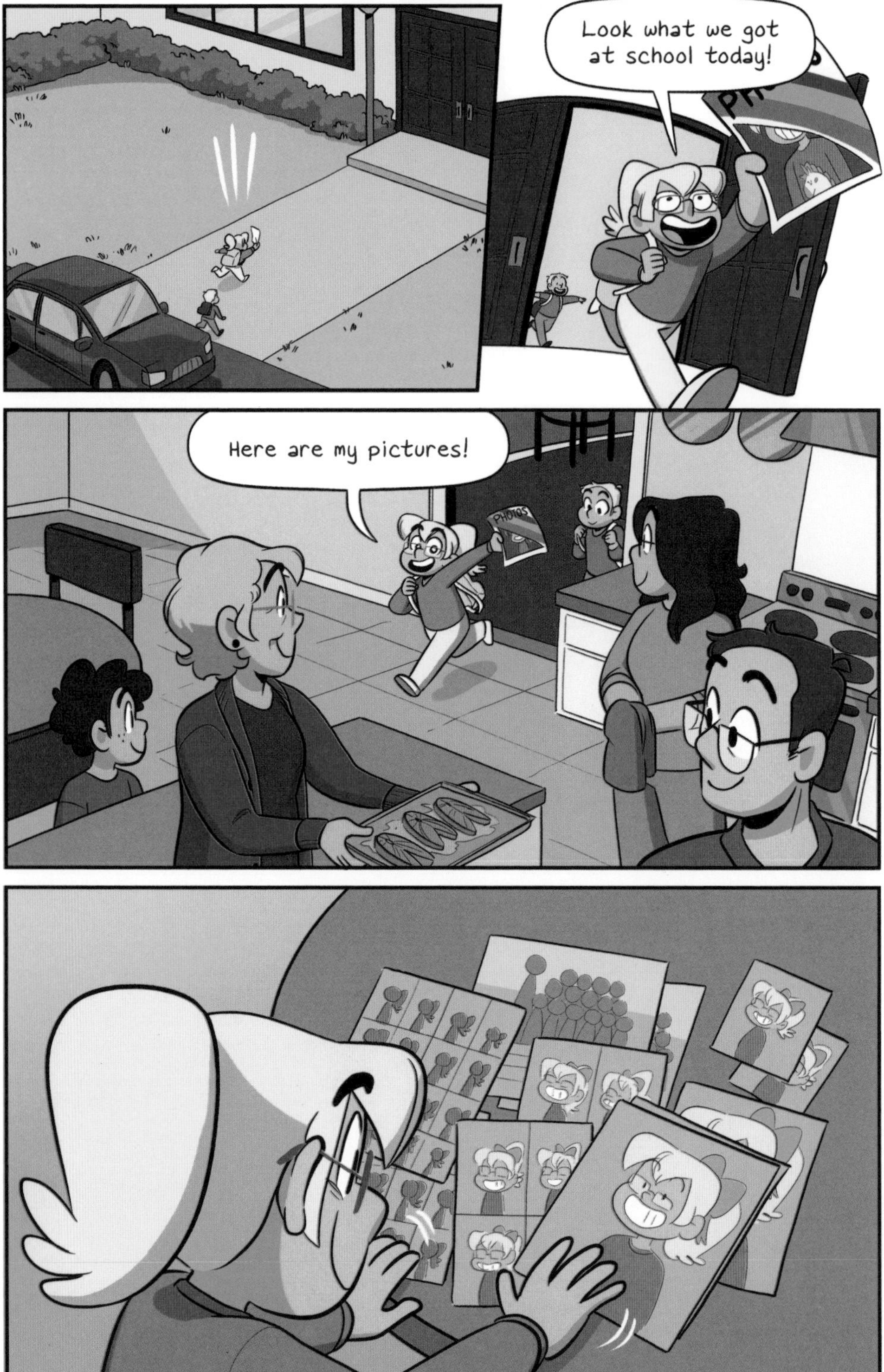
Look what we got at school today!
Here are my pictures!
PHOTOS

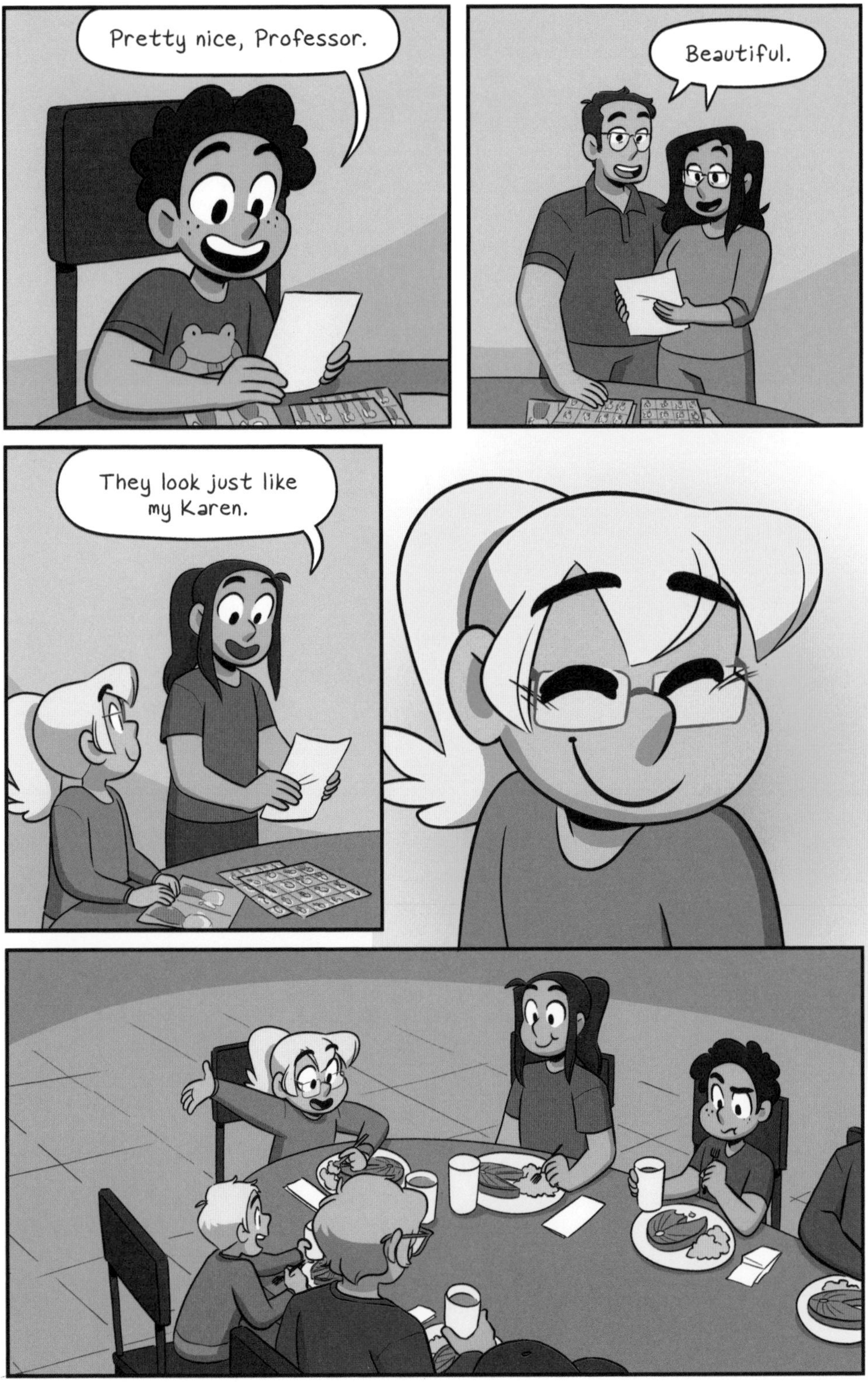
Pretty nice, Professor.
Beautiful.
They look just like my Karen.

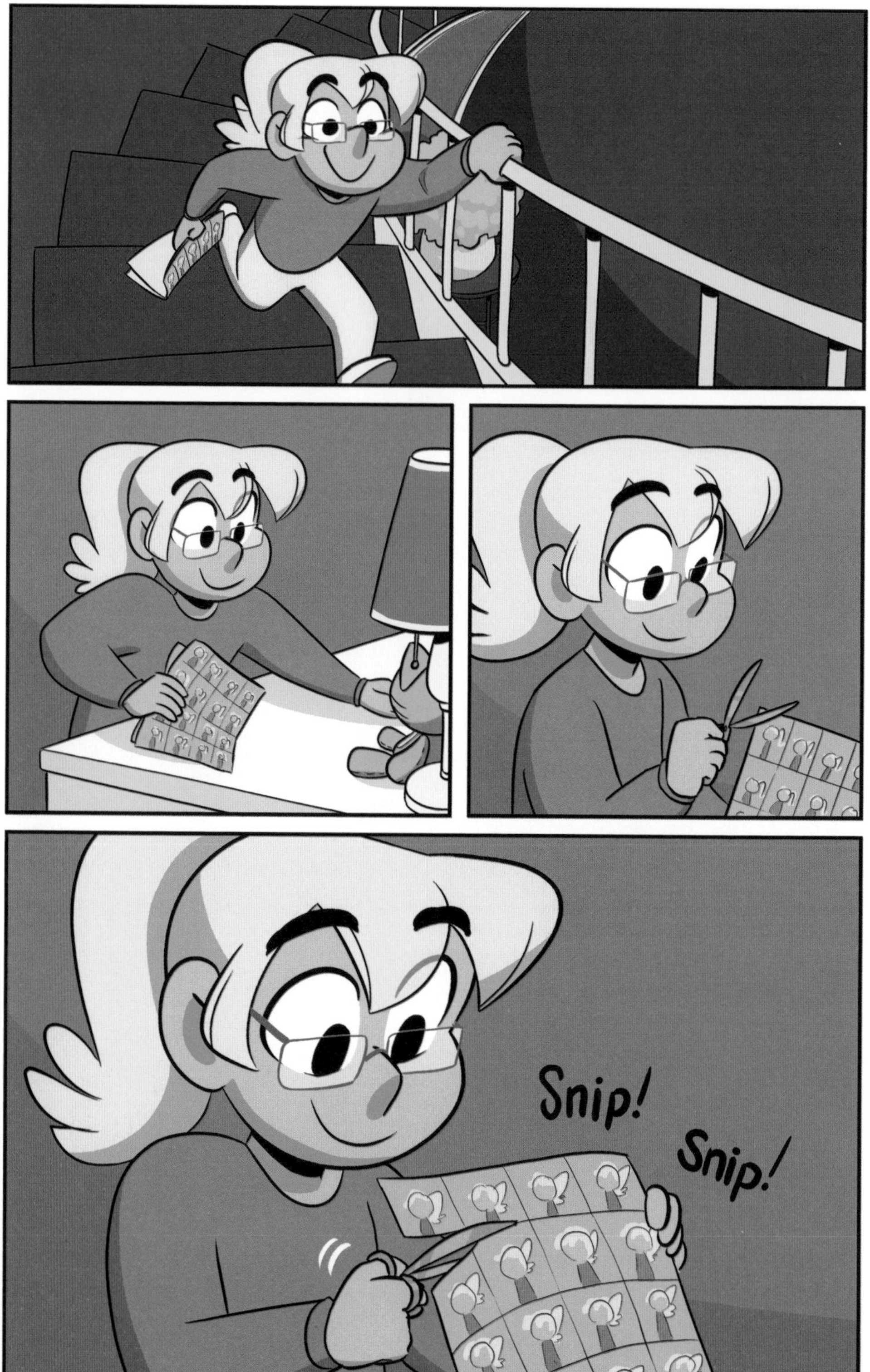
Snip!
Snip!

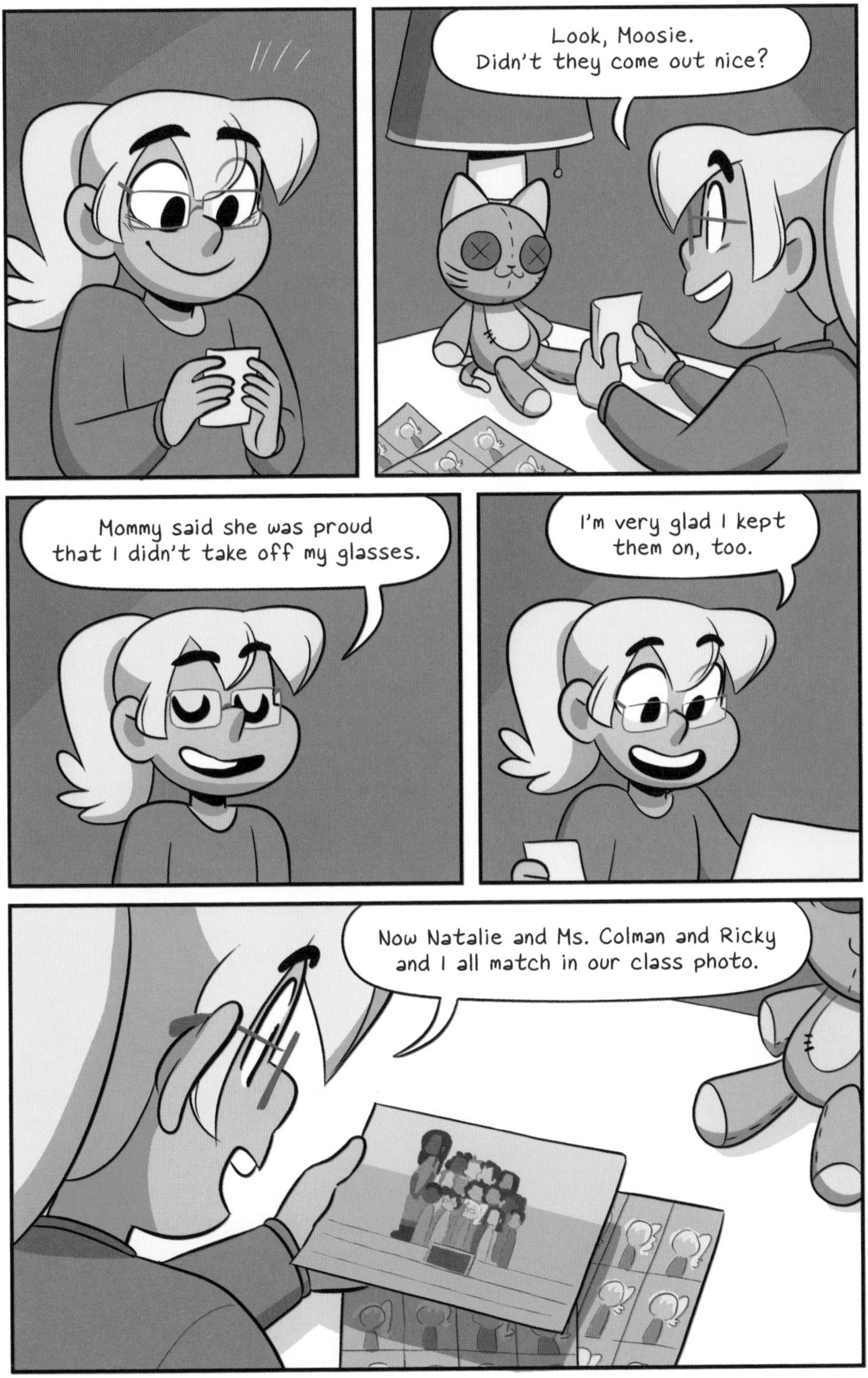
Look, Moosie.
Didn't they come out nice?
Mommy said she was proud that I didn't take off my glasses.
I'm very glad I kept them on, too.
Now Natalie and Ms. Colman and Ricky and I all match in our class photo.

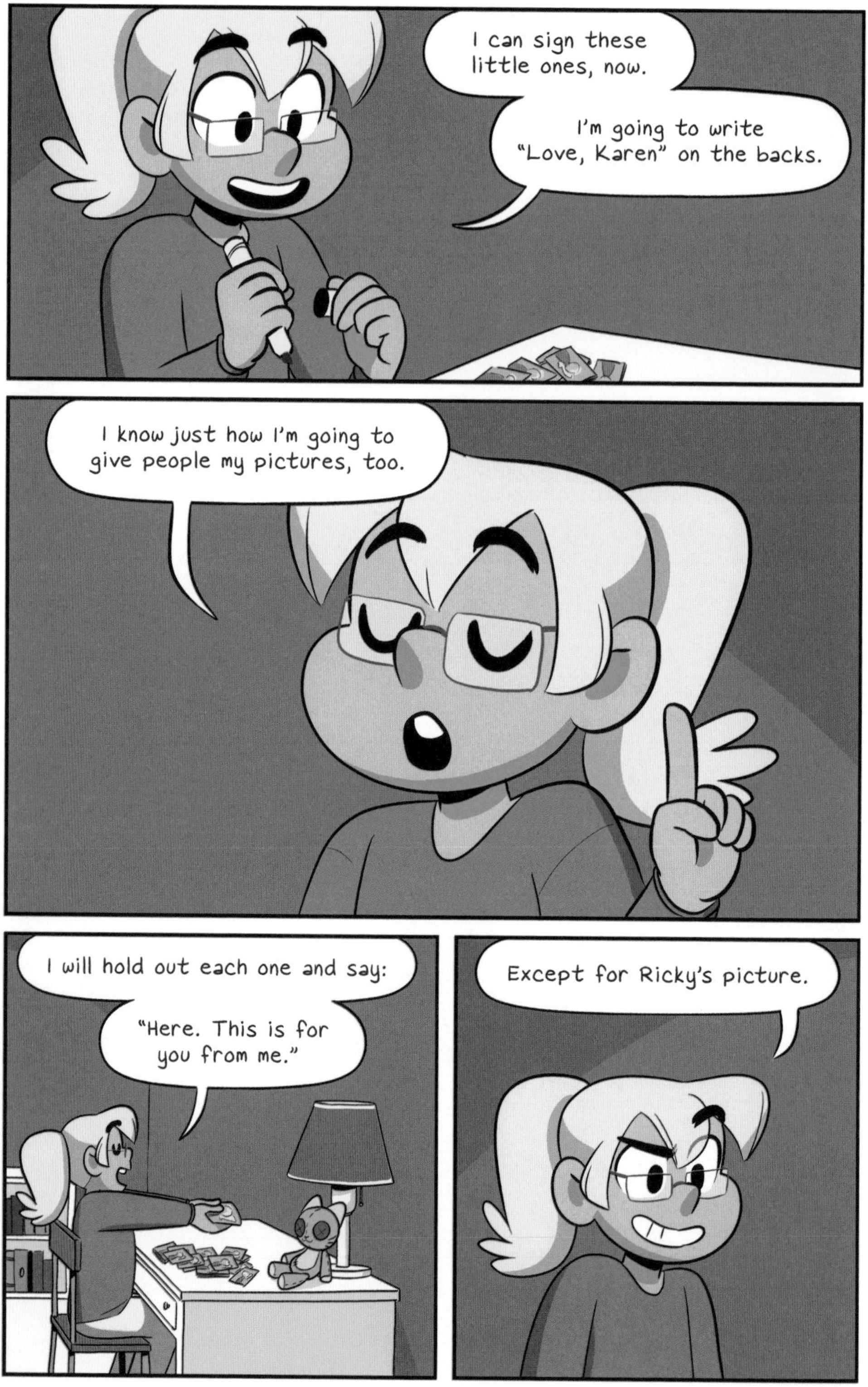
I can sign these little ones, now.
I'm going to write "Love, Karen" on the backs.
I know just how I'm going to give people my pictures, too.
I will hold out each one and say:
"Here. This is for you from me."
Except for Ricky's picture.

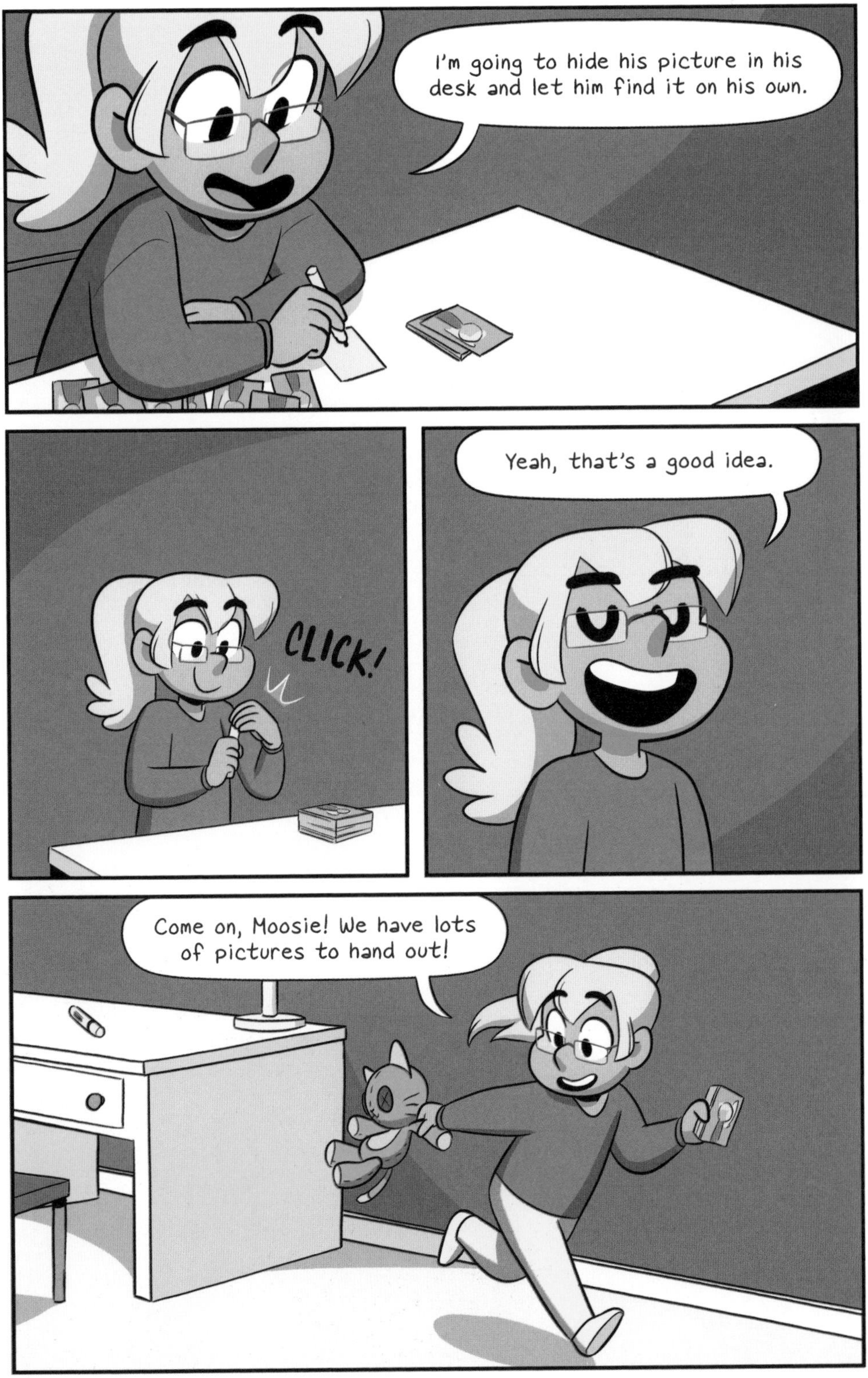
I'm going to hide his picture in his desk and let him find it on his own.
CLICK!
Yeah, that's a good idea.
Come on, Moosie! We have lots of pictures to hand out!

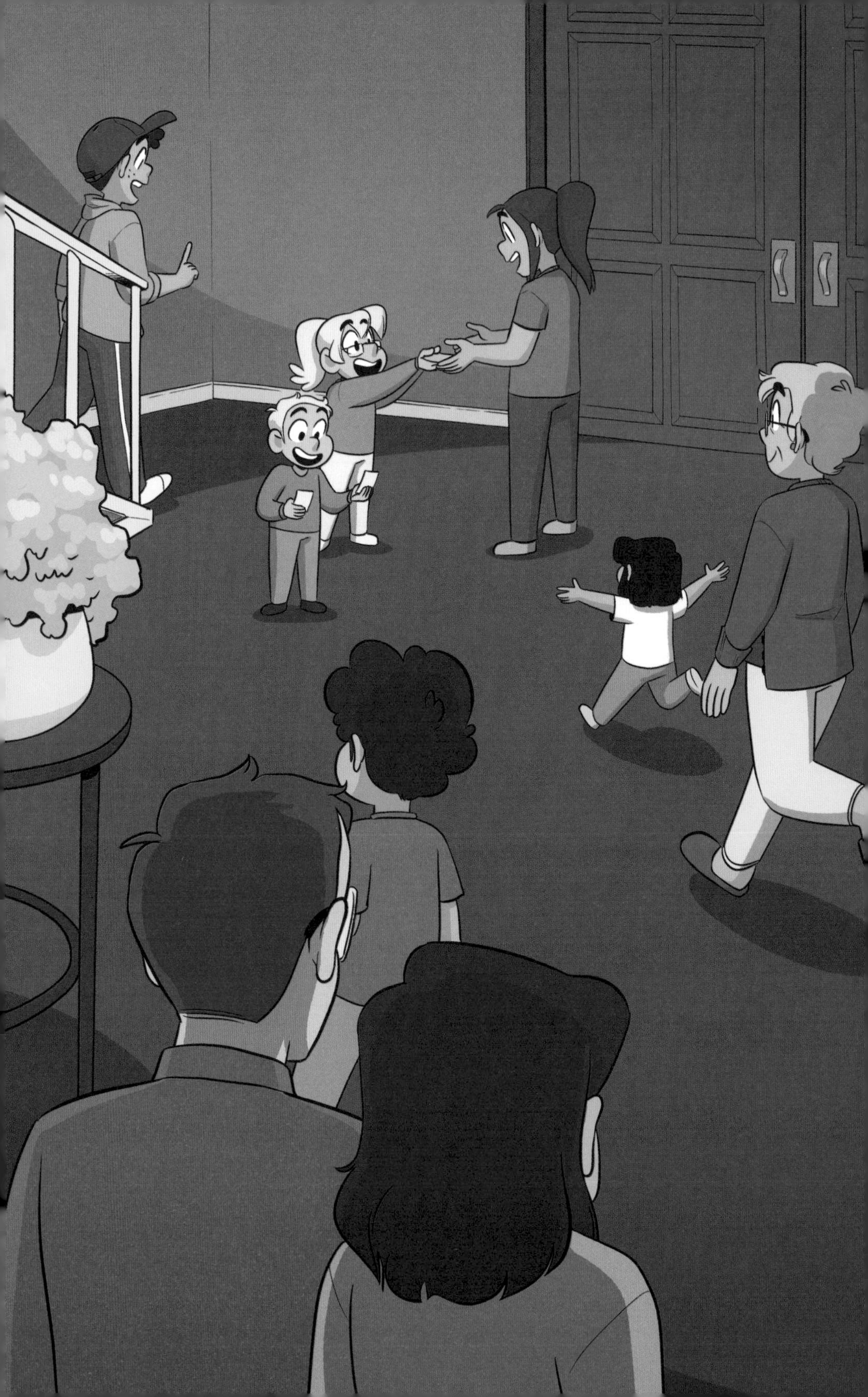

ANN M. MARTIN'S The Baby-sitters Club is one of the most popular series in the history of publishing — with more than 190 million books in print worldwide — and inspired a generation of young readers. Her novels include *Belle Teal*, *A Corner of the Universe* (a Newbery Honor book), *Here Today*, *A Dog's Life*, and *On Christmas Eve*, as well as the much-loved collaborations, *P.S. Longer Letter Later* and *Snail Mail No More*, with Paula Danziger, and *The Doll People* and *The Meanest Doll in the World*, written with Laura Godwin and illustrated by Brian Selznick. Ann lives in upstate New York.

KATY FARINA is the creator of the *New York Times* bestselling graphic novel adaptations of the Baby-sitters Little Sister series by Ann M. Martin, and of an original graphic novel for young readers, *Song of the Court.* Previously, she painted backgrounds for *She-Ra and the Princesses of Power* at DreamWorks TV. Katy lives in Los Angeles with her husband and two rambunctious cats. Visit her online at katyfarina.com

DON'T MISS THE OTHER BABY-SITTERS LITTLE SISTER GRAPHIC NOVELS!

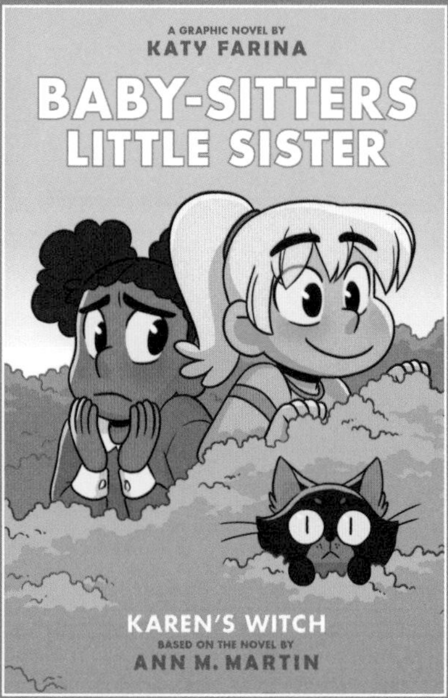
A GRAPHIC NOVEL BY
KATY FARINA
BABY-SITTERS LITTLE SISTER
KAREN'S WITCH
BASED ON THE NOVEL BY
ANN M. MARTIN

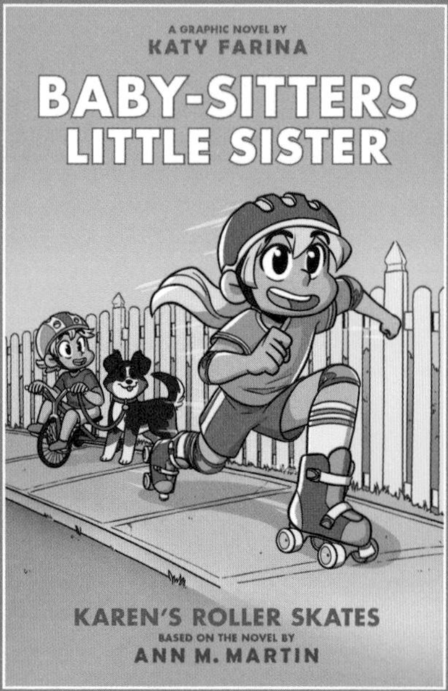
A GRAPHIC NOVEL BY
KATY FARINA
BABY-SITTERS LITTLE SISTER
KAREN'S ROLLER SKATES
BASED ON THE NOVEL BY
ANN M. MARTIN

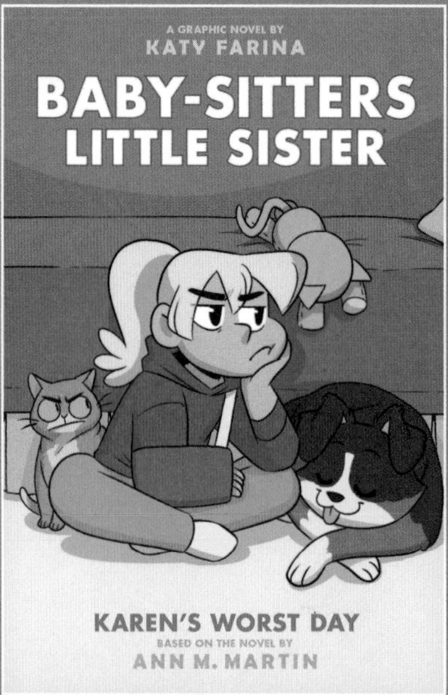
A GRAPHIC NOVEL BY
KATY FARINA
BABY-SITTERS LITTLE SISTER
KAREN'S WORST DAY
BASED ON THE NOVEL BY
ANN M. MARTIN

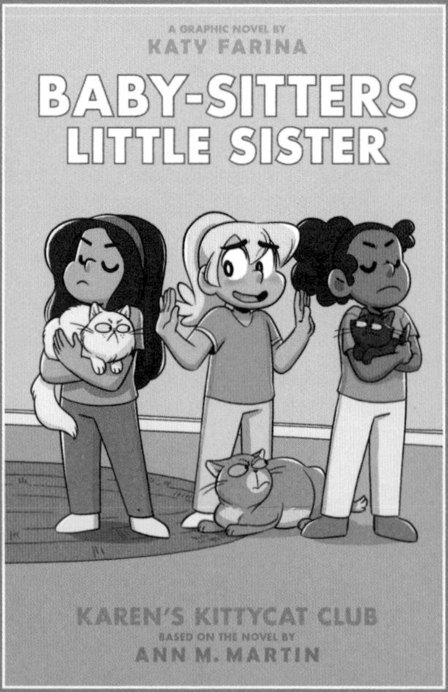
A GRAPHIC NOVEL BY
KATY FARINA
BABY-SITTERS LITTLE SISTER
KAREN'S KITTYCAT CLUB
BASED ON THE NOVEL BY
ANN M. MARTIN